THE FIRST HINT OF THE POWER OF THE FINAL ENCYCLOPEDIA

"Right now," I muttered, but I was merely echoing her words without thought, while listening to my racing mind. "No," I said, "never mind that. What is it I'm supposed to be turning my back on? What special destruction? I'm not planning anything like that—right now."

"Tam!" I felt her hand distantly on my arm, I saw her pale face staring tensely up at me, as if trying to get my attention. But it was as if these things registered on my senses from a long distance away. For if I was right—*if I was right*—then even Padma's calculations were testifying to the dark strength in me, that ability I had worked these five years to harness and drive. And if such power were actually mine, what couldn't I do next?

"But it isn't what you *plan*!" Lisa was saying desperately. "Don't you see, a gun doesn't plan to shoot anyone. But it's in you, Tam, like a gun ready to go off. Only, you don't have to let it go off. You can change yourself while there's still time. You can save yourself, and the Encyclopedia—"

Tor Books by Gordon R. Dickson

NOVELS

Alien Art
The Alien Way
Arcturus Landing
The Far Call
Gremlins, Go Home! (with
    Ben Bova)
Hoka! (with Poul Anderson)
Home from the Shore
The Last Master
Masters of Everon
Mission to Universe
Naked to the Stars
On the Run
Other
Outposter
Planet Run (with Keith
    Laumer)
The Pritcher Mass
Pro
Secrets of the Deep
Sleepwalkers' World
The Space Swimmers
The Space Winners
Spacepaw
Spacial Delivery
Way of the Pilgrim
Wolf and Iron

THE DORSAI SERIES

Necromancer
Tactics of Mistake
Lost Dorsai: The New Dorsai
    Companion
Soldier, Ask Not
The Spirit of Dorsai
Dorsai!
Young Bleys
The Final Encyclopedia,
    vol. 1 (rev. ed.)
The Final Encyclopedia,
    vol. 2 (rev. ed.)
The Chantry Guild

THE DRAGON SERIES

The Dragon Knight
The Dragon and the Gnarly
    King
The Dragon in Lyonesse

COLLECTIONS

Beyond the Dar al-Harb
Guided Tour
Love Not Human
The Man from Earth
The Man the Worlds Rejected
Steel Brother
The Stranger

SOLDIER, ASK NOT

GORDON R. DICKSON

TOR®

A TOM DOHERTY ASSOCIATES BOOK
NEW YORK

SOLDIER, ASK NOT

Copyright © 1967 by Gordon R. Dickson

Cover art by Royo

A Tor Book
Published by Tom Doherty Associates, LLC
175 Fifth Avenue
New York, NY 10010

www.tor.com

Tor® is a registered trademark of Tom Doherty Associates, LLC.

ISBN: 0-812-50400-3

First Tor edition: April 1993

Printed in the United States of America

0 9 8 7 6 5 4 3

CHAPTER 1 ■

Μῆνιν ἄειδε, θεά, Πηληϊάδεω Ἀχιλῆος —*begins* the *Iliad* of Homer, and its story of thirty-four hundred years ago. *This is the story of the wrath of Achilles.* —And this is the story of *my* wrath; I, Earthman, against the people of the two worlds so-called The Friendlies, the conscript, fanatic, black-clad soldiers of Harmony and Association. Nor is it the story of any small anger. For like Achilles, I am a man of Earth.

That does not impress you? Not in these days when the sons of the younger worlds are taller, stronger, more skilled and clever than we of the Old World? Then, how little you know Earth, and the sons of Earth. Leave your younger worlds and come back to the Mother Planet, once, and touch her. She is still here and still the same. Her sun still shines on the waters of the Red Sea that parted before the Children

1 ■

of the Lord. The wind still blows in the Pass of Thermopylae, where Leonidas with the Spartan Three Hundred held back the hosts of Xerxes, King of the Persians, and changed history. Here, men fought and died and bred and buried and built for more than five hundred thousand years before your newer worlds were even dreamed of by man. Do you think those five centuries of tens-of-centuries, generation upon generation, between the same sky and soil left *no* special mark on us in blood and bone and soul?

The men of the Dorsai may be warriors above imagining. The Exotics of Mara and Kultis may be robed magicians who can turn a man inside out and find answers outside philosophy. The researchers in hard sciences on Newton and Venus may have traveled so far beyond ordinary humans that they can talk to us only haltingly, nowadays. But we—we duller, shorter, simpler men of Old Earth still have something more than any of these. For we are still the whole being of man, the basic stock, of which they are only the refined parts—flashing, fine-honed, scintillant parts. But parts.

But, if you still are one of those, like my uncle Mathias Olyn, who think us utterly bypassed, then I direct you to the Exotic-supported Enclave at St. Louis, where forty-two years ago, an Earthman named Mark Torre, a man of great vision, first began the building of what a hundred years from now will be The Final Encyclopedia. Sixty years from now will see it too massive and complicated and delicate to endure Earth's surface. You will start to find it then in orbit about the Mother Planet. A hundred years from now and it will—but no one knows for sure what it will do. Mark Torre's theory is that it will show us the back of our heads—some hidden part of the basic Earth human soul and being that those of the younger worlds have lost, or are not able to know.

But see for yourself. Go there now, to the St. Louis Enclave, and join one of the tours that take you through the chambers and research rooms of the Encyclopedia Project; and finally into the mighty Index Room at their very center, where the vast, curving walls of that chamber are already beginning to be charged with leads to the knowledge of the centuries. When the whole expanse of that great sphere's interior is finally charged, a hundred years from now, connections will be made between bits of knowledge that never have been connected, that never could have been connected, by a human mind before. And in this final knowledge we will see—what?

The back of our heads?

But as I say, never mind that now. Simply visit the Index Room—that is all I ask you to do. Visit it, with the rest of the tour. Stand in the center of it, and do as the guide tells you.

—*Listen*.

Listen. Stand silent and strain your ears. Listen— you will hear nothing. And then finally the guide will break the reaching, almost unendurable silence, and tell you why he asked you to listen.

Only one man or woman in millions ever hears anything. Only one in millions—of those born here on Earth.

But none—*no one*—of all those born on the younger worlds who has ever come here to listen has ever heard a thing.

It still proves nothing, you think? Then you think

3 ■

wrong, my friend. For I have been one of those who *heard*—what there was to hear—and the hearing changed my life, as witness what I have done, arming me with self-knowledge of power with which I later turned in fury to plan the destruction of the peoples of two Friendly worlds.

So do not laugh if I compare my wrath to the wrath of Achilles, bitter and apart among the boats of his Myrmidons, before the walls of Troy. For there are other likenesses between us. Tam Olyn is my name and my ancestry is more Irish than otherwise; but it was on the Peloponnesus of Greece that I, like Achilles, grew to be what I became.

In the very shadow of the ruins of the Parthenon, white over the city of Athens, our souls were darkened by the uncle who should have set them free to grow in the sun. My soul—and that of my younger sister, Eileen.

CHAPTER 2 ■

It was her idea—my sister Eileen's—that we visit the Final Encyclopedia that day, using my new travel pass as a worker in Communications. Ordinarily, perhaps, I might have wondered why she wanted to go there. But in this instance, even as she suggested it, the prospect struck forth a feeling in me, deep and heavy as the sudden note of a gong—a feeling I had never felt before—of something like dread.

But it was not just dread, nothing so simple as that. It was not even wholly unpleasant. Mostly, it resembled that hollow, keyed-up sensation that comes just before the moment of being put to some great test. And yet, it was this—but somehow much more as well. A feeling as of a dragon in my path.

For just a second it touched me; but that was enough. And, because the Encyclopedia, in theory, represented all hope for those Earth-born and my uncle Mathias had always represented to us all hope-lessness, I connected the feeling with him, with the challenge he had posed me during all the years of our living together. And this made me suddenly determined to go, overriding whatever other, little reasons there might be.

Besides, the trip fitted the moment like a celebration. I did not usually take Eileen places; but I had just signed a trainee work-contract with the Interstellar News Services at their Headquarters Unit here on Earth. This, only two weeks after my graduation from the Geneva University of Communications. True, that University was first among those like it on the sixteen worlds of men, including Earth; and my scholastic record there had been the best in its history. But such job offers came to young men straight out of school once in twenty years—if that often.

So I did not stop to question my seventeen-year-old sister as to why she might want me to take her to the Final Encyclopedia, on just that particular day and hour she specified. I suppose perhaps, as I look back on it now, I told myself she only wanted to get away from the dark house of our uncle, for the day. And that, in itself, was reason enough for me.

For it had been Mathias, my father's brother, who had taken us in, Eileen and me, two orphan children after the death of our parents in the same air-car crash. And it was he who had broken us during our growing years that followed. Not that he had ever laid a finger on us physically. Not that he had been guilty of any overt or deliberate cruelty. He did not have to be.

He had only to give us the richest of homes, the choicest of food, clothing and care—and make sure that we shared it all with *him*, whose heart was as sunless as his own great, unpierced block of a house, sunless as a cave below the earth's surface that has never felt the daylight, and whose soul was as cold as a stone within that cave.

His bible was the writings of that old twenty-first century saint or devil, Walter Blunt—whose motto was "DESTRUCT!"—and whose Chantry Guild later gave birth to the Exotic culture on the younger worlds of Mara and Kultis. Never mind that the Exotics had always read Blunt's writings with a difference, seeing the message in them to be one of tearing up the weeds of the present, so that there would be room for the flowers of the future to grow. Mathias, our uncle, saw only as far as the tearing; and day by day, in that dark house, he drummed it into us.

But enough about Mathias. He was perfect in his emptiness and his belief that the younger worlds had already left us of Earth behind them to dwindle and die, like any dead limb or atrophied part. But neither Eileen nor I could match him in that cold philosophy, for all we tried as children. So, each in our own way, we fought to escape from him and it; and our escape routes brought us, that day, together to the Exotic Enclave at St. Louis, and the Final Encyclopedia.

We took a shuttle flight from Athens to St. Louis and the subway from St. Louis to the Enclave. An airbus took us to the Encyclopedia courtyard; and I remember that, somehow, I was last off the bus. As I stepped to the circle of concrete, it struck again, that deep, sudden gong-note of feeling inside me. I stopped dead, like a man struck into a trance.

"—Pardon me?" said a voice behind me. "You're

part of the tour, aren't you? Will you join the rest over here? I'm your guide.''

I turned sharply, and found myself looking down into the brown eyes of a girl in the blue robes of an Exotic. She stood there, as fresh as the sunlight about her—but something in her did not match.

''You're not an Exotic!'' I said suddenly. No more she was. The Exotic-born have their difference plain about them. Their faces are more still than other people's. Their eyes look more deeply into you. They are like Gods of Peace who sit always with one hand on a sleeping thunderbolt they do not seem to know is there.

''I'm a co-worker,'' she answered. ''Lisa Kant's my name.—And you're right. I'm not a born Exotic.'' She did not seem bothered by my penetrating her difference from the robe she wore. She was shorter than my sister, who was tall—as I am tall— for a man from Earth. Eileen was silver-blond, while, even then, my hair was dark. It was the same color as hers when our parents died; but it darkened over the years in Mathias' house. But this girl, Lisa, was brown-haired, pretty and smiling. She intrigued me with her good looks and Exotic robes—and she nettled me a little as well. She seemed so certain of herself.

I watched her, therefore, as she went about rounding up the other people who were waiting for the guided tour through the Encyclopedia; and once the tour itself was underway, I fell into step beside her and got her talking to me, between lecture spots.

She showed no hesitation in speaking about herself. She had been born in the North American Midwest, just outside of St. Louis, she told me. She had

gone to primary and secondary schools in the Enclave and became convinced of the Exotic philoso-
phies. So she had adopted their work and their ways.
I thought it seemed like a waste of a girl as attractive
as herself—and bluntly I told her so.

"How can I be wasting myself," she said, smiling
at me, "when I'm using my energies to the full this
way—and for the best purposes?"

I thought that perhaps she was laughing at me. I
did not like that—even in those days, I was no one
to laugh at.

"What best purposes?" I asked as brutally as I
could. "Contemplating your navel?"

Her smile went away and she looked at me
strangely, so strangely that I always remembered that
look, afterward.

It was as if she had suddenly become aware of
me—as of someone floating and adrift in a nighttime
sea beyond the firm rock shore on which she stood.
And she reached out with her hand, as if she would
touch me, then dropped her hand again, as if suddenly remembering where we were.

"We are always here," she answered me,
strangely. "Remember that. We are always here."

She turned away and led us on through the spread-
out complex of structures that was the Encyclopedia.
These, once moved into space, she said, speaking to
us all now as she led us on, would fold together to
form a roughly spherical shape, in orbit a hundred
and fifty miles above the Earth's surface. She told us
what a vast expense it would be to move the structure
into orbit like that, as one unit. Then she explained
how, expensive as this was, the cost was justified by
the savings during the first hundred years of con-

struction and information-charging, which could be done more economically here on the ground.

For the Final Encyclopedia, she said, was not to be just a storehouse of fact. It would store facts, but only as a means to an end—that end being the establishment and discovery of relationships between those facts. Each knowledge item was to be linked to other knowledge items by energy pulses holding the code of the relationship, until these interconnections were carried to the fullest extent possible. Until, finally, the great interconnected body of man's information about himself and his universe would begin to show its shape as a whole, in a way man had never been able to observe it before.

At this point, Earth would then have in the Encyclopedia a mighty stockpile of immediately available, interrelated information about the human race and its history. This could be traded for the hard science knowledge of worlds like Venus and Newton, for the psychological sciences of the Exotic Worlds—and all the other specialized information of the younger worlds that Earth needed. By this alone, in a multi-world human culture in which the currency between worlds was itself the trading of skilled minds, the Encyclopedia would eventually pay for itself.

But the hope that had led Earth to undertake its building was for more than this. It was Earth's hope—the hope of all the people of Earth, except for such as Mathias, who had given up all hope—that the true payment from the Encyclopedia would come from its use as a tool to explore Mark Torre's theory.

And Torre's theory, as we all should know, was a theory which postulated that there was a dark area in Man's knowledge of himself, an area where man's vision had always failed, as the viewing of any perceptive device fails in the blind area where it, itself, exists. Into man's blind area, Torre theorized, the Final Encyclopedia would be able to explore by inference, from the shape and body of total known knowledge. And in that area, said Torre, we would find something—a quality, ability or strength—in the basic human stock of Earth that was theirs alone, something which had been lost or was not available to the human splinter types on the younger worlds that now seemed to be fast out-stripping our parent breed in strength of body or mind.

Hearing all this, for some reason I found myself remembering the strange look and odd words of Lisa to me earlier. I looked around the strange and crowded rooms, where everything from heavy construction to delicate laboratory work was going on, as we passed; and the odd, dread-like feeling began to come back on me. It not only came back, it stayed and grew, until it was a sort of consciousness, a feeling as if the whole Encyclopedia had become one mighty living organism, with me at its center.

I fought against it, instinctively; for what I had always wanted most in life was to be free—to be swallowed by nothing, human or mechanical. But still it grew on me; and it was still growing as we came at last to the Index Room, which in space would be at the Encyclopedia's exact center.

The room was in the shape of a huge globe so vast that, as we entered it, its farther wall was lost in dimness, except for the faint twinkling of firefly lights that signaled the establishment of new facts and associations of fact within the sensitive recording fabric of its inner surface, that endless surface curving about us which was at once walls, ceiling and floor.

The whole reaching interior of this enormous spherical room was empty; but cantilevered ramps led out and up from the entrances to the room, stretching in graceful curves to a circular platform poised in the midst of the empty space, at the exact center of the chamber.

It was up one of these ramps that Lisa led us now until we came to the platform, which was perhaps twenty feet in diameter.

". . . Here, where we're now standing," said Lisa as we halted on the platform, "is what will be known as the Transit Point. In space, all connections will be made not only around the walls of the Index Room, but also through this central point. And it's from this central point that those handling the Encyclopedia then will try to use it according to Mark Torre's theory, to see if they can uncover the hidden knowledge of our Earth-human minds."

She paused and turned around to locate everyone in the group.

"Gather in closely, please," she said. For a second her gaze brushed mine—and without warning, the wave of feeling inside me about the Encyclopedia suddenly crested. A cold sensation like fear washed through me, and I stiffened.

"Now," she went on, when we were all standing close together, "I want you all to keep absolutely still for sixty seconds and listen. Just listen, and see if you hear anything."

The others stopped talking and the vast, untouchable silence of that huge chamber closed in about us. It wrapped about us, and the feeling in me sang suddenly up to a high pitch of anxiety. I had never been bothered by heights or distances, but suddenly now I was wildly aware of the long emptiness below the platform, of all the space enclosing me. My head began to swim and my heart pounded. I felt dizziness threatening me.

"And what're we supposed to hear?" I broke in loudly, not for the question's sake, but to snap the vertiginous sensation that seemed to be trying to sweep me away. I was standing almost behind Lisa as I said it. She turned and looked up at me. There was a shadow in her eyes again of that strange look she had given me earlier.

"Nothing," she said. And then, still watching me strangely, she hesitated. "Or maybe—something, though the odds are billions to one against it. You'll know if you hear it, and I'll explain after the sixty seconds are up." She touched me lightly, requestingly on the arm with one hand. "Now, please be quiet—for the sake of the others, even if you don't want to listen yourself."

"Oh, I'll listen," I told her.

I turned from her. And suddenly, over her shoulder, behind us, below me, small and far off by that entrance to the Index Room by which we had come in, I saw my sister, no longer with our group. I recognized her at that distance only by the pale color of her hair and her height. She was talking to a dark, slim man dressed all in black, whose face I could not make out at that distance, but who stood close to her.

I was startled and suddenly annoyed. The sight of the thin male figure in black seemed to slap at me like an affront. The very idea that my sister would drop behind our group to speak to someone else after begging me to bring her here—speak to someone who was a complete stranger to me, and speak as earnestly as I could see she was speaking, even at this distance, by the tenseness of her figure and the little movements of her hands—seemed to me like a discourtesy amounting to betrayal. After all, she had talked me into coming.

The hair on the back of my neck rose, a cold wave of anger rose in me. It was ridiculous; at that distance not even the best human ears ever born could have overheard their conversation, but I found myself straining against the enclosing silence of the vast room, trying to make out what it was they could be talking about.

And then—imperceptibly, but growing rapidly louder—I began to hear. Something.

Not my sister's voice, or the voice of the stranger, whoever he was. It was some distant, harsh voice of a man speaking in a language a little like Latin, but with dropped vowels and rolled *r*'s that gave his talk a mutter, like the rapid rolling of the summer thunder that accompanies heat lightning. And it grew, not so much louder, as closer—and then I heard another voice, answering it.

And then another voice. And another, and another and another.

Roaring, shouting, leaping, like an avalanche, the voices leaped suddenly upon me from every direction, growing wildly greater in number every second, doubling and redoubling—all the voices in all the languages of all the world, all the voices that had ever been in the world—and more than that. More—and more—and more.

They shouted in my ear, babbling, crying, laughing, cursing, ordering, submitting—but not merging, as such a multitude should, at last into one voiceless, if mighty, thunder like the roar of a waterfall. More and more as they grew, they still remained all separate. *I heard each one! Each one* of those millions, those billions of men's and women's voices shouted individually in my ears.

And the tumult lifted me at last as a feather is lifted on the breast of a hurricane, swirling me up and away out of my senses into a raging cataract of unconsciousness.

CHAPTER 3 ■

I remember I did not want to wake up. It seemed to me I had been on a far voyage, that I had been away a long time. But when, at last, reluctantly, I opened my eyes, I was lying on the floor of the chamber and only Lisa Kant was bending over me. Some of the others in our party had not yet finished turning around to see what had happened to me.

Lisa was raising my head from the floor.

"You *heard*!" she was saying, urgently and low-voiced, almost in my ear. "What did you hear?"

"Hear?" I shook my head, dazedly, remembering at that, and almost expecting to hear that uncountable horde of voices flooding back in on me. But there was only silence now, and Lisa's question. "Hear?" I said. "—them."

"Them?"

I blinked my eyes up at her and abruptly my mind

cleared. All at once, I remembered my sister Eileen; and I scrambled to my feet, staring off into the distance at the entrance by which I had seen her standing with the man in black. But the entrance and the space about it was empty. The two of them, together—they were gone.

I scrambled to my feet. Shaken, battered, torn loose from my roots of self-confidence by that mighty cataract of voices in which I had been plunged and carried away, the mystery and disappearance of my sister shook me now out of all common sense. I did not answer Lisa, but started at a run down the ramp for the entrance where I had last seen Eileen talking to the stranger in black.

Fast as I was, with my longer legs, Lisa was faster. Even in the blue robes, she was as swift as a track star. She caught up with me, passed me and swung around to bar the entrance as I reached it.

"Where are you going?" she cried. "You can't leave—just yet! If you heard something, I've got to take you to see Mark Torre himself! He has to talk to anyone who ever hears anything!"

I hardly heard her.

"Get out of my way," I muttered, and I pushed her aside, not gently. I plunged on through the entrance into the circular equipment room beyond the entrance. There were technicians at work in their colored smocks, doing incomprehensible things to inconceivable tangles of metal and glass—but no sign of Eileen, or the man in black.

I raced through the room into the corridor beyond. But that, too, was empty. I ran down the corridor and turned right into the first doorway I came to. From desks and tables a few people, reading and transcribing, looked up at me in wonder, but Eileen and the stranger were not among them. I tried another room and another, all without success.

At the fifth room, Lisa caught up with me again.

"Stop!" she said. And this time she took actual hold of me, with a strength that was astonishing for a girl no larger than she was. "Will you stop?—And think for a moment? What's the matter?"

"Matter!" I shouted. "My sister—" and then I stopped. I checked my tongue. All at once it swept over me how foolish it would sound if I told Lisa the object of my search. A seventeen-year-old girl talking to, and even going off from a group with, someone her older brother does not know, is hardly good reason for a wild chase and a frantic search—at least in this day and age. And I was not of any mind to rehearse for Lisa's benefit the cold unhappiness of our upbringing, Eileen's and mine, in the house of my uncle Mathias.

I stood silent.

"You have to come with me," she said urgently after a second. "You don't know how terribly, inconceivably rare it is when someone actually hears something at the Transit Point. You don't know how much it means now to Mark Torre—to Mark Torre, himself—to find someone who's heard!"

I shook my head numbly. I had no wish to talk to anyone about what I had just been through, and least of all to be examined like some freak experimental specimen.

"You have to!" repeated Lisa. "It means so much. Not just to Mark, to the whole project. Think! Don't just run off! Think about what you're doing first!"

The word "think" got through to me. Slowly my

mind cleared. It was quite true what she said. I should think instead of running around like someone out of his wits. Eileen and the black-dressed stranger could be in any one of dozens of rooms or corridors—they could even be on their way out of the Project and the Enclave completely. Besides, what would I have said if I had caught up with them, anyway? Demand that the man identify himself and state his intentions toward my sister? It was probably lucky I had not been able to find them.

Besides, there was something else. I had worked hard to get the contract I had signed three days ago, just out of the University, with the Interstellar News Services. But I had a far way to go yet, to the place of my ambitions. For what I had wanted—so long and so fiercely that it was as if the want was something live with claws and teeth tearing inside me—was freedom. Real freedom, of the kind possessed only by members of planetary governments—and one special group, the working Guild members of the Interstellar News Services. Those workers in the communications field who had signed their oath of nonallegiance and were technically people without a world, in guarantee of the impartiality of the News Services they operated.

For the inhabited worlds of the human race were split—as they had been split for two hundred years now—into two camps, one which held their populations to "tight" contracts and the other who believed in the so-called loose contract. Those on the tight-contract side were the Friendly worlds of Harmony and Association, Newton, Cassida and Venus, and the big new world of Ceta under Tau Ceti. On the loose side were ranged Earth, the Dorsai, the Exotic worlds of Mara and Kultis, New Earth, Freiland, Mars and the small Catholic world of Ste. Marie.

What divided them was a conflict of economic systems—an inheritance of the divided Earth that had originally colonized them. For in our day interplanetary currency was only one thing—and that was the coin of highly trained minds.

The race was now too big for a single planet to train all of its own specialists, particularly when other worlds produced better. Not the best education Earth or any other world could provide could produce a professional soldier to match those turned out by the Dorsai. There were no physicists like the physicists from Newton, no psychologists like those from the Exotics, no conscript hired troops as cheap and careless of casualty losses as those from Harmony and Association—and so on. Consequently, a world trained one kind or type of professional and traded his services by contract to another world for the contract and services of whatever type of other professional the world needed.

And the division between the two camps of worlds was stark. On the "loose" worlds a man's contract belonged in part to him; and he could not be sold or traded to another world without his own consent—except in a case of extreme importance or emergency. On the "tight" worlds the individual lived at the orders of his authorities—his contract might be sold or traded at a moment's notice. When this happened, he had only one duty—and that was to go and work where he was ordered.

So, on all the worlds, there were the non-free and the partly free. On the loose worlds, of which as I say Earth was one, people like myself were partly free. But I wanted full freedom, of the sort only available to me as a Guild member. Once accepted into the Guild, this freedom would be mine. For the contract for my services would belong to the News Services, itself, during the rest of my lifetime.

No world after that would be able to judge me or sell my services, against my will, to some other planet to which it owed a deficit of trained personnel. It was true that Earth, unlike Newton, Cassida, Ceta and some of the others, was proud of the fact that it had never needed to trade off its university graduates in blocks for people with the special trainings of the younger worlds. But, like all the planets, Earth held the right to do so if it should ever become necessary—and there were plenty of stories of individual instances.

So, my goal and my hunger for freedom, which the years under the roof of Mathias had nourished in me, could be filled only by acceptance into the News Services. And in spite of my scholastic record, good as it was, that was still a far, hard, chancy goal to reach. I would need to overlook nothing that could help me to it; and it came to me now that refusing to see Mark Torre might well be to throw away a chance at such help.

"You're right," I said to Lisa. "I'll go and see him. Of course. I'll see him. Where do I go?"

"I'll take you," she answered. "Just let me phone ahead." She went a few steps away from me and spoke quietly into the small phone on her ring finger. Then she came back and led me off.

"What about the others?" I asked, suddenly remembering the rest of our party back in the Index Room.

"I've asked someone else to take them over for the rest of the tour," Lisa answered without looking at me. "This way."

She led me through a doorway off the hall and into a small light-maze. For a moment this surprised me and then I realized that Mark Torre, like anyone in the public eye constantly, would need protection from possibly dangerous crackpots and cranks. We came out of the maze into a small empty room, and stopped.

The room moved—in what direction, I could not say—and then stopped.

"This way," said Lisa again, leading me to one of the walls of the room. At her touch, a section of it folded back and let us into a room furnished like a study, but equipped with a control desk, behind which sat an elderly man. It was Mark Torre, as I had often seen him pictured in the news.

He was not as old in appearance as his age might have made him appear—he was past eighty at the time—but his face was gray and sick-looking. His clothes sat loosely on his big bones, as if he had weighed more once than he did now. His two really extraordinarily large hands lay limply on the little flat space before the console keys, their gray knuckles swollen and enlarged by what I later learned was an obscure disease of the joints called arthritis.

He did not get up when we came in, but his voice was surprisingly clear and young when he spoke and his eyes glowed at me with something like scarcely contained joy. Still he made us sit and wait, until after a few minutes another door to the room opened and there came in a middle-aged man from one of the Exotic worlds—an Exotic-born, with penetrating hazel-colored eyes in his smooth, unlined face under close-cropped white hair, and dressed in blue robes like those Lisa was wearing.

"Mr. Olyn," said Mark Torre, "this is Padma, OutBond from Mara to the St. Louis Enclave. He already knows who you are."

"How do you do?" I said to Padma. He smiled.

"An honor to meet you, Tam Olyn," he said and sat down. His light, hazel-colored eyes did not seem to stare at me in any way—and yet, at the same time, they made me uneasy. There was no strangeness about him—that was the trouble. His gaze, his voice, even the way he sat, seemed to imply that he knew me already as well as anyone could, and better than I would want anyone to know me, whom I did not know as well in return.

For all that I had argued for years against everything my uncle stood for, at that moment I felt the fact of Mathias' bitterness against the peoples of the younger worlds lift its head also inside me, and snarl against the implied superiority in Padma, OutBond from Mara to the Enclave at St. Louis, on Earth. I wrenched my gaze away from him and looked back at the more human, Earth-born eyes of Mark Torre.

"Now that Padma's here," the old man said, leaning forward eagerly toward me over the keys of his control console, "what was it like? Tell us what you heard!"

I shook my head, because there was no good way of describing it as it really had been. Billions of voices, speaking at once, and all distinct, are impossible.

"I heard voices," I said. "All talking at the same time—but separate."

"Many voices?" asked Padma.

I had to look at him again.

"All the voices there are," I heard myself answering. And I tried to describe it. Padma nodded; but, as I talked I looked back at Torre, and saw him sinking into his seat away from me, as if in confusion or disappointment.

"Only . . . voices?" the old man said, half to himself when I was done.

"Why?" I asked, pricked into a little anger. "What was I supposed to hear? What do people usually hear?"

"It's always different," put in the voice of Padma soothingly from the side of my vision. But I would not look at him. I kept my eyes on Mark Torre. "Everyone hears different things."

I turned to Padma at that.

"What did *you* hear?" I challenged. He smiled a little sadly.

"Nothing, Tam," he said.

"Only people who are Earth-born have ever heard anything," said Lisa sharply, as if I should know this without needing to be told.

"You?" I stared at her.

"Me! Of course not!" she replied. "There's not half a dozen people since the Project started who've ever heard anything."

"Less than half a dozen?" I echoed.

"Five," she said. "Mark is one, of course. Of the other four, one is dead and the other three"—she hesitated, staring at me—"weren't fit."

There was a different note to her voice that I heard now for the first time. But I forgot it entirely as, abruptly, the figures she had mentioned struck home.

Five people only, in forty years! Like a body blow the message jarred me that what had happened to me in the Index Room was no small thing; and that this moment with Torre and Padma was not small either, for them as well as myself.

"Oh?" I said; and I looked at Torre. With an effort, I made my voice casual. "What does it mean, then, when someone hears something?"

He did not answer me directly. Instead he leaned forward with his dark old eyes beginning to shine brilliantly again, and stretched out the fingers of his large right hand to me.

"Take hold," he said.

I reached out in my turn and took his hand, feeling his swollen knuckles under my grasp. He gripped my hand hard and held on, staring at me for a long moment, while slowly the brilliance faded and finally went out; and then he let go, sinking back into his chair as if defeated.

"Nothing," he said dully, turning to Padma. "Still—nothing. You'd think he'd feel something—or I would."

"Still," said Padma, quietly, looking at me, "he heard."

He fastened me to my chair with his hazel-colored Exotic eyes.

"Mark is disturbed, Tam," he said, "because what you experienced was only voices, with no overburden of message or understanding."

"What message?" I demanded. "What kind of understanding?"

"That," said Padma, "you'd have to tell us." His glance was so bright on me that I felt uncomfortable, like a bird, an owl, pinned by a searchlight. I felt the hackles of my anger rising in resentment.

"What's this all got to do with you, anyway?" I asked.

He smiled a little.

"Our Exotic funds," he said, "bear most of the financial support of the Encyclopedia Project. But you must understand, it's not *our* Project. It's Earth's. We only feel a responsibility toward all work concerned with the understanding of Man by man, himself. Moreover, between our philosophy and Mark's there's a disagreement."

"Disagreement?" I said. I had a nose for news even then, fresh out of college, and that nose twitched.

But Padma smiled as if he read my mind.

"It's nothing new," he said. "A basic disagreement we've had from the start. Put briefly, and somewhat crudely, we on the Exotics believe that Man is improvable. Our friend Mark, here, believes that Earth man—Basic Man—is already improved, but hasn't been able to uncover his improvement yet and use it."

I stared at him.

"What's that got to do with me?" I asked. "And with what I heard?"

"It's a question of whether you can be useful to him—or to us," answered Padma calmly; and for a second my heart chilled. For if either the Exotics or someone like Mark Torre should put in a demand for my contract from the Earth government, I might as well kiss good-bye all hopes of working my way eventually into the News Services Guild.

"Not to either of you—I think," I said, as indifferently as I could.

"Perhaps. We'll see," said Padma. He held up his hand and extended upward his index finger. "Do you see this finger, Tam?"

I looked at it; and as I looked—suddenly it rushed toward me, growing enormously, blocking out the sight of everything else in the room. For the second time that afternoon, I left the here and now of the real universe for a place of unreality.

Suddenly, I was encompassed by lightnings. I was in darkness but thrown about by lightning strokes—in some vast universe where I was tossed light-years in distance, first this way and then that, as part of some gigantic struggle.

At first I did not understand it, the struggle. Then slowly I woke to the fact that all the lashing of the lightnings was a furious effort for survival and victory in answer to an attempt by the surrounding, ancient, ever-flowing darkness, to quench and kill the lightnings. Nor was this any random battle. Now I saw how there was ambush and defeat, stratagem and tactic, blow and counterblow, between the lightning and the dark.

Then, in that moment, came the memory of the sound of the billions of voices, welling up around me once more in rhythm to the lightnings, to give me the key to what I saw. All at once, in the way a real lightning-flash suddenly reveals in one glimpse all the land for miles around, in a flash of intuition I understood what surrounded me.

It was the centuries-old battle of man to keep his race alive and push forward into the future, the ceaseless, furious struggle of that beastlike, godlike—primitive, sophisticated—savage and civilized—composite organism that was the human race fighting to endure and push onward. Onward, and up, and up again, until the impossible was achieved, all barriers were broken, all pains conquered, all abilities possessed. Until all was lightning and no darkness left.

It was the voices of this continuing struggle down the hundreds of centuries that I had heard in the Index Room. It was this same struggle that the Exotics were attempting to encompass with their strange magics of the psychological and philosophical sciences. *This* struggle that the Final Encyclopedia was designed at last to chart throughout the past centuries of human existence, so that Man's path might be calculated meaningfully into his future.

This was what moved Padma, and Mark Torre—and everyone, including myself. For each human being was caught up in the struggling mass of his fellows and could not avoid the battle of life. Each of us living at this moment was involved in it, as its parts and its plaything.

But with that thought, suddenly, I became conscious that I was different, not just a plaything of this battle. I was something more—potentially an involved power in it, a possible lord of its actions. For the first time, then, I laid hands on the lightnings about me and began to try to drive, to turn and direct their movements, forcing them to my own ends and desires.

Still, I was flung about for unguessable distances. But no longer like a ship adrift upon a storm-wrenched sea, now like a ship close-hauled, using the wind to bear to windward. And in that moment for the first time it came upon me—the feeling of my own strength and power. For the lightnings bent at my grasp and their tossing shaped to my will. I felt it—that sensation of unchained power within me that is beyond description; and it came to me at last that indeed I had never been one of the tossed and buffeted ones. I was a rider, a Master. And I had it in me to shape at least part of all I touched in this battle between the lightnings and the dark.

Only then, at last, I became aware of rare others like myself. Like me they were riders and Masters. They, too, rode the storm that was the rest of the struggling mass of the human race. We would be flung together for a second, then torn measureless eons apart in the next moment. But I saw them. And they saw me. And I became conscious of the fact that they were calling to me, calling on me, not to fight for myself alone, but to join with them in some common effort to bring the whole battle to some future conclusion and order out of chaos.

But everything that was inherent in me rebelled against their call. I had been downtrodden and confounded too long. I had been the lightnings' helplessly buffeted subject for too long. Now I had won to the wild joy of riding where I had been ridden, and I gloried in my power. I did not want the common effort that might lead at last to peace, but only that the intoxicating whirl and surge and conflict should go on with me, like a fury, riding the breast of it. I had been chained and enslaved by my uncle's darkness but now I was free and a Master. Nothing should bring me to put on chains again. I stretched out my grasp on the lightnings and felt that grasp move wider and grow stronger, wider and stronger yet.

—Abruptly, I was back in the office of Mark Torre.

Mark, his aging face set like wood, stared at me. Whitefaced, Lisa also stared in my direction. But, directly before me, Padma sat looking into my eyes with no more expression than he had shown before.

"No," he said, slowly. "You're right, Tam. You can't be any help here on the Encyclopedia."

There was a faint sound from Lisa, a little gasp, almost a tiny cry of pain. But it was drowned in a grunt from Mark Torre, like the grunt of a mortally wounded bear, cornered at last, but turning to raise up on his hind legs and face his attackers.

"Can't?" he said. He had straightened up behind his desk and now he turned to Padma. His swollen right hand was cramped into a great, gray fist on the table. "He must—he has to be! It's been twenty years since anyone heard anything in the Index Room—and I'm getting old!"

"All he heard was the voices; and they touched no special spark in him. You felt nothing when you touched him," said Padma. He spoke softly and distantly, the words coming out one by one, like soldiers marching under orders. "It's because there's nothing there. No identity in him with his fellowman. He has all the machinery, but no empathy—no power source hooked to it."

"You can fix him! Damn it"—the old man's voice rang like a steeple bell, but it was hoarse to the point of tears—"on the Exotics you can heal him!"

Padma shook his head.

"No," he said. "No one can help him but himself. He's not ill or crippled. He's only failed to develop. Once, some time when he was young, he must have turned away from people into some dark, solitary valley of his own, and over the years that valley's grown deeper and darker and more narrow, until now no one can get down there beside him to help him through it. No other mind could go through it and survive—maybe even his can't. But until he does and comes out the other end, he's no good to you or the Encyclopedia; and all it represents for men on Earth and elsewhere. Not only is he no good, he wouldn't take your job if you offered it to him. Look at him.''

The pressure of his gaze all this time, the low, steady utterance of his words, like small stones dropped one after the other into a calm, but bottomless pool of water, had held me paralyzed even while he talked about me as if I were not there. But with his last three words, the pressure from him let up; and I found myself free to speak.

''You hypnotized me!'' I flung at him. ''I didn't give you any permission to put me under—to psychoanalyze me!''

Padma shook his head.

''No one hypnotized you,'' he answered. ''I just opened a window for you to your own inner awareness. And I didn't psychoanalyze you.''

''Then what was it—'' I checked myself, abruptly wary.

''Whatever you saw and felt,'' he said, ''were your own awarenesses and feelings translated into your own symbols. And what those were I've no idea—and no way of finding out, unless you tell me.''

''Then how did you make up your mind to whatever it was you decided here?'' I snarled at him.

"You decided it fast enough. How'd you find out whatever it was made you decide?"

"From you," he answered. "Your looks, your actions, your voice as you talk to me now. A dozen other unconscious signals. These tell me, Tam. A human being communicates with his whole body and being, not just his voice, or his facial expression."

"I don't believe it!" I flared—and then my fury suddenly cooled as caution came on me with the certainty that indeed there must be grounds, even if I could not figure them out at the moment, for my not believing it. "I don't believe it," I repeated, more calmly and coldly. "There had to be more going into your decision than that."

"Yes," he said. "Of course. I had a chance to check the records here. Your personal history, like that of everyone Earthborn who's alive at this moment, is already in the Encyclopedia. I looked at that before I came in."

"More," I said grimly, for I felt I had him on the run now. "There was more to it even than that. I can tell. I know it!"

"Yes," answered Padma and breathed out softly. "Having been through this much, you'd know it, I suppose. In any case, you'd learn it soon enough by yourself." He lifted his eyes to focus squarely on mine, but this time I found myself facing him without any feeling of inferiority.

"It happens, Tam," he said, "that you're what we call an Isolate, a rare pivotal force in the shape of a single individual—a pivotal force in the evolving pattern of human society, not just on Earth, but on all the sixteen worlds, in their road to Man's future.

You're a man with a terrible capability for affecting that future—for good or ill.''

At his words my hands remembered the feel of their grasp on the lightning; and I waited, holding my breath to hear more. But he did not go on.

"And—'' I prompted harshly, at last.

"There is no 'and,' '' said Padma. "That's all there is to it. Have you ever heard of ontogenetics?''

I shook my head.

"It's a name for one of our Exotic calculative techniques,'' he said. "Briefly, there's a continually evolving pattern of events in which all living human beings are caught up. In mass, the strivings and desires of these individuals determine the direction of growth of the pattern into the future. But, again as individuals only, nearly all people are more acted upon, than act effectively upon the pattern.''

He paused, staring at me, as if asking me if I had understood him so far. I had understood—oh, I had understood. But I would not let him know that.

"Go on,'' I said.

"Only now and then, in the case of some rare individual,'' he continued, "do we find a particular combination of factors—of character and the individual's position within the pattern—that combined make him inconceivably more effective than his fellows. When this happens, as in your case, we have an Isolate, a pivotal character, one who has great freedom to act upon the pattern, while being acted upon only to a relatively small degree, himself.''

He stopped again. And this time he folded his hands. The gesture was final and I took a deep breath to calm my racing heart.

"So," I said. "I've got all this—and still you don't want me for whatever it is you want me?"

"Mark wants you to take over from him, eventually, as Controller, building the Encyclopedia," said Padma. "So do we, on the Exotics. For the Encyclopedia is such a device that its full purpose and use, when completed, can only be conceived of by rare individuals; and that conception can only be continually translated into common terms, by a unique individual. Without Mark, or someone like him to see its construction through at least until it is moved into space, the common run of humanity will lose the vision of the Encyclopedia's capabilities when it's finished. The work on it will run into misunderstandings and frustrations. It will slow down, finally stall, and then fall apart."

He paused and looked at me, almost grimly.

"It will never be built," he said, "unless a successor for Mark is found. And without it, Earth-born man may dwindle and die. And if Earth-born man goes, the human strains of the younger worlds may not be viable. But none of this matters to you, does it? Because it's you who don't want us, not the other way around."

He stared across the room with eyes that burned with a hazel flame against me.

"You don't want us," he repeated slowly. "Do you, Tam?"

I shook off the impact of his gaze. But in the same moment I understood what he was driving at, and knew he was right. In that same moment I had seen myself seated in the chair at the console before me, chained there by a sense of duty for the rest of my days. No, I did not want them, or their works, on Encyclopedia or anywhere else. I wanted none of it.

Had I worked this hard, this long, to escape Mathias, only to throw everything aside and become a slave to helpless people—all those in that great mass of the human race who were too weak to fight the lightning for themselves? Should I give up the prospect of my own power and freedom to work for the misty promise of freedom for *them*, someday—for them, who could not earn that freedom for themselves, as I could earn my own, and had? No, I would not—I would not, I would have no part of them, of Torre or his Encyclopedia!

"No!" I said harshly. And Mark Torre made a faint, rattling sound deep in his throat, like a dying echo of the wounded grunt he had given earlier.

"No. That's right," said Padma, nodding. "You see, as I said, you've got no empathy—no soul."

"Soul?" I said. "What's that?"

"Can I describe the color of gold to a man blind from birth?" His eyes were brilliant upon me. "You'll know it if you find it—but you'll find it only if you can fight your way through that valley I mentioned. If you come through that, finally, then maybe you'll find your human soul. You'll know it when you find it."

"Valley," I echoed, at last. "What valley?"

"You know, Tam," said Padma more quietly. "You know, better than I do. That valley of the mind and spirit where all the unique creativity in you is now turned—warped and twisted—toward destruction."

"DESTRUCT!"

There it thundered, in the voice of my uncle, ringing in the ear of my memory, quoting, as Mathias always did, from the writings of Walter Blunt. Suddenly, as if printed in fiery letters on the inner surface of my skull, I saw the power and possibilities of that word to me, on the path I wanted to travel.

And without warning, in my mind's eye, it was as if the valley of which Padma had been speaking became real around me. High black walls rose on either side of me. Straight ahead was my route and narrow—and downward. Abruptly, I was afraid, as of something at the deepest depth, unseen in the farther darkness beyond, some blacker-than-black stirring of amorphous life that lay in wait for me there.

But, even as I shuddered away from this, from somewhere inside me a great, shadowy, but terrible joy swelled up at the thought of meeting it. While, as if from a great distance above me, like a weary bell, came the voice of Mark Torre sadly and hoarsely tolling at Padma.

"No chance for us, then? There's nothing at all we can do? What if he never comes back to us, and the Encyclopedia?"

"You can only wait—and hope he does," Padma's voice was answering. "If he can go on and down and through what he has created for himself, and survive, he may come back. But the choice has always been up to him, heaven or hell, as it is to all of us. Only his choices are greater than ours."

The words pattered like nonsense against my ears, like the sound of a little gust of cold rain against some unfeeling surface like stone or concrete. I felt suddenly a great need to get away from them all, to get off by myself and think. I climbed heavily to my feet.

"How do I get out of here?" I asked thickly.

"Lisa," said Mark Torre, sadly. I saw her get to her feet.

"This way," she said to me. Her face was pale but expressionless, facing me for a moment. Then she turned and went before me.

So she led me out of that room and back the way we had come. Down through the light-maze and the rooms and corridors of the Final Encyclopedia Project and at last to the outer lobby of the Enclave, where our group had first met her. All the way she did not say a word; but when I left her at last, she stopped me unexpectedly, with a hand on my arm. I turned back to face down at her.

"I'm always here," she said. And I saw to my astonishment that her brown eyes were brimming with tears. "Even if no one else is—*I'm* always here!"

Then she turned swiftly and almost ran off. I stared after her, unexpectedly shaken. But so much had happened to me in the past hour or so that I did not have the time or desire to try to discover why, or figure out what the girl could have meant by her strange words, echoing her strange words earlier.

I took the subway back into St. Louis and caught a shuttle flight back to Athens, thinking many things.

So wound up I was in my own thoughts that I entered my uncle's house and walked clear into its library before I was aware of people already there.

Not merely my uncle, seated in his high wing chair, with an old leather-bound book spread open, face down and ignored on his knees, and not only my sister, who had evidently returned before me, standing to one side and facing him, from about ten feet away.

Also in the room was a thin, dark young man some inches shorter than myself. The mark of his Berber ancestry was plain to anyone who, like myself, had been required in college to study ethnic origins. He was dressed all in black, his black hair was cut short above his forehead, and he stood like the upright blade of an unsheathed sword.

He was the stranger I had seen Eileen talking to at the Enclave. And the dark joy of the promised meeting in the valley's depths leaped up again in me. For here, waiting, without my need to summon it, was the first chance to put to use my newly discovered understanding and my strength.

CHAPTER 4 ■

It was a square of conflict.

So much already of the discovery I had made in the place of lightning was already beginning to work in my conscious mind. But almost immediately, this new acuteness of perception in me was momentarily interrupted by recognition of my own personal involvement in the situation.

Eileen threw me one white-faced glance as she saw me, but then looked directly back at Mathias, who sat neither white-featured nor disturbed. His expressionless, spade-shaped face, with its thick eyebrows and thick hair, still uniformly black although he was in his late fifties, was as cold and detached as usual. He, also, looked over at me, but only casually, before turning to meet Eileen's emotional gaze.

"I merely say," he said to her, "that I don't see why you should bother to ask me about it. I've never placed any restraints on you, or Tam. Do what you want.'' And his fingers closed on the book that was face down on his knees as if he would pick it up again and resume reading.

"Tell me what to do!" cried Eileen. She was close to tears and her hands were clenched into fists at her sides.

''There's no point in my telling you what to do,'' said Mathias remotely. ''Whatever you do will make no difference—to you or me, or even to this young man, over here—'' he broke off and turned to me. ''Oh, by the way, Tam. Eileen's forgotten to introduce you. This visitor of ours is Mr. Jamethon Black, from Harmony.''

''Force-Leader Black,'' said the young man turning to me his thin, expressionless face. ''I'm on attaché duty here.''

At that, I identified his origin. He was from one of the worlds called, in sour humor by the people of the other worlds, the Friendlies. He would be one of the religious, spartan-minded zealots who made up the population of those worlds. It was strange, very strange it seemed to me then, that of all the hundreds of types and sorts of human societies which had taken seed on the younger planets, that a society of religious fanatics should turn out, along with the soldier type of the Dorsai World, the philosopher type of the Exotics, and the hard-science-minded people of Newton and Venus, to be one of the few distinct great Splinter Cultures to grow and flourish as human colonies between the stars.

And a distinct Splinter Culture they were. Not of soldiers,· for all that the other fourteen worlds heard of them most often as that. The Dorsai were soldiers—men of war to the bone. The Friendlies were men of Devotion—if grim and hair-shirt devotion—who hired themselves out because their resource-poor worlds had little else to export for the human contractual balances that would allow them to hire needed professionals from other planets.

There was small market for evangelists—and this was the only crop that the Friendlies grew naturally on their thin, stony soil. But they could shoot and obey orders—to the death. And they were cheap. Eldest Bright, First on the Council of Churches ruling Harmony and Association, could underbid any other government in the supplying of mercenaries. Only—never mind the military skill of those mercenaries.

The Dorsai were true men of war. The weapons of battle came to their hands like tame dogs, and fitted their hands like gloves. The common Friendly soldier took up a gun as he might take up an axe or a hoe—as a tool needing to be wielded for his people and his church.

So that those who knew said it was the Dorsai who supplied soldiers to the sixteen worlds. The Friendlies supplied cannon fodder.

However, I did not speculate upon that, then. In that moment my reaction to Jamethon Black was only one of recognition. In the darkness of his appearance and his being, in the stillness of his features, the remoteness, the somehow *impervious* quality like that which Padma possessed—in all these I read him plainly, even without my uncle's introduction, as one of the superior breed from the younger worlds. One of those with whom, as Mathias had always proved to us, it was impossible for an Earth man to compete. But the preternatural alertness from my just-concluded experience at the Encyclopedia Project was back with me again, and it occurred to me with that same dark and inner joy that there were other ways than competition.

". . . Force-Leader Black," Mathias was saying, "has been taking a night course in Earth history—the same course Eileen was in—at Geneva University. He and Eileen met about a month ago. Now, your sister thinks she'd like to marry him, and go back to Harmony with him when he's transferred home at the end of this week."

Mathias' eyes looked over at Eileen.

"I've been telling her it's up to her, of course," he finished.

"But I want someone to help me—help me decide what's right!" burst out Eileen piteously.

Mathias shook his head, slowly.

"I told you," he said, with his usual, lightless calm of voice, "that there's nothing to decide. The decision makes no difference. Go with this man—or not. In the end it'll make no difference either to you or anyone else. You may cling to the absurd notion that what you decide affects the course of events. I don't—and just as I leave you free to do as you want and play at making decisions, I insist you leave me free to do as I want, and engage in no such farce."

With that, he picked up his book, as if he was ready to begin reading again.

The tears began to run down Eileen's cheeks.

"But I don't know—I don't know what to do!" she choked.

"Do nothing then," said our uncle, turning a page of his book. "It's the only civilized course of action, anyway."

She stood, silently weeping. And Jamethon Black spoke to her.

"Eileen," he said, and she turned toward him. He spoke in a low, quiet voice, with just a hint of different rhythm to it. "Do you not want to marry me and make your home on Harmony?"

"Oh, yes, Jamie!" she burst out. "Yes!"

He waited, but she did not move toward him. She burst out again.

"I'm just not sure it's right!" she cried. "Don't you see, Jamie, I want to be sure I'm doing the right thing. And I don't know—I don't *know*!"

She whirled about to face me.

"Tam!" she said. "What should I do? Should I go?"

Her sudden appeal to me rang in my ears like an echo of the voices that had poured in on me in the Index Room. All at once the library in which I stood and the scene within it seemed to lengthen and brighten strangely. The tall walls of bookshelves, my sister, tear-streaked, appealing to me, the silent young man in black—and my uncle, quietly reading, as if the pool of soft light about him from the shelves behind him was some magic island moated off from all human responsibilities and problems—all these seemed suddenly to reveal themselves in an extra dimension.

It was as if I saw through them and around them all in the same moment. Suddenly I understood my uncle as I had never understood him before, understood that for all his pretense of reading he had already worked to decide which way I should jump in answer to Eileen's question.

He knew that had he said "Stay" to my sister, I would have gotten her out of that house by main force if necessary. He knew it was my instinct to oppose him in everything. So, by doing nothing, he was leaving me nothing to fight against. He was retreating into his devil-like (or godlike) indifference, leaving me to be humanly fallible, and decide. And, of course, he believed I would second Eileen's wish to go with Jamethon Black.

But this once he had mistaken me. He did not see the change in me, my new knowledge that pointed the way to me. To him, *"Destruct!"* had been only an empty shell into which he could retreat. But I now, with a sort of fever-brightness of vision, saw it as something far greater—a weapon to be turned even against these superior demons of the younger worlds.

I looked across at Jamethon Black now, and I was not awed by him, as I had ceased to be awed by Padma. Instead, I could not wait to test my strength against him.

"No," I said quietly to Eileen, "I don't think you should go."

She stared at me, and I realized that unconsciously she had reasoned as my uncle had, that I must end up telling her to do what her heart wanted. But I had struck her all adrift now; and I went eagerly ahead to anchor my judgment firmly in those things she believed, choosing my words with care.

They came easily to my mind.

"Harmony's no place for you, Eileen," I said gently. "You know how different they are from us, here on Earth. You'd be out of place. You couldn't measure up to them and their ways. And besides, this man's a Force-Leader." I made myself look across sympathetically at Jamethon Black; and his thin face looked back at me, as free of any resentment or pleading for my favor as the blade of an axe.

"Do you know what that means, on Harmony?" I said. "He's an officer in their military forces. At any moment his contract may be sold, away from you. He may be sent places you can't follow. He may not come back for years—or ever at all, if he's killed, which is likely. Do you want to let yourself in for that?'' And I added brutally, ''Are you strong enough to take that kind of emotional punching, Eileen? I've lived with you all your life and I don't think so. You'd not only let yourself down, you'd let this man down.''

I stopped talking. My uncle had not looked up from his book all this time, and he did not look up now; but I thought—and I took a secret satisfaction from it—that his grip upon its covers trembled a little, in betrayal of feelings he had never admitted having.

As for Eileen, she had been staring at me unbelievingly all the time I talked. Now, she gave one heavy gasp that was almost a sob, and straightened up. She looked toward Jamethon Black.

She did not say anything. But that look was enough. I was watching him, too, for some betraying sign of emotion; but his face only saddened a little, in a gentle way. He took two steps toward her, until he was almost standing at her side. I stiffened, ready to shove myself between them if necessary to back up my opinion. But he only spoke to her, very softly, and in that odd, canting version of ordinary speech that I had read that his people used among themselves, but which had never fallen upon my ears before.

''Thou wilt not come with me, Eileen?'' he said.

She shook, like a light-stemmed plant in unfirm ground when a heavy step comes by, and looked away from him.

''I can't, Jamie,'' she whispered. ''You heard what Tam said. It's true. I'd let you down.''

''It is not true,'' he said, still in the same low voice.

"Do not say you cannot. Say you will not, and I will go."

He waited. But she only continued to stare away from him, refusing to meet his gaze. And then, finally, she shook her head.

He drew a deep breath at that. He had not looked at me or Mathias since I had finished speaking; and he did not look at either of us now. Still without pain or fury visible in his face, he turned and went softly out of the library, and out of the house and my sister's sight forever.

Eileen turned and ran from the room. I looked at Mathias; and he turned a page of his book, not looking up at me. He never referred to Jamethon Black or the incident again, afterward.

Nor did Eileen.

But less than six months later she quietly entered her contract for sale to Cassida and was shipped off to a job on that world. A few months after she arrived she married a young man, a native of the planet named David Long Hall. Neither Mathias nor I heard about it until some months after the marriage had taken place, and then from another source. She, herself, did not write.

But by that time I was as little concerned with the news of it as was Mathias, for my success with Jamethon Black and my sister in that moment in the library had pointed me the way I wanted. My new perception was beginning to harden in me. I had begun to evolve techniques to put it to work to manipulate people, as I had manipulated Eileen, to gain what I wanted; and already I was hot on the road to my personal goal of power and freedom.

CHAPTER 5 ■

Yet, it turned out that the scene in the library was to stick in my mind like a burr, after all.

For five years, while I climbed through the ranks of the News Service like a man born to succeed, I had no word from Eileen. She still did not write Mathias; and she did not write me. The few letters I wrote her went unanswered. I knew many people, but I could not say I had any friends—and Mathias was nothing. Distantly, in one corner of me, I became slowly aware that I was alone in the world; and that in the first feverish flush of my discovered ability for manipulating people I might well have chosen a different target than the one person on sixteen worlds who might have had some reason to love me.

It was this, five years later, that brought me to a hillside on New Earth, recently torn up by heavy artillery. I was walking down it, for the hillside was part of a battlefield occupied only a few hours since by the mutually engaged forces of the North and South Partitions of Altland, New Earth. The military both of the North and the South consisted of only a nucleus of native forces. That of the rebellious North was over eighty percent of mercenary Commands, hired from the Friendlies. That of the South was more than sixty-five percent of Cassidan levies, hired on contractual balance by the New Earth authorities from Cassida—and it was this latter fact that had me picking my way down among the torn earth and exploded tree trunks on the hillside. Among the levies in this particular command was a young Groupman named Dave Hall—the man my sister had married on Cassida.

My guide was a foot soldier of the loyal, or South Partition Forces. Not a Cassidan but a native New Earthman, a cadreman-runner. He was a skinny individual, in his thirties and naturally sour-minded—as I gathered from the secret pleasure he seemed to take in getting my city boots and Newsman's cloak dirtied up in the earth and underbrush. Now, five years after my moment at the Final Encyclopedia, my personal skills had begun to harden in me, and by taking a few minutes out, I could have entirely rebuilt his opinion of me. But it was not worth it.

He brought me at last to a small message center at the foot of the hill, and turned me over to a heavy-jawed officer in his forties, with dark circles under his eyes. The officer was overage for such a field command and the fatigues of middle age were showing. Moreover, the grim Friendly legions had lately been having a good deal of pleasure with the half-trained Cassidan levies opposing them. It was small wonder he looked on me as sourly as had my guide.

Only, in the Commander's case his attitude posed a problem. I would have to change it to get what I was after. And the rub in changing it was that I had come out practically without data concerning this man. But there had been rumors of a new Friendly push and as time was short I had come here on the spur of the moment. I would have to make up my arguments as I went.

"Commandant Hal Frane!" He introduced himself without waiting for me to speak, and held out a square, somewhat dirty hand brusquely. "Your papers!"

I produced them. He looked them over with no softening of expression. "Oh?" he said. "Probationary?"

The question was tantamount to an insult. It was none of his business whether I was a full-fledged member of the Newsman's Guild, or still on trial as an Apprentice. The point he was making implied that I was probably still so wet behind the ears that I would be a potential danger to him and his men, up here in the front lines.

However, if he had only known it, by that question he had not so much attacked a soft spot in my own personal defenses, as revealed such a spot in his own.

"Right," I said calmly, taking the papers back from him. And I improvised on the basis of what he had just given away about himself. "Now, about your promotion—"

"Promotion!"

He stared at me. The tone of his voice confirmed all I had deduced, one of the little ways people betray themselves by their choice of the accusations they bring to bear on others. The man who hints that you are a thief is almost sure to have a large, vulnerable area of dishonesty in his own inner self; and in this case, Frane's attempt to needle me about my status undoubtedly assumed I was sensitive where he was sensitive. This attempt to insult, coupled with the fact that he was overage for the rank he held, indicated that he had been passed over at least once for promotion, and was vulnerable on the subject.

It was an opening wedge only—but all I needed, now, after five years of practicing my skills on people's minds.

"Aren't you up for promotion to Major?" I asked. "I thought—" I broke off abruptly, and grinned at him. "My mistake, I guess. I must have mixed you up with somebody else." I changed the subject, looking around the hillside. "I see you and your people had a rough time here, earlier today."

He broke in on me.

"Where'd you hear I'd been promoted?" he demanded, scowling at me. I saw it was time to apply a touch of the lash.

"Why, I don't think I remember, Commandant," I said, looking squarely back at him. I paused a minute to let that sink in. "And if I did, I don't suppose I'd be free to tell you. A Newsman's sources are privileged—they have to be, in my business. Just as the military has to have its secrecy."

That brought him to heel. Suddenly he was reminded that I was not one of his infantrymen. He had no authority to order me to tell him anything I didn't wish to tell him. I was a case calling for the velvet glove rather than the iron fist, if he wanted to get anything from me.

"Yes," he said, struggling to make the transition from scowling to smiling as gracefully as possible.

"Yes, of course. You've got to forgive me. We've been under fire a lot here."

"I can see that," I said more sympathetically. "Of course, that's not the sort of thing that leaves your nerves lying limp and easy."

"No." He managed a smile. "You—can't tell me anything about any promotion affecting me, then?"

"I'm afraid not," I said. Our eyes met again. And held.

"I see." He looked away, a little sourly. "Well, what can we do for you, Newsman?"

"Why, you can tell me about yourself," I answered. "I'd like to get some background on you."

He faced back at me suddenly.

"Me?" he said, staring.

"Why, yes," I said. "Just a notion of mine. A human-interest story—the campaign as seen from the viewpoint of one of the experienced officers in the field. You know."

He knew. I thought he did. I could see the light coming back into his eyes, and all but see the wheels turning in the back of his mind. We were at the point where a man of clear conscience would have once again demanded—"Why *me*, for a human-interest story, instead of some other officer of higher rank or more decorations?"

But Frane was not about to ask it. He thought he knew why *him*. His own buried hopes had led him to put two and two together to get what he thought was four. He was thinking that he must indeed be up for a promotion—a battlefield promotion. Somehow, although he could not right now think why, his recent conduct in the field must have put him in line for an extra grade in rank; and I was out here to make my human-interest story out of that. Being nothing but a civilian, he was reasoning, it would not have occurred to me that he, himself, might not yet have heard of the pending promotion; and my ignorance had caused me thoughtlessly to spill the beans on first meeting him.

It was a little disgusting the way his voice and attitude changed, once he had finished working this out to his own satisfaction. Like some people of inferior ability, he had spent his lifetime storing up reasons and excuses to prove that he was really possessed of extraordinary qualities, but that chance and prejudice had combined until now to keep him from his rightful rewards.

He proceeded then to tell me all these reasons and excuses, in the process of informing me about himself; and if I had been actually interviewing him for purposes of reportage I could have convicted him of his small soul and little worth, out of his own words, a dozen times over. There was a whine to his story as he told it. The real money in soldiering was in work as a mercenary, but all the good mercenary opportunities went either to men of the Friendlies, or the Dorsai. Frane did not have either the guts or the conviction to live the hair-shirt life of even a commissioned officer among the Friendlies. And, of course, the only way anyone could be a Dorsai was to be born one. That left only garrison work, cadre-work, officering the standby forces of worlds or political areas—only to be shoved aside for the top command posts when war did come, by the mercenaries born or built and imported for the actual fighting.

And garrison work, needless to say, paid a pittance compared to mercenary wages. A government could sign second-class officer material like Frane to long-term contracts at low salaries and hold them to it. But when the same government wanted mercenaries, it *needed* mercenaries; and every time it needed mercenaries, then quite naturally those who were in the business of laying their lives on the line for cash, drove hard bargains.

But enough about Commandant Frane, who was not that important. He was a little man who had now convinced himself that he was about to be recognized—in the Interstellar News Services at that—as a potentially big man. Like most of his kind he had a wildly inflated view of the usefulness of publicity in furthering a man's career. He told me all about himself, he showed me about the positions on the hillside where his men were dug in; and by the time I was ready to leave, I had him reacting like a well-tuned machine to my every suggestion. So, just as I was about to head back behind the lines, I made it— the one real suggestion I had come here to make.

"You know, I've just had an idea," I said, turning back to him. "Battle Headquarters has given me permission to pick out one of the enlisted men to assist me during the rest of the campaign. I was going to pick out one of the men from Headquarters Pool, but you know, it might be better to get one of the men from your Command."

"One of my men?" He blinked.

"That's right," I said. "Then if there's a request for a follow-up story on you or they want expansion of the original details about the campaign as you've seen it here, I could get the information from him. It wouldn't be practical to chase you all over the battlefield for things like that; otherwise I'd simply have to message back advising that follow-up or expansion wasn't possible.''

"I see," he said; and his face cleared. Then he frowned again. "It'll take a week or two to get a replacement up here so that I can let someone go, though. I don't see how—''

"Oh, that's all right," I said, and fished a paper out of my pocket. "I've got authority to pick up anyone I want without waiting for his replacement—if the Commandant lets him go, of course. You'd be a man short for a few days, naturally, but—''

I let him think about it. And for a moment he *was* thinking—with all the nonsense gone out of his head—just like any other military commander in such a position. All the Commands in this sector were understrength after the last few weeks of battle. Another man out meant a hole in Frane's line, and he was reacting to the prospect with the conditioned reflexes of any officer in the field.

Then I saw the prospect of promotion and publicity fight its way back to his attention, and the battle was joined in his head.

"Who?" he said at last, almost more to himself than to me. What he was asking himself was where he could best spare someone. But I took him up on it, as if the question had been all for me.

"There's a boy in your Command called Dave Hall—''

His head came up like a shot. Suspicion leaped into being, plain and short and ugly in his face. There are two ways to deal with suspicion—one is to protest your innocence, the other, and better, is to plead guilty to a lesser charge.

"I noticed his name on the Command roster when I was looking you up at Battle Headquarters, before I came up here to see you," I said. "To tell the truth, it was one of the reasons I *chose*"—I emphasized the word a little, so that he shouldn't miss it—"you for this writeup. He's a sort of shirt-tail relative of mine, this Dave Hall, and I thought I might as well kill two birds with one stone. The family's been after me to do something for the boy."

Frane stared at me.

"Of course," I said, "I know you're short-handed. If he's that valuable to you—"

If he's that valuable to you, my tone of voice hinted, *I won't think of arguing that you give him up. On the other hand, I'm the man who's going to be writing you up as a hero-type for the sixteen worlds to read, and if I sit down to my vocoder feeling you could have released my relative from the front lines, and didn't—*

He got the message.

"Who? Hall?" he said. "No, I can spare him, all right." He turned to his command post and barked, "Runner! Get Hall in here—full pack, weapons and equipment, ready to move out."

Frane turned back to me as the runner left.

"Take about five minutes to get him ready and up here," he said.

It took closer to ten. But I didn't mind waiting. Twelve minutes later, with our Groupman guide, we were on our way back to Battle Headquarters, Dave and I.

CHAPTER 6 ■

Dave had never seen me before, of course. But Ei-
leen must have described me, and it was plain he
recognized my name the minute the Commandant
turned him over to me. At that, though, he had sense
enough not to ask me any foolish questions until we
had made it back to Battle Headquarters and gotten
rid of that Groupman guiding us.

As a result I had a chance to study him myself on
the way in. He did not assay too highly on my first
examination of him. He was smaller than I, and
looked a good deal younger than the difference in
our ages should have made him. He had one of those
round, open faces under taffy-colored hair which
seem to look boyish right up into middle age. About
the only thing that I could see that he seemed to have
in common with my sister was a sort of inborn innocence and gentleness—that innocence and gentle-

ness of weak creatures who know they are too weak
to fight for their rights and win, and so try to make
the best of it by the willingness of their dependence
on the good will of others.

Or maybe I was being harsh. I was no denizen of
the sheepfold myself. You would rather find me outside, slinking along the fence and cocking a thoughtful eye at the inmates.

But it is true, Dave seemed nothing great to me as
far as appearance and character were concerned. I
do not think, either, that he was any great shakes
mentally. He had been an ordinary programmer when
Eileen had married him; and he had worked part
time, and she full time, these last five years trying
to get him through a Cassidan University schedule in
shift mechanics. He had had three years yet of work
to go when he fell below the seventy-percentile me-
dian on a competitive examination. It was his bad
luck that this should happen just at that moment when
Cassida was raising its levies for sale to New Earth
in the present campaign to put down the North Partition rebels. Away he went, in uniform.

You might think that Eileen had immediately ap-
pealed to me for help. No such thing—though the
fact that she had not, puzzled me, when I finally
heard of it. Though it should not have. She told me,
eventually, and the telling stripped my soul and left
its bare bones for the winds of rage and madness to
howl through. But that was later. Actually, the way
I found out about Dave going with the levies for New
Earth was because our uncle Mathias, quietly and
unexpectedly, died; and I was required to get in touch
with Eileen on Cassida about the estate.

Her small share of the estate (contemptuously, even

sneeringly, Mathias had left the bulk of his considerable fortune to The Final Encyclopedia Project as testimony that he thought any project concerning Earth and Earthmen so futile that no help could make it succeed) was no use to her unless I could make a private deal for her with some Earth-working Cassidan who had a family back on Cassida. Only governments or great organizations could translate planetary wealth into the human work-contracts that were actually transferable from one world to another. It was so that I learned that Dave had already left her and his native world for the ruckus on New Earth.

Even then, Eileen did not ask me for help. It was I who thought of asking for Dave as my assistant during the campaign and went ahead with it, merely writing to let her know what I was doing. Now that I had begun the deal, I was not at all sure why, myself, and even a little uncomfortable about it, as when Dave tried to thank me, after we finally got rid of our guide and headed in toward Molon, the nearest large city behind the lines.

"Save it!" I snapped at him. "All I've done for you so far's been the easy part. You're going to have to go into those lines with me as a noncombatant, carrying no weapons. And to do that, you've got to have a pass signed by both sides. That isn't going to be easy, for someone who was laying the sights of his spring-rifle on Friendly soldiers less than eight hours ago!"

He shut up at that. He was abashed. He was plainly hurt by the fact that I wouldn't let him thank me. But it stopped him talking and that was all I cared about.

We got orders cut by his Battle Headquarters, assigning him permanently to me; and then finished our ride by platform into Molon, where I left him in a hotel room with my gear, explaining that I'd be back for him in the morning.

"I'm to stay in the room?" he asked, as I was leaving.

"Do what you want, damn it!" I said. "I'm not your Groupman. Just be here by nine in the morning, local time, when I get back."

I went out. It was only after I closed the door behind me that I realized both what was driving him and eating me. He thought we might spend a few hours getting to know each other as brothers-in-law, and something in me set my teeth on edge at the prospect. I'd save his life for him for Eileen's sake, but that was no reason why I had to associate with him.

New Earth and Freiland, as everyone knows, are brother planets under the sun of Sirius. That makes them close—not so close as Venus-Earth-Mars clumping, naturally—but close enough so that from orbit New Earth you can make orbit Freiland in a single shift jump with a good but not excellent statistical chance of reaching your goal with minimum error. For those, then, who aren't afraid of a little risk in travel between the worlds, you can go from one planet to the other in about an hour—half an hour up to orbit station, no time at all for the jump, and half an hour down to surface at the end of the trip.

That was the way I went, and two hours after leaving my brother-in-law, I was showing my hard-wangled invitation to the doorman at the entrance of the establishment of Hendrik Galt, First Marshal of Freiland's battle forces.

The invitation was to a party being held for a man not so well known then as he has since become, a Dorsai (as Galt of course was a Dorsai) Space Sub-Patrol Chief named Donal Graeme. This was Graeme's first emergence into the public eye. He had just completed an utterly foolhardy attack on the planetary defenses of Newton, with something like four or five ships—an attack that had been lucky enough to relieve Newtonian pressure on Oriente, an uninhabited sister world of Freiland and New Earth, and get Galt's planetary forces out of a bad tactical hole.

He was, I judged at the time, a wild-eyed military gambler of some sort—his kind usually were. But my business, happily, was not with him, anyway. It was with some of the influential people who should be at this party of his.

In particular, I wanted the co-signature of the Freiland News Services Department Chief on Dave's papers—not that this would imply any actual protection extended to my brother-in-law by the News Services. That type of protection was extended only to Guild members and, with reservations, to apprentices on trial like myself. But to the uninitiate, like a soldier in the field, it might well look as if News Service protection was implied. Then, in addition, I wanted the signature of someone ranking among the Friendly mercenaries, for Dave's protection, in case he and I should fall in with some of their soldiers on the battlefield during the campaign.

I found the News Services Department Chief, a reasonable pleasant Earthman named Nuy Snelling, without difficulty. He gave me no trouble about noting on Dave's pass that the News Services agreed to Dave's assisting me and signing the message.

"Of course you know," he said, "this isn't worth a hoot." He eyed me curiously, as he handed the pass back. "This Dave Hall some friend of yours?"

"Brother-in-law," I answered.

"Hmm," he said, raising his eyebrows. "Well, good luck." And he turned away to talk to an Exotic in blue robes—who, with a sudden shock, I recognized as Padma.

The shock was severe enough so that I committed an imprudence I had not been guilty of for several years, at least, that of speaking without thinking.

"Padma—OutBond!" I said, the words jolted from me. "What are you doing here?"

Snelling, stepping back so as to have both of us in view at once, raised his eyebrows again. But Padma answered before my superior in the Services could take me to task for a pretty obvious rudeness. Padma was under no compulsion to account to me for his whereabouts. But he did not seem to take offense.

"I could ask you the same thing, Tam," he said, smiling.

I had my wits back by that time.

"I go where the news is," I answered. It was the stock News Services answer. But Padma chose to take it literally.

"And, in a sense, so do I," he said. "Remember I spoke to you once about a pattern, Tam? This place and moment is a locus."

I did not know what he was talking about; but having begun the conversation, I could not let go of it easily.

"Is that so?" I said smiling. "Nothing to do with me, I hope?"

"Yes," he said. And all at once I was aware once more of his hazel eyes, looking at and deep into me. "But more with Donal Graeme."

"That's only fair, I suppose," I said, "since the party's in his honor." And I laughed, while trying to think of some excuse to escape. Padma's presence was making the skin crawl at the back of my neck. It was as if he had some occult effect on me, so that I could not think clearly when he was present. "By the way, whatever happened to that girl who brought me to Mark Torre's office that day? Lisa . . . Kant, I think her name was."

"Yes, Lisa," said Padma, his eyes steady on me. "She's here with me. She's my personal secretary now. I imagine you'll bump into her shortly. She's concerned about saving you."

"Saving him?" put in Snelling, lightly, but interestedly enough. It was his job, as it was the job of all full Guild members, to observe the Apprentices for anything that might affect their acceptability into the Guild.

"From himself," said Padma, his hazel eyes still watching me, as smoky and yellow as the eyes of a god or a demon.

"Then, I'd better see if I can't look her up myself and let her get on with it," I said lightly in my turn, grasping at the opportunity to get away. "I'll see you both later perhaps."

"Perhaps," said Snelling. And I went off.

As soon as I had lost myself in the crowd, I ducked toward one of the entrances to the stairways leading up to the small balconies that looked down around the walls of the room, like opera boxes in a theater. It was no plan of mine to be trapped by that strange girl, Lisa Kant, whom I remembered with too much vividness anyway. Five years before, after the occasion at the Final Encyclopedia, I had been bothered, time and again, by the desire to go back to the Enclave and look her up. And, time and again, something like a fear had stopped me.

I knew what the fear was. Deep in me was the irrational feeling that the perception and ability I had been evolving for handling people, as I had first handled my sister in the library with Jamethon Black, and as I had later handled all who got in my path right up to Commandant Frane, earlier that same day and a world away—deep in me, I say, was the fear that something would rob me of this power in the face of any attempt of mine to handle Lisa Kant.

Therefore, I found a stairway and ran up it, onto a little, deserted balcony with a few chairs around a circular table. From here I should be able to spot Eldest Bright, Chief Elder of the Joint Church Council that ruled both Friendly worlds of Harmony and Association. Bright was a Militant—one of the ruling Friendly churchmen who believed most strongly in war as a means to any end—and he had been paying a brief visit to New Earth to see how the Friendly mercenaries were working out for their New Earth employers. A scribble from him on Dave's pass would be better protection for my brother-in-law from the Friendly troops than five Commands of Cassidan armor.

I spotted him, after only a few minutes of searching the crowd milling about fifteen feet below me. He was clear across the large room, talking to a white-haired man—a Venusian or Newtonian by the look of him. I knew the appearance of Eldest Bright, as I knew the appearance of most interstellarly newsworthy people on the sixteen inhabited worlds. Just because I had made my way this far and fast by my own special talents, did not mean I had not also worked to learn my job. But, in spite of my knowledge, my first sight of Eldest Bright was still a shock.

I had not realized how strangely powerful for a churchman he would look in the flesh. Bigger than myself, with shoulders like a barn door and—though he was middle-aged—a waist like a sprinter. He stood, dressed all in black, with his back to me and his legs a little spread, the weight of him on the balls of his feet like a trained fighter. Altogether, there was something about the man, like a black flame of strength, that at the same time chilled me and made me eager to match wits with him.

One thing was certain, he would be no Commandant Frane to dance eagerly at the end of a string of words.

I turned to go down to him—and chance stopped me. If it *was* chance. I shall never know for sure. Perhaps it was a hypersensitivity planted in me by Padma's remark that this place and moment was a locus in the human pattern of development to which he had responsibility. I had affected too many people myself by just such subtle but apposite suggestion, to doubt that it might have been done to me, in this case. But I suddenly caught sight of a little knot of people almost below me.

One of the group was William of Ceta, Chief Entrepreneur of that huge, commercial, low-gravity planet under the sun of Tau Ceti. Another was a tall,

beautiful, quite good-looking girl named Anea Mar-
livana, who was the Select of Kultis for her generation, chief jewel of generations of Exotic breeding.
There was also Hendrik Galt, massive in his Marshal's dress uniform, and his niece Elvine. And there
was also another man, who could only be Donal
Graeme.

He was a young man in the uniform of a Sub-
Patrol Chief, an obvious Dorsai with the black hair
and strange efficiency of movement that character-
izes those people who are born to war. But he was
small for a Dorsai—no taller than I would have been,
standing next to him—and slim, almost unobtrusive.
Yet he caught my eye out of all that group; and, in
the same instant, glancing up, he saw me.

Our eyes met for a second. We were close enough
so that I should have been able to see the color of
his eyes—and that is what stopped me.

For their color was no color, no one color. They
were gray, or green, or blue, depending on what
shade you looked for in them. Graeme looked away
again, almost in the same instant. But I was held,
caught by the strangeness of eyes like that, in a moment of surprise and transferred attention; and the
delay of that moment was enough.

When I shook myself out of my trance and looked
back to where I had seen Eldest Bright, I discovered
him now drawn away from the white-haired man by
the appearance of an aide, a figure strangely familiar-
looking to me in its shape and posture, who was
talking animatedly to the Eldest of the Friendly
Worlds.

And, as I still stood watching, Bright spun about
on his heel; and, following the familiar-looking aide,

went rapidly from the room through a doorway which I knew led to the front hall and the entrance to Galt's establishment. He was leaving and I would lose my chance at him. I turned quickly, to rush down the stairs from the balcony and follow him before he could get away.

But my way was blocked. My moment of trans-fixed staring at Donal Graeme had tripped me up. Just coming up the stairs and reaching the balcony as I turned to leave was Lisa Kant.

CHAPTER 7 ∎

"Tam!" she said. "Wait! Don't go!"

I could not, without crowding past her. She blocked the narrow stairway. I stopped, irresolute, glancing over at the far entrance through which Bright and his aide had already disappeared. At once it became plain to me that I was already too late. The two of them had been moving fast. By the time I could get downstairs and across the crowded room, they would have already reached their transportation outside the establishment and been gone.

Possibly, if I had moved the second I saw Bright turn to leave—But probably, catching him, even then, would have been a lost cause. Not Lisa's arrival, but my own moment of wandered attention, on seeing the unusual eyes of Donal Graeme, had cost me my chance to obtain Bright's signature on Dave's pass.

I looked back at Lisa. Oddly, now that she had

actually caught up with me and we were face to face once more, I was glad of it, though I still had that fear which I mentioned earlier, that she would somehow render me ineffective.

"How'd you know I was here?" I demanded.

"Padma said you'd be trying to avoid me," she said. "You couldn't very well avoid me down on the main floor there. You had to be out of the way someplace, and there weren't any out-of-the-way places but these balconies. I saw you standing at the railing of this one just now, looking down."

She was a little out of breath from hurrying up the stairs, and her words came out in a rush.

"All right," I said. "You've found me. What do you want?"

She was getting her breath back now, but the flush of effort from her run up the stairs still colored her cheeks. Seen like this, she was beautiful, and I could not ignore the fact. But I was still afraid of her.

"Tam!" she said. "Mark Torre has to talk to you!"

My fear of her whined sharply upward in me, like the mounting siren of an alarm signal. I saw the source of her dangerousness to me in that moment. Either instinct or knowledge had armed her. Anyone else would have worked up to that demand slowly. But an instinctive wisdom in her knew the danger of giving me time to assess a situation, so that I could twist it to my own ends.

But I could be direct, too. I started to go around her, without answering. She stepped in my way, and I had to stop.

"What about?" I said harshly.

"He didn't tell me."

I saw a way of handling her attack then. I started laughing at her. She stared at me for a second, then flushed again and began to look very angry indeed.

"I'm sorry." I throttled down on the laughter; and at the same time, secretly, I was in fact truly sorry. For all I was forced to fight her off, I liked Lisa Kant too well to laugh so at her. "But what else could we talk about except the old business of my taking over on the Final Encyclopedia again? Don't you remember? Padma said you couldn't use me. I was all oriented toward"—I tasted the word, as it went out of my mouth—*"destruction."*

"We'll just have to take our chance on that." She looked stubborn. "Besides, it isn't Padma who decides for the Encyclopedia. It's Mark Torre, and he's getting old. He knows better than anyone else how dangerous it would be if he dropped the reins and there was no one there quickly to pick them up. In a year, in six months, the Project could founder. Or be wrecked by people outside it. Do you think your uncle was the only person on Earth who felt about Earth and the younger worlds' people the way he did?"

I stiffened, and a cold feeling came into my mind. She had made a mistake, mentioning Mathias. My face must have changed, too; because I saw her own face change, looking at me.

"What've you been doing?" Fury burst out in me all of a sudden. "Studying up on me? Putting tracers on my comings and goings?" I took a step forward and she backed instinctively. I caught her by the arm and held her from moving further. "Why chase me down *now*, after five years? How'd you know I was going to be here anyway?"

She stopped trying to pull away and stood still, with dignity.

"Let go of me," she said quietly. I did and she stepped back. "Padma told me you'd be here. He said that it was my last chance at you—he calculated it. You remember, he told you about ontogenetics."

I stared at her for a second, then snorted with harsh laughter.

"Come on, now!" I said. "I'm willing to swallow a lot about your Exotics. But don't tell me they can calculate exactly where anyone in the sixteen worlds is going to be ahead of time!"

"Not anyone!" she answered angrily. "*You.* You and a few like you—because you're a maker, not a made part of the pattern. The influences operating on someone who's moved about by the pattern are too far reaching, and too complicated to calculate. But *you* aren't at the mercy of outside influences. You have *choice*, overriding the pressures people and events bring to bear on you. Padma told you that five years ago!"

"And that makes me easier to predict instead of harder? Let's hear another joke."

"Oh, Tam!" she said, exasperated. "Of course it makes you easier. It doesn't take ontogenetics, hardly. You can almost do it yourself. You've been working for five years now to get Membership in the Newsman's Guild, haven't you? Do you suppose that hasn't been obvious?"

Of course, she was right. I had made no secret of my ambitions. There had been no reason to keep them secret. She read the admission in my expression.

"All right," she went on. "So now you've worked

your way up to Apprentice. Next, what's the quickest
and surest way for an Apprentice to win his way into
full Guild membership? To make a habit of being
where the most interesting news is breaking, isn't
that right? And what's the most interesting—if not
important—news on the sixteen worlds right now?
The war between the North and South Partitions on
New Earth. News of a war is always dramatic. So
you were bound to arrange to get yourself assigned
to cover this one, if you could. And you seem to be
able to get most things you want.''

I looked at her closely. All that she said was true
and reasonable. But, if so, why hadn't it occurred to
me before this that I could be so predictable? It was
like finding myself suddenly under observation by
someone with high-powered binoculars, someone
whose spying I had not even slightly suspected. Then
I realized something.

''But you've only explained why I'd be on New
Earth,'' I said slowly. ''Why would I be here,
though, at this particular party on Freiland?''

For the first time she faltered. She no longer
seemed sure in her knowledge.

''Padma . . .'' she said, and hesitated. ''Padma
says this place and moment is a locus. And, being
what you are you can perceive, and are drawn to,
loci—by your own desire to use them for your own
purposes.''

I stared at her, slowly absorbing this. And then,
as suddenly as a sheet of flame across my mind
leaped the connection between what she had just said
and what I had heard earlier.

''Locus—yes!'' I said tightly, taking a step toward
her again in my excitement. ''Padma said it was a

locus here. For Graeme—but for me, too! Why? What does it mean for me?''

"I . . ." she hesitated. "I don't know exactly, Tam. I don't think even Padma knows.''

"But something about it, and me, brought you here! Isn't that right?" I almost shouted at her. My mind was closing on the truth like a fox on a winded rabbit. "Why did you come hunting me now then? At this particular place and moment, as you call it! Tell me!''

"Padma . . ." she faltered. I saw then with the almost blinding light of my sudden understanding that she would have liked to lie about this, but something in her would not let her. "Padma . . . only found out everything he knows now because of the way the Encyclopedia's grown able to help him. It has given him extra data to use in his calculations. And recently, when he used that data, the results showed everything up as more complex—and important. The Encyclopedia's more important, to the whole human race, than he thought five years ago. And the danger of the Encyclopedia's never being finished is greater. And your own power of destruction . . .''

She ran down and looked at me, almost pleadingly as if asking me to excuse her from finishing what she had started to say. But my mind was racing, and my heart pounded with excitement.

"Go on!" I told her harshly.

"The power in you for destruction was greater than he had dreamed. But, Tam''—she broke in on herself quickly, almost frantically—"there was something else. You remember five years ago how Padma thought you had no choice but to go through that dark valley of yours to its very end? Well, that's not quite true. There *is* a chance—at this point in the pattern, here at this locus. If you'll think, and choose, and turn aside, there's a narrow way for you up out of the darkness. But you've got to turn sharply right now! You've got to give up this assignment you're on, no matter what it costs, and come back to Earth to talk to Mark Torre, right now!''

''Right now,'' I muttered, but I was merely echoing her words without thought, while listening to my racing mind. ''No,'' I said, ''never mind that. What is it I'm supposed to be turning my back on? What special destruction? I'm not planning anything like that—right now.''

''Tam!'' I felt her hand distantly on my arm, I saw her pale face staring tensely up at me, as if trying to get my attention. But it was as if these things registered on my senses from a long distance away. For if I was right—*if I was right*—then even Padma's calculations were testifying to the dark strength in me, that ability I had worked these five years to harness and drive. And if such power were actually mine, what couldn't I do next?

''But it isn't what you *plan*!'' Lisa was saying desperately. ''Don't you see, a gun doesn't plan to shoot anyone. But it's in you, Tam, like a gun ready to go off. Only, you don't have to let it go off. You can change yourself while there's still time. You can save yourself, and the Encyclopedia—''

The last word rang suddenly through me, with a million echoes. It rang like the uncounted voices I had heard five years ago at the Transit Point of the Index Room in the Encyclopedia itself. Suddenly, through all the excitement holding me, it reached and touched me as sharply as the point of a spear. Like a brilliant shaft of light it pierced through the dark walls that had been building triumphantly in my mind on either side of me, as they had built in my mind that day in Mark Torre's office. Like an unbearable illumination it opened the darkness for a second, and showed me a picture—myself, in the rain; and Padma, facing me; and a dead man who lay between us.

But I flung myself away from that moment of imagination, flung myself clear back into the comforting darkness, and the sense of my power and strength came back on me.

"I don't need the Encyclopedia!" I said loudly.

"But you do!" she cried. "Everybody who's Earth-born—and if Padma's right, all the people in the future on the sixteen worlds—are going to need it. And only you can make sure they get it. Tam, you *have to*—"

"Have to!"

I took a step back from her, myself, this time. I had gone fiercely cold all over with the same sort of fury Mathias had been able to raise in me once, but it was mixed now with my feeling of triumph and of power. "I don't *'have to'* anything! Don't lump me in with the rest of you Earth worms. Maybe *they* need your Encyclopedia. But not me!"

I went around her with that, using my strength finally to shove her physically aside. I heard her still calling after me as I went down the stairs. But I shut my mind to the sense of her voice and refused to hear it. To this day I do not know what the last words she called after me were. I left the balcony and her calling behind me, and threaded my way through the people of the floor below toward the same exit through which Bright had disappeared. With the Friendly leader gone, there was no point in my hanging around. And with the newly rearoused sense of my power in me, abruptly I could not bear them close around me. Most of them, nearly all of them, were people from the younger worlds; and Lisa's voice rang on and on, it seemed, in my ear, telling me I needed the Encyclopedia, reechoing all Mathias' bitter lesson-giving about the relative helplessness and ineffectuality of Earthmen.

As I had suspected, once I gained the open air of the cool and moonless Freiland night outside, Eldest Bright, and whoever had called him from the party, had disappeared. The parking-lot attendant told me that they had left.

There was no point in my trying to find them, now. They might be headed anywhere on the planet, if not to a spacefield off-world entirely, back to Harmony or Association. Let them go, I thought, still bitter from the implication of my Earth-born ineffectiveness that I thought I had read in Lisa's words. Let them go. I alone could handle any trouble Dave might get in with the Friendlies, as a result of having a pass unsigned by one of their authorities.

I headed back to the spacefield and took the first shuttle to orbit and shift back to New Earth. But on the way, I had a chance to cool down. I faced the fact that it was still worthwhile getting Dave's pass signed. I might have to send him off for some reason of his own. An accident might even separate us on the battlefield. Any one of a number of things could occur to put him in trouble where I would not be around to save him.

With Eldest Bright a lost cause, I was left with the only option of heading to military headquarters of the Friendly troops in North Partition, to seek the signature for Dave's pass there. Accordingly, as soon as I hit orbit New Earth, I changed my ticket for Contrevale, the North Partition city right behind the lines of the Friendly mercenaries.

All this took some little time. It was after midnight by the time I had gotten from Contrevale to Battle Headquarters of the North Partition Forces. My Newsman's pass got me admission to the Headquarters' area, which seemed strangely deserted even for this time of night. But, when I pulled in at last before the Command building, I was surprised at the number of floaters parked there in the Officers' area.

Once again, my pass got me past a silent-faced, black-clothed guard with spring-rifle at the ready. I stepped into the reception room, with its long counter clipping it in half before me and the tall wall transparencies showing the full parking area under its night lights behind me. Only one man was behind the counter at one of the desks there, a Groupman hardly older than myself, but with his face already hardened into the lines of grim and merciless self-discipline to be observed on some of these people.

He got up from his desk and came to the other side of the counter as I approached the near side.

"I'm a Newsman of the Interstellar News Service," I began. "I'm looking for—"

"Thy papers!"

The interruption was harsh and nasal. The black eyes in the bony face stared into mine; and the archaic choice of the pronoun was all but flung in my face. Grim contempt, amounting nearly to a hatred on sight, leaped like a spark from him to me, as he held out his hand for the papers he had requested— and like a lion roused from slumber by the roar of an enemy, my own hatred leaped back at him, instinctively, before I could leash it with cooler reflection and wisdom.

I had heard of his breed of Friendly, but never until this moment had I come face to face with one. This was one of those from Harmony or Association who used the canting version of their private speech not just privately among themselves, but indifferently toward all men and women. He was one of those who avoided all personal joy in life, as he avoided any softness of bed or fullness of belly. His life was a trial-at-arms, antechamber only for the life to come, that life to come that was possible only to those who had kept the true faith—and to only those who, in keeping the true faith, had in addition been Chosen of the Lord.

It did not matter to this man that he was no more than a noncommissioned officer, a lesser functionary among thousands such, from a poor and stony planet, and I was one of only a few hundred on sixteen inhabited worlds intensively educated, trained and privileged to wear the Newsman's cloak. It made no difference to him that I was a member or Apprentice of the Guild, that I could talk with the rulers of planets. It did not even matter that I knew him to be half a madman and he knew me to be a product of education and training many times his own. None of this mattered, for he was one of God's Elect, and I was without the shadow of his church; and so he looked on me as an emperor might look at a dog to be kicked from his path.

And I looked back at him. There is a counter for every human emotional blow, deliberately given. Who knew this better than I? And I knew well the counter to anyone who tries to look down his nose at you. That counter is laughter. There never was a throne yet built so high that it could not be rocked by laughter from below. But I looked at this Groupman now, and I could not laugh.

I could not laugh for a very simple reason. For half-mad as he was, narrow-minded, limited as he was, yet *he* would have calmly let himself be burned at the stake rather than give up the lightest tenet of his beliefs. While *I* could not have held one finger in a match flame one minute to uphold the greatest of my own.

And he knew I knew that was true of him. And he knew I knew he knew what was true of me. Our mutual knowledge was plain as the counter between us. And so I could not laugh at him, and win my self-respect back. And I hated him for it.

I gave him my papers. He looked them over. Then he handed them back to me.

"Thy papers are in order," he said, high in his nose. "What brings thee here?"

"A pass," I said, putting my own papers away and digging out Dave's. "For my assistant. You see, we move back and forth on both sides of the battle line and—"

"Behind our lines and across them, no pass is necessary. Thy Newsman's papers are sufficient." He turned as if to go back to his desk.

"But this assistant of mine"—I kept my voice level—"doesn't have Newsman's papers. I just took him on earlier today and I haven't had time to make arrangements for him. What I'd like would be a temporary pass, signed by one of your Headquarters' officers here—''

He had turned back to the counter.

"Thy assistant is no Newsman?"

"Not officially. No. But—"

"Then he hath no leave or freedom to move across our battle lines. No pass can be issued."

"Oh, I don't know," I said carefully. "I was going to get one from your Eldest Bright, at a party on Freiland, just a few hours back, but he left before I had a chance to get it from him." I stopped, for the Groupman was grimly shaking his head.

"*Brother* Bright," he said, and in his choice of title I saw at last that he would be immovable. Only the purest of the fanatics among the Friendlies scorned the necessities of rank amongst themselves. *Eldest* Bright might order my Groupman to charge an enemy gun emplacement bare-handed and my Groupman would not hesitate to obey. But that did not mean that my Groupman considered Bright, or Brother Bright's opinion of the rightness of things, to be better than his own.

The reason was a very simple one. Bright's rank and title were of this present life, and therefore, in my Groupman's eyes, no more than toys and dross and tinkling cymbals. They did not weigh with the fact that as Brothers of the Elect, he and the Groupman were equal in the sight of the Lord.

"*Brother* Bright," he said, "could not have issued a pass to one not qualified to go and come among our numbers and perhaps be a spy upon us to the favor of our enemies."

There was one last card to play, and it was, I knew, a losing card; but I might as well play it anyway.

"If you don't mind," I said. "I'd like to get an answer on this from one of your superior officers. Please call one—the Officer of the Day, if no one else's available."

But he turned and went back to sit down at his desk.

"The Officer of the Day," he said, with finality, returning to some papers he had been working on, "can give thee no other answer. Neither will I summon him from his duties to repeat what I have already told thee."

It was like the crashing down of an iron portcullis upon my plans to get that pass signed. But there was nothing to be gained by arguing further with this man. I turned about and left the building.

CHAPTER 8 ◼

As the door shut behind me, I paused on the top of the three steps leading up it, to try to think what I could do next. What I would do next. I had gone over, under, or around what seemed to be immovable barriers of human decision too many times to give up so easily. Somewhere, there must be a back entrance to what I wanted, a trapdoor, a crack in the wall. I glanced again at the officers' parking area, jammed with floaters.

And then, suddenly, it came to me. All at once the bits and pieces floated together to give me a completed picture; and I kicked myself mentally for not having seen it before.

Item, the strange look of familiarity about the aide who had come to take Eldest Bright from the party of Donal Graeme. Item, Bright's own precipitate departure following the aide's appearance. Finally, the unusually deserted Headquarters' area, contrasted with the crowded parking lot here, the empty office within, and the refusal of the Groupman on duty reception even to call the Officer of the Day.

Either Bright himself, or his presence in the war area, had triggered some unusual plan for military action on the part of the Friendly mercenaries. A surprise blow, crushing the Cassidan forces and ending the war suddenly would be excellent publicity for the Eldest's attempts to hire out his Friendly commands of mercenaries in the face of some public dislike on the other worlds of their fanatic behavior and attitudes.

Not that all Friendlies were dislikable, I had been told. But, having met the Groupman inside, I could see where it would not take many like him to prejudice people against the black-clad soldiers as a group.

Therefore, I would bet my boots that Bright was inside the Command Post now with his top brass, preparing some military action to take the Cassidan levies by surprise. And with him would be the aide who had summoned him from Donal Graeme's party—and unless my highly trained professional memory was misleading me, I had a hunch who that aide might be.

I went quickly back down to my own floater, got in it and turned on its phone. Central at Contrevale looked abruptly at me out of the screen, with the face of a pretty, young blonde girl.

I gave her the number of my floater, which of course was a rented vehicle.

"I'd like to speak to a Jamethon Black," I said. "He's an officer with the Friendly forces; I believe he's right now at their Headquarters' Unit near Contrevale. I'm not sure what his rank is—at least Force-Leader, though he may be a Commandant. It's something of an emergency. If you can contact him, would you put him through to me on this phone?''

"Yes, sir," said Central. "Please hold on, I'll report in a minute." The screen blanked out and the voice was replaced by the soft hum that indicated the channel was open and holding.

I sat back against the cushions of the floater, and waited. Less than forty seconds later, the face returned.

"I have reached your party and he will be in contact with you in a few seconds. Will you hold, please?''

"Certainly," I said.

"Thank you, sir." The face disappeared. There was another half minute or so of hum and the screen lit up once more, this time with the face of Jamethon.

"Hello, Force-Leader Black?" I said. "Probably you don't remember me. I'm Newsman Tam Olyn. You used to know my sister, Eileen Olyn."

His eyes had already told me that he remembered me. Evidently I had not changed as much as I thought I had; or else his memory was a very good one. He himself had changed also, but not in any way that would make him unrecognizable. Above the tabs on the lapels of his uniform that showed his rank was still the same, his face had strengthened and deepened. But it was the same still face I remembered from my uncle's library that day. Only—it was older, of course.

I remembered how I had thought of him then, as

83 ■

a boy. Whatever he was now, however, he was a boy no longer. Nor ever could be again.

"What can I do for you, Mr. Olyn?" he asked. His voice was perfectly even and calm, a little deeper than I remembered it. "The operator said your call was an emergency."

"In a way it is," I said, and paused. "I don't want to take you from anything important; but I'm in your Headquarters Area here, in the officers' parking lot just outside the Headquarters Command Building. If you're not too far from there, maybe you can step over here and speak to me for a moment." I hesitated again. "Of course, if you're on duty at the moment—"

"My duty at the moment can spare me for a few minutes," he said. "You're in the parking lot of the Command Building?"

"In a rental floater, green, with transparent top."

"I will be right down, Mr. Olyn."

The screen went blank.

I waited. A couple of minutes later, the same door by which I myself had entered the Command Building to talk with the Groupman behind the counter opened. A dark, slim figure was momentarily silhouetted against the light there; then it came down the three steps toward the lot.

I opened the door of the floater as he got close and slid around on the seat so that he could step in and sit down himself.

"Mr. Olyn?" he said, putting his head in.

"That's right. Join me."

"Thank you."

He stepped in and sat down, leaving the door open behind him. It was a warm spring night for that season and latitude on New Earth; and the soft scents of trees and grasses blew past him into my face.

"What is this emergency?" he asked.

"I've got an assistant I need a pass for." I told him the situation, omitting the fact that Dave was Eileen's husband.

When I was through, he sat silent for a moment, a silhouette against the lights of the lot and the Command Building, with the soft night airs blowing past him.

"If your assistant's not a Newsman, Mr. Olyn," he said at last, in his quiet voice, "I don't see how we can authorize his coming and going behind and through our lines."

"He *is* a Newsman—for this campaign at least," I said. "I'm responsible for him, and the Guild is responsible for me, as it is for any Newsman. Our impartiality is guaranteed between the stars. That impartiality of course includes my assistant."

He shook his head slowly in the darkness.

"It would be easy enough for you to disown him, if he should turn out to be a spy. You could say simply that he was pushed upon you as an assistant, without your knowledge."

I turned my head to look full into his darkened features. I had led him to this point in our talk for just this reason.

"No, I wouldn't find it easy at all," I said. "Because he wasn't pushed on me. I went to a great deal of trouble to get him. He's my brother-in-law. He's the boy Eileen finally married; and by using him as my assistant, I'm keeping him out of the lines where he's likely to get killed." I paused to let that sink in.

"I'm trying to save his life for Eileen, and I'm asking you to try and help me save it."

He did not move or answer immediately. In the darkness, I could not see any change of expression on his features. But I do not think there would have been any change to see even if I had had light to see by, because he was a product of his own spartan culture, and I had just dealt him a heavy, double blow.

For, as you have seen, that was how I handled men—and women. Deep in every intelligent, living individual are things too great, too secret or too fearful for questioning. Faiths, or loves, or hates or fears or guilts. All I needed ever was to discover these things, and then anchor my argument for the answer I wanted in one of these deep, unself-questionable areas of the individual psyche, so that to question the rightness of what I argued, a man must needs question the secret, unquestionable place in himself as well.

In Jamethon Black's case, I had anchored my request both in that area of him which had been capable of love for Eileen in the first place; and in that part of every prideful man (and pride was in the very bone of the religion of these Friendlies) that required him to be above nourishing a long-held resentment for a past and (as far as he knew) a fair defeat.

To refuse the pass to Dave, now that I had spoken as I did, was tantamount to sending Dave forth to be killed, and who could think this was not done on purpose, now that I had shown Jamethon the emotional lines connecting it to his inner pride and lost love?

He stirred now, on the seat of the floater.

"Give me the pass, Mr. Olyn," he said. "I'll see what can be done."

I gave it to him, and he left me.

In a couple of minutes, he was back. He did not enter the floater this time, but he bent down to the open door and passed in the paper I had given him.

"You did not tell me," he said in his quiet voice, "that you had already applied for a pass, and been refused."

I stopped dead, still clutching the paper in midair, staring up and out at him.

"Who? That Groupman in there?" I said. "But he's just a noncommissioned officer. And you're not only a commissioned officer but an aide."

"Nonetheless," he said, "a refusal has been given. I cannot alter a decision already made. I'm sorry. No pass is possible for your brother-in-law."

It was only then I realized that the paper he had handed me back was unsigned. I stared at it, as if I could read it in the darkness and will a signature into being on the blank area where it should have gone. Then fury boiled up in me almost beyond control. I jerked my gaze up from the paper and stared out the open door of the floater at Jamethon Black.

"So that's your way of getting out of it!" I said. "That's how you excuse yourself for sending Eileen's husband to his death! Don't think I don't see through you, Black—because I do!"

With his back to the light, with his face in darkness, I still could not see his face and any change that might have come over it at my words. But something like a light sigh, a faint, sad breath, came from him; and he answered in the same, even tones.

"You see only the man, Mr. Olyn," he said. "Not

the Vessel of the Lord. I must get back to my duties now. Good morning.''

With that he swung closed the door of the floater, turned and went away across the lot. I sat, staring after him, boiling inside at the line of cant he had thrown at me in leaving by way of what I took to be excuse. Then I woke to what I was doing. As the door of the Command Building opened, his dark figure was silhouetted there for an instant, and then disappeared, taking the light with it as the door closed again. I kicked the floater into movement, swung it about and headed out of the military area.

As I drove out past the gateyard, they were changing guards for the three-A.M. watch; and the dismissed watch were drawn up in a dark clump, still under weapons, engaged in some ritual of their special worship.

As I passed them, they began to sing—chant rather—one of their hymns. I was not listening for the words, but the three beginning ones stuck in my ear in spite of me. *"Soldier, ask not—"* were the first three words, of what I later learned was their special battle hymn, sung at times of special rejoicing, or on the very eve of combat.

"Soldier, ask not—" It continued to ring in my ears, mockingly it seemed to me, as I drove away with Dave's pass still unsigned in my pocket. And once more the fury rose in me; and once more I swore that Dave would need no pass. I would not let him from my side for an instant during the coming day between the battle lines; and in my presence he would find his protection and his utter safety.

CHAPTER 9 ■

It was six-thirty in the morning when I stepped out of the tube from the port into the lobby of my hotel in Molon. There was a gritty feeling to my nerves and a dryness to my eyes and mouth, for I had not slept for twenty-four hours. The day coming up was to be a big one, so that I could probably not look forward to rest for another twenty-four. But going two or three days without sleep is an occupational hazard of Newswork. You get hold of something, with the situation about to break at a second's warning; and you simply have to stay with it until it does.

I would be alert enough; and if it came right down to the wire, I had medication to see me through. As it happened, though, at the desk I found something that knocked the need for sleep cheerfully right out of my head.

It was a letter from Eileen. I stepped aside and pressed it open.

Dearest Tam: [she wrote]
　　Your letter about your plan to take Dave out of the battle lines and keep him with you as your assistant just reached here. I'm so happy I can't tell you how I feel. It never occurred to me that someone like you, from Earth, and still only an Apprentice in the Newsman's Guild, could do something like that for us.

How can I thank you? And how can you forgive me after the way I've been, not writing, or not caring what happened to you all these last five years? I haven't been very much like a sister to you. But it was because I knew how useless and helpless I was; and ever since I was a little girl I've felt you were secretly ashamed of me and just putting up with me.

And then when you told me that day in the library how it would never work out for me to marry Jamethon Black—I knew you were right, even at the time, you were only telling me the truth about myself—but I couldn't help hating you for it. It seemed to me then that you were actually *proud* of the fact you could stop me from going away with Jamie.

But how wrong I was, as this thing you are doing to protect Dave shows me now; and how bitterly, bitterly sorry I am for feeling the way I did. You were the only one I had left to love after Mother and Daddy died, and I did love you, Tam; but most of the time it seemed to me you didn't want me to, any more than Uncle Mathias did.

Anyway, all that has changed now, since I met

Dave and he married me. Someday you must come to Alban, on Cassida, and see our apartment. We were very lucky to get one this big. It is my first real home of my own, and I think you may be a little surprised at how well we've fixed it up. Dave will tell you all about it, if you ask him—don't you think he's wonderful, for someone like me to marry, I mean? He is so kind, and so loyal. Do you know he wanted me to let you know about our marriage at the time it happened, in spite of the way I felt? But I wouldn't do it. Only of course he was right. He is always right, just as I am nearly always wrong—as you know, Tam.

But thank you, thank you again for what you're doing for Dave; and all my love goes with both of you. Tell Dave I'm writing him, too, at this same time; but I suppose his army mail won't reach him as fast as yours does you.

> All my love,
> Eileen

I tucked the letter and its envelope away in my pocket and went up to my room. I had meant to show him the letter; but on the way up the tube I found myself unexpectedly embarrassed at the thought of the fullness of her thanks expressed in it, and the way she had accused herself of not being the best possible sister. I had not been the best possible brother, either; and what I was doing for Dave now might look big to her, but it was nothing great really. Hardly more than the sort of thing I might do for a total stranger, by way of returning a professional favor.

She had me, in fact, feeling somewhat ashamed of

myself, absurdly warmed by having heard from her so. Maybe we could turn out to exist like normal people after all. The way she and Dave felt about each other, I would undoubtedly be having nephews or nieces one of these days. Who knew—I might even end up married myself (the thought of Lisa floated inexplicably through my mind) and with children. And we might all end up with relations spread over half a dozen worlds like most of the ordinary family groups, nowadays.

Thus I refute Mathias! I thought to myself. *And Padma, too.*

I was daydreaming in this absurd but cheerful fashion when I reached the door of my hotel suite and remembered the question of showing Dave the letter. Better to let him wait and read his own letter, which Eileen had said was on the way, I decided. I pushed open the door and went in.

He was already up, dressed, and packed. He grinned at the sight of me; and this puzzled me for a split second until I realized that I must have come in with a smile on my own face.

"I heard from Eileen," I said. "Just a note. She says a letter's on its way to you, but it may take a day or so to catch up from being forwarded on from your army unit."

He beamed at that; and we went down to breakfast. The food helped to wake me up; and we took off the moment we were done, for Battle Headquarters of the Cassidan and local troops. Dave was handling my recording and other equipment. There was no real bulk or weight to it. I often carried it myself without hardly noticing it. But theoretically his caring for it left me free to concentrate on finer matters of reportage.

Battle Headquarters had promised me a military air-car, one of the small two-man reconnaissance jobs. When I got to the Transport Pool, however, I found myself in line behind a Field Commander who was waiting for his command car to be specially equipped. My first impulse was to put up a squawk on principle at being kept waiting. My second thought was decidedly to do no such thing. This was no ordinary Field Commander.

He was a lean, tall man with black, slightly coarse, slightly curly hair above a big-boned, but open and smiling face. I have mentioned before that I am tall, for an Earth-born man. This Field Commander was tall for a Dorsai, which of course he was. In addition he had that—that quality for which there is no name, which is the birthright of his people. Something beyond just strength, or fearsomeness, or courage. Something almost the opposite of those keyed-up qualities.

It is calmness, even; a thing beyond argument, beyond time, beyond life itself. I have been on the Dorsai planet since then, and I have seen it as well among the half-grown boys there, and in some of the children. These people can be killed—all who are born of women are mortal—but staining them through, like a dye, is the undeniable fact that together, or as individuals, they cannot be conquered. By anything. Conquest of the Dorsai character is not merely unthinkable. It is somehow not—possible.

So, all this my Field Commander automatically had, in addition to his magnificent military mind and body. But there was something strange, over and above it all. Something that did not seem to belong in with the rest of the Dorsai character at all.

It was an odd, powerful, sunny warmth of character that lapped even upon me, standing several yards away and outside the knot of officers and men that surrounded him like elm saplings in the wind-shelter of an oak. A joy of life seemed to fountain up in this Dorsai officer, so brightly that it forced the kindling of a similar joy in those around him. Even in me, standing to one side and not—I would have said—normally too much liable to such influence.

But it may have been that Eileen's letter was making me particularly vulnerable that morning. That could have been it.

There was another thing which my professional eye was quick to spot; and which had nothing to do with character qualities. That was the fact that his uniform was of the field-blue color and narrow cut that identified it as issue, not of the Cassidan, but of the Exotic forces. The Exotics, rich and powerful, and philosophically committed not to do violence in their own proper persons, hired the best mercenary troops to be had between the stars. And, of course, that meant that an unusually high proportion of those troops, or at least of their officers, were Dorsai. So what was a Dorsai Field Commander doing here with a New Earth shoulder patch hastily added to his Exotic-cut uniform, and surrounded by New Earth and Cassidan staff officers?

If he was newly come to the battered New Earth South Partition Forces, it was indeed a fortunate co-incidence that he should show up on the very morning following a night I happened to know had been occupied by busy planning on the part of the Friendly Battle Headquarters at Contrevale.

But, was it coincidence? It was hard to believe that the Cassidans could already have found out about the Friendly tactical session. The Cadre of the New Earth Intelligence Forces staffed by men like Commandant Frane, were poor in the spying department; and it was part of the Mercenaries Code, under which professional soldiers of all worlds hired out, that a mercenary could not operate out of uniform on any intelligence mission. But coincidence seemed too easy an answer, all the same.

"Stay here," I told Dave.

I started forward to penetrate the crowd of staff officers around this unusual Dorsai Field Commander, and find out something about him from his own lips. But at that moment his command car came up, and he got in, taking off before I could reach him. I noted he headed south into the battle lines.

The officers he had left behind dispersed. I let them go, keeping my questions instead for the enlisted New Earth cadreman who brought up my own aircar. He would be likely to know almost as much as the officers and a lot less likely to have been cautioned not to tell it to me. The Field Commander, I learned, had indeed been loaned to the South Partition Forces just the day before, on the orders of an Exotic OutBond called Patma, or Padma. Oddly, this Exotic officer was a relative of that same Donal Graeme whose party I had attended—although Donal was, as far as I knew, in Freiland, not Exotic employ, and under the command of Hendrik Galt.

"Kensie Graeme, that's the name of this one," said the Transport Pool cadreman. "And he's a twin, do you know that? By the way, you know how to drive one of these cars?''

''Yes,'' I said. I was already behind the stick and Dave was in the seat beside me. I touched the lift button and we rose on our eight-inch cushion of air. ''Is his twin here, too?''

''No, still back on Kultis, I guess,'' said the cadreman. ''He's just as sour as this one's happy, I hear. They've each got two men's dose of being one way or the other. Outside of that, they say, you can't tell them apart—other one's a Field Commander, too.''

''What's the other one's name?'' I asked, with my hand on the stick, ready to pull out.

He frowned, thought for a minute, shook his head.

''Can't remember,'' he said. ''Something short— Ian, I think.''

''Thanks, anyhow,'' I said, and I took off. It was a temptation to head south in the direction Kensie Graeme had gone; but I had made my plans on my way back from Friendly Battle Headquarters the night before; and when you're short on sleep, it's a bad practice to go changing plans without strong reason. Often the fuzzy-headedness that comes from sleeplessness is just enough to make you forget some strong reason you had for making the original plan. Some strong reason which later on—too late—you will remember to your regret.

So, I make it a principle not to change plans on the spur of the moment, unless I can be sure my mind is in top working order. It's a principle that pays off more often than not. Though, of course, no principle is perfect.

We lifted the air-car to about six hundred feet of altitude and cruised north along the Cassidan lines, our News Service colors on the air-car body glowing in the sunlight and our warning beeper beaming a neutral signal at the same time. Banner and beeper together should be enough, I figured, to make us safe at this altitude as long as there was no active shooting going on. Once the fighting really started, we would be smarter to head for ground cover like a wounded bird.

Meanwhile, while it was still safe to do so from the air, I meant to coast the lines first to the north (where they angled back toward the Friendly Battle HQ and Contrevale) and then to the south—and see if I couldn't figure out just what Bright, or Bright's black-clad officers, could have in mind for their plan.

Between the two enemy camps of Contrevale and Dhores, a direct line would have run almost due north and south. The present actual battle line struck across this imaginary north-south line at an angle, its northern end leaning toward Contrevale and the Friendly HQ, and its southern end all but touching the outskirts of Dhores, which was a city of about sixty-odd thousand people.

So the battle line as a whole was much closer to Dhores than to Contrevale—which put the Cassidan-New Earth Forces at a disadvantage. They could not fall back at their south end into the city proper and still be able to preserve a straight front of battle line and the communication necessary for effective defense. By so much had the Friendly troops already pushed their opponents into bad field position.

On the other hand, the angle of the battle line was acute enough so that a major share of the Friendly troops toward the south were inside the northern end of the Cassidan line. Given more reserves in the way of troops and bolder leadership, I thought determined sallies from the north end of the Cassidan line could have cut communications between the southern and forward elements of the Friendly line—and the Friendly HQ, back toward Contrevale.

This would at least have had the advantage of introducing confusion into the Friendly ranks, out of which a determined Cassidan field command might have made some capital.

They had shown no signs of doing so, however. Now, with a Dorsai as Field Commander, some such thing might still be attempted by the Cassidans—if there was still time and men available. But it seemed unlikely to me that the Friendlies, after sitting up all night, planning, were going to sit still today while the Cassidans made attempts to cut enemy communications.

The big question was, what did the Friendlies have in mind? I could see what I have just mentioned as a possible tactic for the Cassidans. But I could not imagine just how the Friendlies planned to take advantage of the present positions and tactical situation.

The south end of the line, on the outskirts of Dhores, was pretty much open country, farmland planted in corn, or cattle pasture on rolling glaciated hills. To the north, there were also the hills, but covered with wooded patches, groves of towering yellow birch, which had found a fine, alien home in the moist, glacial uplands of the South Partition, here on New Earth, so that here they rose to nearly double their Earthly heights—nearly two hundred feet—and clustered their tops so densely that no undergrowth but a native, mosslike groundcover could exist beneath them. Consequently, it was a sort of dim, Robin Hood-like country that existed beneath their branches, with great, peeling, silver-gold and gray, four-to-six-foot trunks reaching straight up like pillars in the dimness to the darkness of sun-shot leaves overhead.

It was not until, looking at them, I remembered all this of how it was underneath them, that it struck me that any number of troops could be at movement under their cover and I—up here in my air-car—would not be aware of rifle or helmet of them. In short, the Friendlies could be developing a major push under the cover of the trees below me and I would have no suspicion of it.

No sooner thought than acted upon. I blamed my lack of sleep for a fuzziness of perception that had not made me suspect something like this before. I swung the air-car wide to the edge of one of the groves, where there was a fortified Cassidan emplacement with the ringed muzzle of a sonic cannon poking out of it, and parked. Out here in the open, there was too much sun for the mosslike ground-cover, but a knee-high native grass was everywhere, leaning to the little wind that was blowing it in ripples, like the surface of a lake.

I got out and waded through it to the entrance of the bushes masking the gun emplacement. The day was getting hot already.

"Any sign of Friendly movement around here, or in the woods over there?" I asked the Senior Groupman in charge of the emplacement.

"Nothing, far as we know," he answered. He was a slim, high-keyed young fellow, gone half-bald considerably before his time. His uniform jacket was unclipped at the throat. "Patrols are out."

"Hmm," I said. "I'll try up forward a bit. Thanks."

I got back in the air-car and took off again, just six inches above ground obstacles now, and into the woods. Here it was cooler. The patch of trees we entered led to another and that to another. In the third patch we were challenged, and found we had come up on a Cassidan patrol. Its members were flat on the ground, out of sight and covering us at the time we were challenged; and I did not spot a single man until a square-faced Force-Leader rose up almost beside the car, spring-rifle in his hand and visor of his helmet down.

"What the hell are you doing here?" he said, shoving the visor up.

"Newsman. I've got permissions to be in and across the battle lines. Want to see them?"

"You know what you can do with your permissions," he said. "If it was up to me, you'd do it, too. Not that your being here makes this business any more of a damn Sunday picnic than it is now. But we've got trouble enough trying to keep the men acting halfway like soldiers in a battle zone without people like you wandering around."

"Why?" I asked innocently. "Are you having some kind of trouble besides that? What trouble?"

"We haven't seen a black helmet since dawn, that's what trouble!" he said. "Their forward gun emplacements are empty—and they weren't yesterday, that's what trouble. Shoot an antenna down into bedrock and listen for five seconds and you can hear armor—heavy armor and lots of it—moving not more than fifteen, twenty kilometers from here. That's what trouble! Now, why don't you get back behind the lines, friend, so we don't have to worry about you on top of everything else?''

"Which direction did you hear the armor?"

He pointed ahead, into Friendly territory.

"Then that's where we're headed ourselves," I said, leaning back into the seat of the air-car and getting ready to close the overhead.

"Hold it!" His voice stopped me before I got the overhead shut. "If you're determined to cross over toward the enemy, I can't stop you. But it's my duty to warn you that you head that way on your own responsibility. That's between the lines, out there; and your chances of running into automatic weapons are better than not."

"Sure, sure. Consider us cautioned!" I slid the overhead shut with a bang. It may have been my own lack of sleep making me irritable, but it seemed to me at the time that he was giving us an unnecessarily hard time. I saw his face staring grimly at us as I started up the car and pulled away.

But maybe I did him an injustice. We slid forward between the trees and in a few seconds he was lost to sight behind us. We moved on, through forests and across small glades, over gently rolling territory for about half an hour more, without encountering anything. I was just figuring that we could not be more than two or three kilometers short of where the Force-Leader had estimated the sound of Friendly armor to be coming from when it happened.

There was a sudden swift sound and blow that seemed to tilt the instrument panel suddenly into my face, smashing me into unconsciousness.

I blinked and opened my eyes. His round face concerned, Dave was out of his own seat harness and bent over me, unfastening mine.

"What?" I muttered. But he paid no attention, merely getting me loose and getting me out of the air-car.

He wanted me to lie down on the moss; but by the time we were outside the vehicle, my head had cleared. I had been, I thought, almost more dazed than out. But, when I turned to look back at the air-car, I felt grateful that that had been the worst to happen to me.

We had run across a vibration mine. Of course the air-car, like any vehicle designed for use around battlefields, had sensor rods projecting out of it at odd angles; and one of these had set off the mine while we were still a dozen feet from it. But still the air-car now had a tangle of junk for a front end, and the instrument panel was pretty well wrecked by my head; so much so that it was surprising I had not even a cut on my forehead to show for it, though a rather considerable bruise was already rising there.

"I'm all right—*I'm all right!*" I said irritably to Dave. And then I swore at the air-car for a few minutes to relieve my feelings.

"What do we do now?" asked Dave when I was finished.

"Head for the Friendly lines on foot. They're the closest!" I growled. The warning of the Force-Leader came back to my mind, and I swore again. Then, because I had to take it out on somebody, I snapped at Dave. "We're still out here to get a newsstory, remember?"

I turned and stalked away in the direction the air-car had been headed. There were probably other vibration mines around, but walking on foot, I would not have the weight or disturbance to spring them. After a moment Dave caught up with me and we walked along in silence together over the mosslike groundcover, between the enormous tree trunks, until glancing back, I saw that the air-car was out of sight behind us.

It was only then, when it was too late, that it occurred to me that I had forgotten to check my wrist director with the direction indicator in the air-car. I glanced at the director on my wrist now. It seemed to indicate the Friendly lines as just ahead. If it had kept correlation with the direction indicator in the air-car, all was well. If not—among these huge pillars of tree trunks, on this soft, unending, mossy carpet, every direction looked alike. Turning back to search for the air-car to correct the correlation could make us lost in a real sense.

Well, there was nothing to be done about it now. The important thing was to keep on in a straight line forward through the dimness and silence of the forest. I locked the wrist director to our present line of march and hoped for the best. We kept on—toward the Friendly battle line, I hoped, wherever that might be.

CHAPTER 10 ■

I had seen enough of this part of the territory from the air-car to be fairly sure that whatever was going on, either in the movement of Friendly or Cassidan forces, was not taking place in the open. So we stuck to the trees, moving from one grove to another.

Necessarily, this meant that we were not able to go straight in the direction the patrol's Force-Leader had pointed, but zigzagged to it as the wooded cover permitted. It was slow going, on foot.

By noon, disgusted, I sat down with Dave to eat the cold lunch we had packed along. By noon we had seen no one since the Cassidan patrol earlier, heard nothing, discovered nothing. We had moved forward from the point where we left the air-car only about three kilometers, but because of the arrangement of the wooded patches, we had angled south about five kilometers.

"Maybe they've gone home—the Friendlies, I mean," suggested Dave.

He was joking, with a grin on his face that I saw as I jerked up my head from my sandwich to stare at him. I managed a grin in return, feeling I owed him at least that. The truth of the matter was that he had been an unusually good assistant, keeping his mouth shut and avoiding the making of suggestions born in ignorance not only of warfare but of News-work.

"No," I said, "something's up—but I was an idiot to let myself get separated from that air-car. We just can't cover enough territory on foot. The Friendlies have pulled back for some reason, at least at this end of the front. Probably it was to draw the Cassidan levies in after them, would be my guess. But why we haven't seen black uniforms counterattacking before now—"

"Listen!" said Dave.

He had turned his head and held up his hand to stop me talking. I broke off and listened. Sure enough, at some distance off, I heard a *wump*, a muffled, innocuous sound like a blanket snapping, as if it were being shaken out by an energetic housewife.

"Sonics!" I said, scrambling to my feet and leaving the rest of our picnic lunch lying. "By God, they're starting to get some action on after all! Let's see." I pivoted, trying to aim myself at the direction the noise had come from. "That sounded about a couple of hundred meters off, and over to our right—"

I never finished speaking. Suddenly, Dave and I were caught in the heart of a thunderclap. I found myself lying on the moss without remembering how I had got there. Five feet away, Dave was lying sprawled out; and less than forty feet away was a shallow, scooped area of torn-up earth, surrounded by trees that appeared to have exploded from internal pressure, with the white wood of their insides showing splintered and spread.

"Dave!" I got to him, and turned him over. He was breathing, and, as I watched, his eyes opened. His eyes were bloodshot, and he was bleeding from the nose. At the sight of his blood I became conscious of a wetness of my own upper lip, a salt taste in my mouth, and, putting up my hand, felt the blood dripping from my own nose.

I wiped it away with one hand. With the other hand, I pulled Dave to his feet.

"Barrage!" I said. "Come on, Dave! We've got to get out of here." For the first time, the reaction of Eileen if I should fail to bring him safely home to her presented itself to my mind in vivid image. I had been sure of the protection my skilled mind and tongue could provide for Dave between the battle lines. But you cannot argue with a sonic cannon, firing from five to fifty kilometers away.

He made it to his feet. He had been closer to the "burst" of the sonic capsule than I had, but luckily the effective zone of a sonic explosion is bell-shaped, with the wide mouth of the bell-area downward. So we had both been in the rim-part of that sudden imbalance of internal and external pressures. He was only a little more dazed than I was. And shortly, recovering somewhat as we went, we were both legging it away from the area, back at an angle toward where figuring from my wrist director indicated the Cassidan lines should be.

We stopped, finally, out of breath, and sat down for a moment, panting. We could hear the *wump, wump* of the barrage bursts continuing, some little distance behind us.

"—'s all right," I panted to Dave. "They'll lift the barrage and send in troops before they follow up with armor. Troops we can talk sense to. With sonic cannon and armored vehicles we'd never have a chance. Might as well sit here and pull ourselves together, then strike sideways along the lines to join up with either a Cassidan force, or the first wave of Friendlies—whichever we run into first."

I saw him looking at me with an expression I could not fathom at first. Then, to my astonishment, I recognized it as admiration.

"You saved my life back there," he said.

"Saved your—" I broke off. "Look, Dave, I'm the last man to turn down credit when credit is due. But that sonic only knocked you out for a second."

"But you knew what to do when we came to," he said. "And you didn't just think of doing it for yourself. You waited to get me on my feet and help me get out of there, too."

I shook my head, and let it go at that. If he had accused me instead of deliberately trying to save myself first, I would not have thought it worth the trouble to change his mind. So, since he had chosen to go the other way in his opinion, why should I bother to change that, either? If he liked to consider me a selfless-minded hero, let him.

"Suit yourself," I said. "Let's go."

We got back on our feet a little shakily—there was

no doubt that same burst had taken it out of us both—
and moved off southward at an angle that ought to
cut the line of any Cassidan resistance, if indeed we
were as far forward of their main posts as our earlier
encounter with the patrol had indicated.

After a little while the *wump, wump* of the barrage
moved away from our right on ahead of us and finally
died out into the distance. In spite of myself, I found
myself sweating a little and hoping we would come
upon Cassidans before the Friendly infantry swept
over us. The business of the sonic capsule had reminded me of how big a part chance plays in the
matter of death and wounds on a battlefield. I would
like to get Dave safely under the protective shell of
a gun emplacement, so that there would be a chance
to talk to any of the black-uniformed men we came
upon before any shooting began.

For myself, there was no danger. My billowing
Newsman's cloak, the colors of which I had this day
set on a dazzling white and scarlet, advertised me as
a noncombatant as far as I could be seen. Dave, on
the other hand, was still wearing a Cassidan's field-
gray uniform, though without insignia or decorations
and with a noncombatant's white armband. I crossed
my fingers, for luck.

The luck worked; but not to the extent of bringing
us to a Cassidan gun-emplacement shell. A small
neck of woods running up the spine of a hill brought
us to its top and a red-yellow flare, blinding in the
dimness under the trees, burst in warning half a
dozen feet in front of us. I literally knocked Dave to
the ground with a hand in the middle of his back and
skidded to a stop myself, waving my arms.

"Newsman!" I shouted. "Newsman! I'm a non-combatant!"

"I know you're a goddam Newsman!" called back a voice tense with anger and stifled with caution. "Get on over here, both of you, and keep your voices down!"

I gave Dave a hand up, and we went, still half-blinded, toward the voice. As we moved, my vision cleared; and twenty steps farther on I found myself behind the eight-foot-thick trunk of an enormous yellow birch, face to face once more with the Cassidan Force-Leader who had warned me about going on toward the Friendly line.

"You again!" we both said in the same second. But then our reactions varied. Because he began telling me in a low, fervent, and determined voice, just what he thought of civilians like myself who got themselves mixed up in the front lines of a battle.

Meanwhile, I was paying little attention and using the seconds to pull my own wits together. Anger is a luxury—the Force-Leader might be a good soldier, but he had not yet learned that elemental fact in all occupations. He ran down finally.

"The point is," he said grimly, "you *are* on my hands. And what am I going to do with you?"

"Nothing," I answered. "We're here at our own risk, to observe. And observe we will. Tell us where we can dig in out of your way, and that'll be the last you'll have to think of us."

"I'll bet!" he said sourly, but it was merely a last spark of his anger sputtering out. "All right. Over there. Behind the men dug in between those two trees. And stay in your spot once you pick it!"

"All right," I said. "But before we take off, would

you answer me one other question? What're you supposed to be doing on this hill?''

He glared at me as if he would not answer. Then, the emotion inside him forced the answer out.

''Holding it!'' he said. And he looked as if he would have liked to spit, to clean the taste of those two words out of his mouth.

''Holding it? With a patrol?'' I stared at him. ''You can't hold a position like this with a dozen or so men if the Friendlies are moving in!'' I waited, but he said nothing. ''Or can you?''

''No,'' he answered. And this time he did spit. ''But we're going to try. Better lay that cloak out where the black helmets can see it when they come up the hill.'' He turned away to the man beside him wearing the message unit. ''Get Command HQ,'' I heard him say. ''Tell him we've got a couple of Newsmen up here with us!''

I got the name, and unit, and the names of the men in his patrol; then I took Dave off to the spot the Force-Leader had indicated, and we started digging in just like the soldiers around us. Nor did I forget to spread my cloak out in front of our two foxholes as the Force-Leader had said. Pride runs a very slow second to the desire to remain alive.

From our holes, once we were in them, we could look down the steeper slope of the wooded hill toward the direction of the Friendly lines. The trees went all the way down the hill and continued on to the next hill beyond. But halfway down, there was the scar of an old landslip, like a miniature cliff, breaking the even roof of treetops, so that we could look out between the pillars of those tree trunks rising from the upper edge of the landslip and see over the tops of the trees at the bottom edge, and thus get a view of the whole panorama of wooded slope and open field toward the far green horizon under which probably sat the Friendly sonic cannon Dave and I had run from earlier.

It was our first good look at the general field since I had brought the air-car down to ground level, and I was busy studying it through glasses, when I saw what seemed to be a flicker of movement among the tree trunks at the bottom of the divide between our hill and the next. The flicker was not enough for me to pick out anything definite, but at the same time I saw movement in both of the foxholes ahead of us and knew that the soldiers in them had been alerted by whichever one of them carried the patrol's heat-sensing unit. The screens of which would now be showing the blips of the body heat of men, starting to mix in with the earth vegetation, and other heat of the ground area before us.

The Friendlies had found us. In a few seconds, there was no question of it, for even my glasses picked out flickers of black as their soldiers began to work their way up the slope of the hill toward our front and the weapons of the Cassidan patrol began to whicker and snap in response.

"Down!" I said to Dave.

He had been trying to raise up and see. I suppose he thought that because I was raising up to get a better view and so exposing myself, he could too. It was true that the Newsman's cloak was spread out in front of both our holes; but I also had my beret color controls set on scarlet and white, and in addition I had more faith in my ability to survive than he. All men have such moments when they feel invulnerable; and the moment in that foxhole, with the Friendly troops attacking, was one of mine. Besides, I was expecting the current Friendly attack on us to die down and quit in a moment.

And sure enough, it did.

CHAPTER 11 ■

There was no great mystery about the pause that came then in the Friendly attack. The men who had come into momentary contact with us were little more than a skirmish line out in front of the main Friendly forces. It had been their job to push the Cassidan opposition ahead of them, until it dug in and showed signs of fighting. When that happened the first line of skirmishers had, predictably, backed off, sent messages for reinforcements, and waited.

It was a military tactic older than Julius Caesar— assuming Julius Caesar were still alive.

But it, and the rest of the circumstances that had brought Dave and me to this place and moment, provided me with the mental ammunition to draw a couple of conclusions.

The first was that all of us—I included the Friendly forces as well as the Cassidan, and the whole war right down to its involved individuals, like Dave and myself—were being shoved around by the plannings of forces outside and beyond the battlefield. And it was not too hard to figure who those manipulating forces might be. One, clearly, was Eldest Bright and his concern with whether the Friendly mercenaries wrapped up their assignment in such a way as to attract further employers to their employment. Bright, like one chess player facing another, had planned and set in motion some kind of move aimed at wrapping up the war in one bold tactical strike.

But that strike had been, if not foreseen, at least precalculated by his opponent. And that opponent could only be Padma, with his ontogenetics.

For if Padma, with his calculations, could figure that I would put in an appearance at the party of Donal Graeme on Freiland, then with the same ontogenetics he would have been able to calculate that Bright would make some swift move with the Friendly forces to destroy the Cassidan levies opposing them. His calculation of this was deducible from the fact that he had lent one of his own best tacticians from the Exotic forces—Kensie Graeme—to frustrate what Bright had planned. Without that explanation Kensie's appearance here on the battlefield at the crucial moment made no sense.

But the interesting question to me, behind all this, was why Padma should automatically oppose himself to Bright in any case. As far as I knew the Exotics had no stake in this civil war on New Earth—important enough to the world on which it was occurring, but small compared to other matters between the sixteen worlds and the stars.

The answer might lie somewhere in the tangle of

contractual agreements that controlled the ebb and flow of trained personnel between the worlds. The Exotics, like Earth, Mars, Freiland, Dorsai, and the little Catholic Christian world of Ste. Marie, did not draft their trained young graduates en bloc, and trade off their contracts to other worlds without consulting the wishes of the individual. They were therefore known as "loose" worlds; in automatic opposition to "tight" worlds like Ceta, the Friendlies, Venus, Newton, and the rest who bartered their skilled personnel without concern for individual rights or desires.

The Exotics, therefore, being "loose" worlds, were automatically in opposition to the "tight" worlds of the Friendlies. But this alone was not reason enough for their choosing up sides in a conflict on some third world gratuitously. There might be some secret tangle of contractual balances concerning the Exotics and the Friendlies I knew nothing about. Otherwise, I was at a loss to understand Padma's taking a hand in the current situation.

But it showed me, who was concerned with manipulating my environment by manipulating those immediately around me, that forces could be brought into play outside the charmed circle of my tongue, which could frustrate anything I could do, simply because they were from outside. In short, there were wider areas to be considered in the handling of men and events to some individually desired end than I had thought of before this.

I filed that discovery away for future reference.

The second conclusion that came to mind now had to do with the immediate matter of our defending this hill as soon as the Friendlies could bring up reinforcements. For it was no place to defend with a couple of dozen men. Even a civilian like myself could see that.

If I could see it, certainly the Friendlies could see it, to say nothing of the Force-Leader of the patrol, himself. Obviously he was holding it under orders from his Headquarters, a good deal farther back behind the lines. For the first time I began to see some excuse for this unwelcoming attitude where Dave and I were concerned. He obviously had his troubles—including some superior officer back at Headquarters who would ask him and his patrol to hold such a place as this hill. I began to feel more kindly toward the Force-Leader. Wise, panic-stricken, or foolish his orders might be; but he was soldier enough to do his best to carry them out.

It would make a great story, his hopeless attempt to defend this hill, with no support on either side or behind him and the whole Friendly army in front. And between the lines of my writing, I could have my say about the kind of command who had put him there. And then I looked around the slope and saw the enlisted men of his patrol dug in and a cool, sickly feeling knotted my stomach right under my breastbone. For they were in this, too, and they did not know the price they were about to pay in order to become heroes in my newsstory.

Dave punched me in the side.

"Look there—over there—" he breathed in my ear. I looked.

There was a stir among the Friendlies hidden in the trees at the bottom of the hill. But they were clearly only picking up extra strength and grouping for an actual assault on the hill. Nothing would happen for a few minutes yet, and I was about to tell Dave so, when he jogged me again.

"No!" he said, low-voiced, but urgently. "Out there. Away out. Near the horizon."

I looked. And I saw what he meant. Out there among the trees that finally met the sky, now turning hot and blue, some ten kilometers, or about six miles, off, there were firefly-like flickers. Little yellow flashes among the green and occasionally a little upward plume of something white or dark that dissipated on the breeze.

But no fireflies ever flickered so as to be seen in broad daylight like that, and at a distance of over six miles. They were heat beams we were looking at.

"Armor!" I said.

"They're coming this way," said Dave, staring fascinated at the flashes, looking so small and trivial at that distance. Flashes that were in reality swords of searing light, forty thousand degrees centigrade at the core, that could topple the huge trees around us as a razor blade might slice through a bed of standing asparagus.

They were coming on unopposed, for there were no infantry worthy of the name in their way to take them out with plastics or sonic hand-weapons. Missiles, the classic defense against armor, had been outdated nearly fifty years by counter-missilery advanced to the point where reaction speeds of half-light made their use on planetary surfaces impossible. They were coming on slowly, but unstoppably, burning out on principle any likely hiding spots for infantry they passed.

Their coming made our defense of the hill a mockery. For if the Friendly infantry did not sweep over

us before the armor got here, we would be fried in
our foxholes. It was plain to me—and plain to the
men of the platoon as well, for I heard a little hum-
ming moan move along the hillside as the soldiers in
the other holes spotted the flashes.

"Silence!" snapped the Force-Leader from his.
"Hold your positions. If you don't—"

But he had no time to finish, for, at that moment,
the first serious assault of the Friendly infantry
mounted the slope against us.

And a sliver from a spring-gun took the Force-
Leader high in the chest, just at the base of the neck,
so that he fell back, choking on his own blood.

But the rest of the patrol had no time to notice
this, for the assaulting Friendly spring-gunmen, wave
on wave of them, were halfway up the slope to them.
Low in their foxholes, the Cassidans fired back; and
either the hopelessness of their position or an unusual amount of battle experience was paying off for
them, for I did not see a single man who was paralyzed by combat fear and not using his gun.

They had all the advantage of it. The slope steep-
ened as the top of the hill was approached. The
Friendlies slowed and were shot down easily as they
came closer. They broke and ran once more for the
bottom of the hill. And once again, there was a pause
in the firing.

I scrambled out of my foxhole and ran over toward
the Force-Leader, to find out if he was still alive. It
was a foolish thing to do, standing up in plain sight
like that, Newsman's cape or not; and I paid for it
accordingly. The retreating Friendlies had lost friends
and fellow soldiers on the hill. Now one of them
reacted. Just a few steps short of the Force-Leader's

foxhole, something chopped my left leg out from under me and I went down, skidding, on my face.

The next thing I knew I was in the command foxhole beside the Force-Leader, and Dave was leaning over me, crowding the narrow space which also held two Groupmen, who must have been the Force-Leader's noncoms.

"What's going on . . ." I began, and tried to get to my feet. Dave moved to push me back; but I had already tried to put some of my weight on my left leg; and a tiger's-tooth of pain drove through it, so that I slumped again, half-fainting, and soaked in my own sweat.

"Got to fall back," one of the Groupmen was saying to the other. "Got to get out of here, Akke. Next time they'll get us, or if we wait twenty minutes the armor'll do it for them!"

"No," croaked the Force-Leader beside me. I had thought him dead; but when I turned to look, I saw someone had set a pressure bandage against his wound, and released the trigger, so that its fibers would be inside the hole in him now, sealing apertures and clotting the blood flow. All the same he was dying. I could see it in his eyes. The Groupman ignored him.

"Listen to me, Akke," said the Groupman who had just spoken. "You're in command now. Got to move!"

"No." The Force-Leader could barely whisper, but whisper he did. "Orders. Hold at all—costs—"

The Groupman evidently called Akke looked uncertain. His face was pale and he turned to look at the communications unit beside him in the foxhole. The other Groupman saw the direction of his glance and the spring-rifle across his knees went off, as if by accident. There was a smash and a tinkle inside the communications unit and I could see the ready light on its instrument panel go dark.

"I order you," the Force-Leader was saying: but then the terrible jaws of pain closed upon my knee once more and my head swam. When my vision cleared again, I could see that Dave had ripped my left pant's leg up above the knee and just finished setting a neat, white pressure bandage around the knee.

"It's all right, Tam," he was saying to me. "The spring-rifle sliver went all the way through. It's all right."

I looked around. The Force-Leader still sat beside me, now with his side-arm half drawn. There was another spring-rifle wound, this time in his forehead and he was quite dead. Of the two Groupmen, there was no sign.

"They've gone, Tam," said Dave. "We've got to get out of here, too." He pointed down the hill. "The Friendly troops decided we weren't worth it. They pulled out. But their armor's getting close—and you can't move fast with that knee. Try to stand up, now."

I tried. It was like standing with one knee resting on the needle-point of a stake and bearing half my weight on that. But I stood. Dave helped me out of the foxhole; and we began our limping retreat down the back way of the hill, away from the armor.

I had likened those woods earlier in my thoughts to a Robin Hood-like forest, in their openness, dimness and color finding them fancifully attractive. Now, as I struggled through them, with each step, or hop rather, feeling as if a red-hot nail was being driven into my knee, my image of the tree groves began to change. They became darkling, ominous, hateful and full of cruelty, in the fact that they held us trapped in their shadow where the Friendly armor would seek us out and destroy us either with heat beams or falling trees before we had a chance to explain who we were.

I had hoped desperately that we would catch sight of an open area. For the armored vehicles floating up behind us were hunting the woods, not the open spaces; and particularly out in the open knee-high grass, it would be hard for even an armored pilot to see and identify my cape before shooting at us.

But we had evidently moved into an area where there were much more trees than open spaces. Also, as I had noticed before, all directions among those tree trunks looked alike. Our only way of being sure we would not be traveling in circles, but of keeping in a straight line away from the pursuing tanks, was to follow back along the direction we had come. This direction we could follow because we could be guided back along it by my wrist director. But that direction, that line of march that had brought us here, had been deliberately through all the treed areas I could find.

Meanwhile, we were moving at so slow a pace because of my knee that even the relatively slow-moving armor must soon catch up with us. I had been badly shaken by the sonic explosion earlier. Now, the continual jab-jabbing of the brilliant pain through my knee goaded me into a sort of feverish frenzy. It was like some calculated torture—and it happens that I am not a stoic when it comes to pain.

Neither am I cowardly, though I do not think it would be fair to call me brave, either. It is simply that I am so constructed that my response to pain beyond a certain level is fury. And the greater the pain the greater my rage. Some ancient berserker blood, perhaps, filtering down through the Irish in my veins, if you want to be romantic about it. But there it is—the fact. And now, as we hobbled through the eternal twilight ·between those gold-and-silver, peeling tree trunks, I exploded inside.

In my rage, I had no fear of the Friendly armor. I was certain of the fact that they would see my white and scarlet cloak in time not to fire at me. I was positive that if they did fire, both their beam and any falling tree trunks or limbs would miss me. In short I was convinced of my own invulnerability—and the only thing that concerned me was that Dave was being slowed down by being with me and that if anything happened to him Eileen would never get over it.

I raved at him, I cursed him. I told him to go on and leave me, and save his own neck, that I was in no danger by myself.

His only answer was that I had not abandoned him when the sonic barrage caught us both; and he would not abandon me. I was Eileen's brother and it was his duty to take care of me. It was just as she had said in her letter, he was loyal. He was too damn loyal, he was a loyal damn fool—and I told him so, obscenely and at length. I tried valiantly to pull away from him; but hopping on one leg, tottering on one leg rather, it was no use. I sank down on the ground and refused to go any farther; but he actually outwrestled me and got me up on his back, piggy-back, and tried to carry me that way.

That was even worse. I had to promise to go along with him, if he would let me down. He was already tottering himself from weariness when he let me. By that time, half-insane with my pain and my fury, I was ready to do anything to save him from himself. I began to yell for help as loudly as I could in spite of his efforts to shut me up.

It worked. In less than five minutes after he got me quiet we found ourselves staring down the pin-hole muzzles of the spring-rifles in the hands of two young Friendly skirmishers, attracted by my shouts.

CHAPTER 12 ■

I had expected them to appear in answer to my shouts
even more quickly. The Friendly skirmishers were
naturally all around us almost from the moment we
left the hill to its dead, under the command of their
dead Force-Leader. These two might have been
among the same Friendlies who had discovered the
patrol dug in on the hill in the first place. But, having
found it, they had moved on.

For it was their job to discover important pockets
of Cassidan resistance, so that they could call for
strength to eliminate those points. They would be
carrying listening devices as part of their equipment,
but they would pay little attention if those devices
picked up merely the sound of two men arguing. Two
men were game too small for their orders to concern
themselves with.

But one man deliberately calling for help—that was

an occurrence unusual enough to be worth investigating. A Soldier of the Lord should not be weak enough to be so calling, whether he needed personal assistance or not. And why should a Cassidan be appealing for aid in this area where no fighting had been going on? And who other than Soldiers of the Lord or their weaponed enemies might be in this zone of battle?

Now they knew who might be—a Newsman and his assistant. Both noncombatants, as I was quick to point out to them. Nevertheless the spring-rifles remained steadily aimed at us.

"Damn your eyes!" I told them. "Can't you see I need medical attention? Get me to one of your field hospitals right away!"

They looked back at me with startlingly innocent eyes in smooth young faces. The one on the right wore the single collar mark of a lance-private, the other was an ordinary battle-class private soldier. Neither one of them was out of his teens.

"We have no orders to turn aside and return to a field hospital," said the lance-private, speaking for both of them, as the—barely—superior in rank. "I can only conduct you to a gathering spot for prisoners, where no doubt other measures will be taken for your care." He stepped back, his rifle still aimed at us. "Do thou help the other to aid this wounded man along, Greten," he said dropping into the cant to speak to his partner. "Take his other side and I will follow with both our weapons."

The other soldier passed over his spring-rifle and between him and Dave, I began getting over the ground a little more comfortably, although the rage still seethed and bubbled in me. They brought us to a clearing finally, not an actual grass-filled clearing exposed to the sun, but a spot where one huge tree had fallen and left open a sort of glade among the other giants. Here, there were perhaps twenty or so dejected-looking Cassidans, disarmed and being held under guard by four young Friendlies like those who had captured us.

Dave and the young Friendly soldier sat me down carefully with my back to the stump of the huge fallen tree. Then Dave was herded over to join the rest of the uniformed Cassidans, who were backed against the tall trunk of the fallen and moldering tree itself, with the four armed Friendly guards facing them. I shouted that Dave should be left with me as a non-combatant, pointing out his white armband and lack of insignia. But all six of the men in black uniforms ignored me.

"Who hath rank here?" asked the lance-private of the four guards.

"I am senior," answered one of them, "but my rank is less than thine."

He was, in fact, a plain battle-private. However, he was well into his twenties, plainly older than the rest of them, and his quick disclaimer of authority had the ring of the experienced soldier, who has learned not to volunteer for things.

"This man is a Newsman," said the lance-private, indicating me, "and does claim the other under his protection. Certain the Newsman needeth medical attention; and though none of us can take him to the nearest field hospital, maybe thou canst call his case to the attention of higher authority over thy communicator."

"We have none," said the older soldier. "Message center is two hundred meters distant."

"I and Greten will remain to assist thy guard while one of you go to your message center."

"There was no provision"—the older, battle-private looked stubborn—"in our orders for one of us to leave for such a purpose."

"Surely this is a special case and situation?"

"There was no provision."

"But—"

"I tell thee, there was no provision made for this!" the battle-private shouted at him. "We can do nothing until an officer or a Groupman comes!"

"Will he come shortly?" The lance-private had been shaken by the vehemence of the objections of the older man. He glanced over at me worriedly; and I thought that perhaps he was beginning to think he had made a mistake in even mentioning medical help for us. But I had underestimated him. His face was a little pale, but he spoke evenly enough to the older man.

"I do not know," answered the other.

"Then I myself will go to your message center. Wait here, Greten."

He shouldered his spring-rifle and went off. We never saw him again.

Meanwhile, the fury and the body adrenalin that had helped me fight the pain of the hole drilled through my kneecap and the flesh and nerves and bone beyond it were beginning to wear off. I no longer felt the recurrent stab of agony as I tried to move the leg, but a swelling, steady ache was beginning to send billows of pain up my thigh from it—or so it seemed—and this was making me lightheaded. I began to wonder if I could stand it—and then, suddenly, with the feeling of stupidity that hits you when you realize all at once that what you have been searching for has been right before your eyes all this time, I remembered my belt.

Clipped to my belt, as to the belt of all soldiers, was a field-medication kit. Almost ready to laugh in spite of the pain, I reached for it now, fumbled it open, thumbed out two of the octagonal pills I found there—unaccountably, it was growing dark under the trees where we were, so that I could not make out their red color, but their shape was identity enough. It had been designed for just that purpose.

I chewed and swallowed them dry. Off in the distance, it seemed, I heard Dave's voice, unaccountably shouting. But, swift as cyanide on the tongue, the anesthetic, tranquilizing effect of the pain pills was sweeping through me. The pain was washed away before it, leaving me feeling whole, and clean and new—and unconcerned about anything beyond the peace and comfort of my own body.

Once more I heard Dave shouting. This time I understood him, but the message of his shouting had no power to disturb me. He was calling that he had already given me the pain pills from his own kit, when I had passed out twice before. He was shouting that I had now taken an overdose, that someone should help me. Distant, also, at the same time, the grove grew quite dark and there was a roll like thunder overhead, and then I heard, as one hears some distant, charming symphony, the patter of millions of raindrops on the millions of leaves far overhead.

And I went away into comforting nothingness.

* * *

When I came back to myself again, for a while I paid very little attention to anything around me, for I was cramped and nauseated, with the aftereffects of the drug overdose. My knee no longer hurt if it was not moved, but it had swollen and grown stiff as a steel rod; and the slightest movement of it brought a jolt of pain that shook me like a blow.

I vomited and began slowly to feel better internally. Slowly, I began to be aware once more of what was going on around me. I was wet to the skin, for the rain, after being held up a little by the leaves overhead, had worked its way down to us. Off a little way by the trees, both the prisoners and the guards made a sodden group. There was a newcomer in the black uniform of the Friendlies. He was a Groupman, middle-aged, lean and lined heavily in the face; and he had taken the battle-private called Greten aside in my direction, evidently to argue with him.

Above us, in the little openings between the tree branches that had been left by the falling of the giant tree that had produced the forest glade, the sky had lightened after the thunderstorm; but though it was cloudless, it was all flushed now with the crimson of sunset. To my drug-distorted vision, that red came down and painted the outlines of the wet-dark figures of the gray-clad prisoners, and glittered the soaked black uniforms of the Friendlies.

Red and black, black and red, they were like some figures in a stained-glass window, under the huge, over-arching frame of the shadow-dark giants that were the trees. I sat there, chilled by my own heavy, damp clothes, staring at the Groupman and the battle-private in their argument. And gradually their words, low-pitched so that they would not carry to the prisoners, but plain to my closer ears, began to make sense to me.

"Thou art a child!" the Groupman was snarling. He lifted his head a little with the vehemence of his emotion; and the sunset sky reached down to illuminate his face with red, so that I saw it clearly for the first time—and saw in its starved features and graven lines the same sort of harsh and utter fanaticism I had found in the Groupman at Friendly Battle Headquarters who had turned down the chance of a pass for Dave.

"Thou art a child!" he repeated. "Young thou art! What dost thou know of the struggle to gain sustenance, generation on generation, on our harsh and stony worlds, as I have known it? What dost thou know of hunger and want, even to the women and babes, I say it, among the Children of the Lord? What dost thou know of the purposes of them who send us to battle, that our people may live and flourish when all men elsewhere would gladly see us dead and our faith dead and buried with us?"

"I know something," retorted the younger soldier, though his voice showed its youth and trembled a little even as he answered. "I know that we have a duty to the right, and that we have sworn to the Mercenaries' Code, and—"

"Shut thy milk-babe mouth!" hissed the Groupman. "What are Codes before the Code of the Almighty? What are oaths other than our oath to the God of Battles? Lo, our Eldest of our Council of Elders, he who is called Bright, hath said that this day bears hard upon the future of our people, and the winning of this day's war is a need that we must meet. Therefore shall we win! And nothing else!"

"But still I tell thee—"

"Thou shalt tell me nothing! I am thy superior! I tell *thee*. Our orders are to regroup for another attack upon the enemy. Thou and these four with thee are to report *now*, to their message center. It recks not that thou art not of their unit. Thou hast been called and will obey!"

"Then we shall take the prisoners safely with us—"

"Thou shalt obey!" The Groupman was carrying his spring-gun slung under one arm. He swung it around into his grasp so that the barrel pointed at the private. The Groupman's thumb pushed the control of the weapon to automatic fire. I saw Greten's eyes close for a second and his throat worked; but when his voice came out, it was still steady.

"Yet all my life have I walked in the shadow of the Lord which is truth and faith—" I heard him say, and the barrel came up. I shouted at the Groupman.

"You! Hey, you—Groupman!"

He jerked about like a timber wolf at the sound of a snapping twig under a hunter's boot—and I was looking down the pinhole muzzle of his automatic-set spring-rifle myself. Then he came toward me, gun still aimed, and the axe blade of his starved fanatic's face above it looked down at me.

"Thou art sensible, then?" he said. And the words were like a sneer. I read in them a contempt for anyone weak enough to take a pain-killer for the relief of any physical discomfort.

"Sensible enough to tell you a few things," I croaked. My throat was dry and my leg was beginning to stir to an ache again, but he was good medicine for me, reawakening my anger, so that the returning hurt could feed the fury that rose easily in me. "Listen to me. I'm a Newsman. You've been around long enough to know that nobody wears this cape and beret who isn't entitled to them. But just to make sure"—I dug into my jacket and produced them—"here are my papers. Look them over."

He took them and glanced through them.

"All right now," I said, when he had looked at the last of them. "I'm a Newsman and you're a Groupman. And I'm not asking you anything—I'm telling you! I want transportation to a field hospital immediately, and I want my assistant over there"—and I pointed at Dave—"returned to me. Now! Not ten minutes from now, or two minutes from now; but now! These privates who've been on guard here may not think they have the authority to get me and my assistant out of here and me to a hospital, but you know you have. And I want it done!"

He stared from the papers to me and there came over his face a peculiar grimness of cast, the sort of look a man might get as he shakes off the grasp of those escorting him to a gallows and strides forward to the place of his execution contemptuously under his own power.

"Thou art a Newsman," he said, and drew a deep breath. "Aye, thou art one of Anarch's breed, who with lies and false report spreads hatred of our people and our faith throughout the worlds of men. I know thee well, Newsman"—he stared at me with black, hollowed eyes—"and thy papers to me are but trash and nonsense. But I will humor thee, and show thee how little thou weighest in the balance, with all thy foul reports. I will give thee a story to write, and thou shalt write it, and thou shalt see how it is less than dry leaves blowing before the marching feet of the Anointed of the Lord.''

"Get me to a field hospital," I said.

"Thou shalt wait for that," he said. "Further" —and he waved the papers at me—"I see here thy pass, but no pass signed by one of authority in our ranks that gives free passage to the one thou callest thy assistant. Therefore he shall not come to thee, but remain with those prisoners of like uniform, to meet what the Lord shall send them."

He threw the papers down into my lap, turned and stalked off, back toward the prisoners. I shouted after him, telling him to come back; but he paid me no attention.

But Greten ran after him, caught him by the arm and murmured something in his ear, meanwhile gesturing sharply toward the group of prisoners. The Groupman shoved him off with a thrust of his arm that sent Greten staggering.

"Are they of the Chosen?" the Groupman shouted. "Are *they* Chosen of God?"

And he whirled about in fury, with his spring-rifle still set on automatic menacing not merely Greten, but the other guards as well.

"Fall in!" he shouted.

Some slowly, some hastily, they left off guarding the prisoners and fell into line, facing the Groupman.

"You shall all report to the Message Center— now!" the Groupman snapped. "Right face!" And they turned. *"Move out!"*

And so they left us, moving off out of my sight among the shadows of the trees.

The Groupman watched after them for a second,

then turned his attention and his rifle back on the Cassidan prisoners. They shrank a little from him; and I saw the white, indistinct outline of Dave's face turned momentarily in my direction.

"Now, your guards are gone," the Groupman said to them slowly and grimly. "For an assault begins that will wipe your forces from the field. In that assault every soldier of the Lord is needed, for a call has been placed upon us by our Eldest in Council. Even I must go—and I cannot leave enemies like yourselves unguarded behind our lines, to do mischief against our victory. Therefore, I send you now to a place from which you cannot harm the Anointed of the Lord."

In that moment, in that moment only, for the first time, I understood what he meant. And I opened my mouth to shout; but nothing came out. I tried to rise, but my stiff leg would not let me. And I hung there, mouth open, frozen in the act of half-rising.

He opened fire at full automatic upon the unarmed men before him. And they fell—Dave among them— they dropped and fell, and died.

CHAPTER 13 ■

I am not clear in my mind exactly how things went after that. I remember, when there was no longer any stir or movement among the fallen bodies, how the Groupman turned and came toward me, holding his rifle in one hand.

He seemed, though he strode swiftly, to come slowly, slowly but inexorably. It was as if I watched him on a treadmill growing ever bigger as he loomed closer to me with the black rifle in his hand and the red sky behind his head. Until, at last, he reached me and stopped, standing over me.

I also tried to shrink from him, but could not; for the great stump of the tree was behind me and my damaged leg, itself stiff as a dead stick of wood, anchored me. But he did not lift his rifle against me; and he did not shoot me.

"There," he said, looking at me. His voice was

deep and calm, but his eyes were strange. "Thou hast thy story, Newsman. And thou shalt live to report it. Perhaps they will let thee come when I am led before a firing squad—unless the Lord decrees otherwise, so that I fall in the assault now beginning. But though they executed me a million times over, thy writing will avail thee nothing. For I, who am the fingers of the Lord, have writ His will upon these men, and that writing thou cannot erase. So shalt thou know at last how little is *thy* writing in the face of that which is written by the God of Battles."

He stepped back from me one step without turning his back. It was almost as if I were some dark altar from which he retreated with ironic respect.

"Now, farewell, Newsman," he said, and a hard smile twisted his lips. "Fear not, for they will find thee. And save thy life."

He turned and went. I saw him go, black into the blackness of the deeper shadows; and then I was alone.

I was alone—alone with the still dripping leaves ticking occasionally upon the forest floor. Alone with the red-darkening sky, showing in its tiny patches between the growing black masses of the treetops. Alone with the day's end and the dead.

I do not know how I did it, but after a while I began to crawl, dragging my useless leg along with me, over the wet forest floor until I came to the still heap of bodies. In the little light that remained I hunted through them until I found Dave. A line of slivers had stitched themselves across the lower part of his chest, and from there on down his jacket was soaked with blood. But his eyelids fluttered as I got my arm around his shoulders and lifted him up so that I could support his head on my good knee. His face was as white and smooth as the face of a child in sleep.

"Eileen?" he said faintly but clearly as I lifted him. But he did not open his eyes.

I opened my mouth to say something, but at first no sound would come out. Then, when I could make my vocal cords work, they sounded strange.

"She'll be here in a minute," I said.

The answer seemed to soothe him. He lay still, hardly breathing. The calmness of his face made it seem as if he were not in any pain. I heard a steady sound of dripping that at first I took to be the rain dripping still from some leaf overhead; but then I put down my hand and felt the falling of dampness on its palm. The dripping was of his blood, from the lower part of his soaked jacket, onto the forest earth below where the mosslike groundcover had been scuffed away by the scrabbling of dying men, leaving the bare earth.

I hunted around as best I could for wound dressings on the bodies near us, without disturbing Dave upon my knee. I found three of them, and tried to stop his wounds with them, but it was no use. He was bleeding from half a dozen places. By trying to put the bandages on I disturbed him, rousing him a little.

"Eileen?" he asked.

"She'll be here in a minute," I told him, again.

And, later on, after I had given up and was just sitting, holding him, he asked again.

"Eileen?"

"She'll be here in a minute."

But by the time the full dark passed and the moon rose high enough to send its silver light down through the little opening into the trees, so that I could see his face again, he was dead.

CHAPTER 14 ◼

I was found just after sunrise, not by Friendly, but by Cassidan troops. Kensie Graeme had fallen back at the south end of his battle line before Bright's well-laid plan of an attack to crush the Cassidan defenses there and cut them up in the streets of Dhores. But Kensie, foreseeing this, had robbed the southern end of his line and sent the armor and infantry so acquired swinging wide around to reinforce the north end of his line, where Dave and I had been.

The result was that his line pivoted about a central point, which was just about at the motor pool where I had first caught sight of him. The advancing reinforced north end of it, the following morning, swept around and down, cutting the Friendly communications and crashing in upon the rear of those Friendly troops that thought they had most of the Cassidan levies penned and broken up within the city.

Dhores, which was to have been a rock on which the Cassidan levies were broken up, became instead the rock on which the Friendly forces themselves were broken. The black-clad warriors fought with their usual fierceness and reckless bravery on being trapped; but they were between the barrage of Kensie's sonic cannon to the west of the city and his fresh forces piling in upon their rear. Finally, the Friendly Command, rather than lose any more of the valuable battle units in human shape that were their soldiers, surrendered—and the civil war between the North and South Partitions of New Earth was over, won by the Cassidan levies.

But I cared nothing about this. I was taken, half-conscious from medication, back to Molon for hospitalization. The wound in my knee had complicated itself from lack of attention—I do not know the details; but, though they were able to heal it, it remained stiff. The only cure for that, the medicians told me, was surgery and a whole new, completely artificial knee—and they advised against that. The original flesh and blood, they said, was still better than anything man could build to replace it.

For my part, I did not care. They had caught and tried the Groupman who had perpetrated the massacre; and—as he himself had predicted—he had been executed by firing squad under the provisions of the Mercenaries' Code with respect to the treatment of prisoners. But I did not care even about that.

Because—again as he himself had said—his execution did not alter things. What he had written upon Dave and the other prisoners with his spring-rifle was past the power of me, or any other man, to erase; and by this much he had done something to me.

I was like a clock with a broken part in it that does not keep it from running, but which you can hear rattling away, if you pick the clock up and shake it. I had been broken, inside; and not even the commendation that came from the Interstellar News Service and my acceptance into full membership in the Guild could mend me. But the wealth and power of the Guild was caring for me, now that I was a full member; and they did what few private organizations would have been able to do—they sent me to the wizards of mental mending on Kultis, the larger of the two Exotic Worlds, for treatment.

On Kultis, they enticed me into mending myself—but they could not force the manner in which I chose to mend. First, because they did not have the power (though I am not sure if they actually realized how limited they were, in my particular case) and secondly, because their basic philosophy forbade the use of force in their own proper persons, and also forbade them any attempt to control the individual's self-will. They could only beckon me down the road they wished I would go.

And the instrument they chose to beckon me down that road was a powerful one. It was Lisa Kant.

"—But you're not a psychiatrist!" I said in astonishment to Lisa when she first appeared in the place on Kultis to which I had been brought—one of their many-purposed indoor-outdoor structures. I had been lying by a swimming pool, ostensibly soaking up sun and relaxing, when she showed up suddenly beside me and replied, in answer to my question, that Padma had recommended she be the person to work with me in getting my emotional strength back.

"How do you know what I am?" she snapped

back, not at all with the calm self-control of a born Exotic. "It's been five years since I first met you in the Encyclopedia, and I'd already been a student then for years!"

I lay blinking at her, as she stood over me. Slowly, something that had been dormant in me began to come back to life and began to tick and move once more. I got to my feet. Here was I, who had been able to choose the proper words to make people dance like puppets, making a blundering assumption like that.

"Then you actually are a psychiatrist?" I asked.

"Yes and no," she answered me quietly. Suddenly she smiled at me. "Anyway, you don't need a psychiatrist."

The moment she said this, I woke to the fact that this was exactly my own thought, that it had been my own thought all along, but encased in my own misery I had let the Guild plow to its own conclusions. Suddenly, all through the machinery of my mental awareness, little relays began to click over and perceptions to light up again.

If she knew that much, how much more did she know? At once, the alarms were ringing throughout the mental citadel I had spent these last five years in building, and defenses were rushing to their post.

"Maybe you're right," I said, suddenly wary; and I grinned at her. "Why don't we sit down and talk it over?"

"Why not?" she said.

And so we did sit down and talk—unimportant make-conversation to begin with, while I sized her up. There was a strange echo about her. I can describe it no other way. Everything she said, every gesture or movement of her, seemed to ring with special meaning for me, a meaning I could not quite interpret.

"Why did Padma think you could—I mean, think that you ought to come here and see me?" I asked cautiously after a while.

"Not just see you—work with you," she corrected me. She was wearing not the Exotic robes, but some ordinary, short street dress of white. Above it her eyes were a darker brown than I had ever seen them. Suddenly she darted a glance at me as challenging and sharp as a spear. "Because he believes I'm one of the two portals by which you can still be reached, Tam."

The glance and the words shook me. If it had not been for that strange echo about her, I might have fallen into the error of thinking she was inviting me. But it was something bigger than that.

I could have asked her then and there what she meant; but I was just newly reawakened and cautious. I changed the subject—I think I invited her to join me for a swim or something—and I did not come back to the subject until several days later.

By that time, aroused and wary, I had had a chance to look around me and see where the echo came from, to see what was being done to me by Exotic methods. I was being worked on subtly, by a skillful coordination of total environmental pressure, pressure that did not try to steer me in one direction or another, but which continually urged me to take hold of the tiller of my own being and steer myself. Briefly, the structure that housed me, the weather that bathed it, the very walls and furniture and colors and shapes that inhabited it, were so designed that they subtly combined to urge me to live—not only to live, but to live actively, fully and joyously. It was not merely a happy dwelling—it was an exciting dwelling, a stimulating environment that wrapped me around.

And Lisa was a working part of it.

I began to notice that as I roused from my depression, not only did the colors and shapes of the furniture and of the dwelling itself alter day by day, but her choice of conversational subjects, her tone of voice, her laughter changed as well, to continue to exert maximum pressure upon my own shifting and developing feelings. I do not think even Lisa herself understood how the parts combined to produce the gestalt effect. It would have taken a native Exotic to understand that. But she understood—consciously or subconsciously—her own part in it. And played it.

I did not care. Automatically, inevitably, as I healed myself I was falling in love with her.

Women had never been hard for me to find, from the time I broke loose from my uncle's house and began to feel my own powers of mind and body. Especially the beautiful ones, in whom there was often a strange hunger for affection that often ran unsatisfied. But before Lisa they had all, beautiful or not, broken, and turned hollow on me. It was as if I were continually capturing song-sparrows and bringing them home, only to find the following morning that they had become common sparrows overnight and their wild song had dwindled to a single chirp.

Then I would realize that it was my own fault—it was I who had made song-sparrows of them. Some chance trait or element in them had touched me off like a skyrocket, so that my imagination had soared, and my tongue with it, so that I had lifted us both up with words and carried us off to a place of pure light and air and green grass and running water. And there I had built us a castle full of light and air and promise and beauty.

They always liked my castle. They would come gladly up on the wings of my imagination, and I would believe that we flew together. But later, on a different day, I would wake to the fact that the light was gone, the song was muted. For they had not really believed in my castle. It was well enough to dream of such a thing, but not to think of translating it into ordinary stone, and wood, and glass and tile. When it came to these matters of reality, a castle was madness; and I should put the thought aside for some real dwelling. Perhaps of poured concrete like the home of my uncle Mathias. With practical vision screen instead of windows, with economic roof, not soaring turrets, and weathered-glassed porches, not open loggias. And so we parted.

But Lisa did not leave me as the others always had when at last I fell in love with her. She soared with me and soared again on her own. And then, for the first time I knew why she was different, why she would never retreat earthward like the others.

It was because she had built castles of her own, before I ever met her. So she needed no help from me to lift her to the land of enchantment, for she had reached there before on her own strong wings. We were sky-matched, though our castles were different.

It was that difference in castles which stopped me, which came at last to shatter the Exotic shell. Because when finally I would have made love to her, she stopped me.

"No, Tam," she said, and she fended me off. "Not yet."

"Not yet" might have meant "not this minute," or "not until tomorrow"; but, looking at the change that had come into her face, the way her eyes looked a little away from mine, suddenly I knew better. Something stood like a barred gate half-ajar between us, and my mind leaped to name it.

"The Encyclopedia," I said. "You still want me to come back and work on it." I stared at her. "All right. Ask me again."

She shook her head.

"No," she said, in a low voice. "Padma told me before I hunted you out at the Donal Graeme party that you would never come just because I asked you. But I didn't believe him then. I believe him now." She turned her face back to look me squarely in the eyes. "If I did ask now, and told you to take a moment to think about it before answering, you'd say no all over again, even now."

She sat, staring at me, by the side of the pool where we were, in the sunlight, with a bush of great yellow roses behind her, and the light of the flowers upon her.

"Wouldn't you, Tam?" she asked.

I opened my mouth, and then I closed it again. Because, like the stone hand of some heathen god, all that I had forgotten while I mended here, all of that which Mathias and then the Friendly Groupman had carved upon my soul, came back heavily down upon me.

The barred gate slammed shut then between Lisa

and me, and its closing echoed in the inmost depths of my being.

"That's right," I admitted hollowly. "You're right. I'd say no."

I looked at Lisa, sitting among the shatters of our mutual dream. And I remembered something.

"When you first came here," I said slowly but unsparingly, for she was almost my enemy again now, "you mentioned something about Padma saying you were one of the two portals by which I could be reached. What was the other one? I didn't ask you then."

"But now you can't wait to stop up the other one, can you, Tam?" she said a little bitterly. "All right— tell me something." She picked up a petal fallen from one of the flowers behind her and tossed it onto the still waters of the pool, where it floated like some fragile yellow boat. "Have you gotten in touch with your sister?"

Her words crashed in upon me like a bar of iron. All the matter of Eileen and Dave, and Dave's death after I had promised Eileen to keep him safe, came swarming back on me. I found myself on my feet without knowing how I had gotten there, and a cold sweat had sprung out all over me.

"I haven't been able—" I started to answer; but my voice failed me. It strangled itself in the tightness of my throat and I stood face to face in my own soul with the knowledge of my own cowardice.

"*They've* notified her!" I shouted, turning furiously on Lisa where she still sat watching up at me. "The Cassidan authorities will have told her all about it! What's the matter—don't you think she knows what happened to Dave?"

But Lisa said nothing. She only sat, looking up at me. Then I realized that she would go on saying nothing. No more than the Exotics who had trained her almost from the cradle would she tell me what to do.

But she did not have to. The Devil had been raised again in my soul; and he stood, laughing on the far side of a river of glowing coals, daring me to come over and tangle with him. And neither man nor Devil has ever challenged me in vain.

I turned from Lisa, and I went.

CHAPTER 15 ■

As a full member of the Guild, I no longer had to produce an assignment as a reason for drawing travel money. The currency between worlds was knowledge and skills wrapped up in the human packages that conveyed these things. In the same way, a credit easily convertible into this currency was the information collected and transferred by the skilled Communications people of the Interstellar News Guild—which was no less necessary to the individual worlds between the stars. So the Guild was not poor; and the two hundred or so full members had funds to draw upon on each one of the sixteen worlds that might have made a government leader envious.

The curious result of which in my case, I discovered, was that money as such ceased to have any meaning for me. In that corner of my mind which before this had concerned itself with spendables, there was now a void—and rushing in to fill that void, it seemed, through the long flight from Kultis to Cassida, were memories. Memories of Eileen.

I had not thought that she had been so important a part of my young life, both before our parents' death, and especially after. But now, as our space ship shifted, and paused, and shifted again between the stars, moments and scenes came thronging to my mind as I sat alone in my first-class compartment. Or for that matter, still alone in the lounge, for I was in no mood for company.

They were not dramatic memories. They were recollections of gifts she had given me on this birthday or that. They were moments in which she had helped me to bear up under the unendurable empty pressure of Mathias upon my soul. There were unhappy moments of her own that I recalled now as well, that I now realized had been unhappy and lonely, but that I had not understood at the time, because of being so bound up in my own unhappiness. Suddenly it came to me that I could remember any number of times when she had ignored her own troubles to do something about mine; and never—there was no single instance I could recall—had I ever forgotten mine even to consider hers.

As all this came back to me, my very guts shrank up into a cold, hard knot of guilt and unhappiness. I tried between one set of shifts to see if I could not drink the memories away. But I found I had no taste either for the liquor or for that as a way out.

And so I came to Cassida.

A poorer, smaller planetary counterpart of Newton, with whom it shared a double-sun system, Cassida lacked the other world's academic link with and consequently the rarefied supply of scientific and mathematical minds that had made the earlier-settled world of Newton a rich one. From Cassida's capital-city spaceport of Moro, I took a shuttle flight to Alban, the Newton-sponsored University City where Dave had been studying shift mechanics, and where both he and Eileen had held supportive jobs while he did so.

It was an efficient ant-hill of a city on various levels. Not that there had been any lack of land on which to build it, but because most of it had been built by Newtonian credit; and the building method most economical of that credit had been one that clustered all necessary quarters together in the smallest practical space.

I picked up a direction rod at the shuttleport and set it for the address Eileen had given me in that one letter received the morning of Dave's death. It pointed me the way through a series of vertical and horizontal tubes and passageways to a housing-complex unit that was above ground level—but that was about the best you could say for it.

As I turned into the final hallway that led to the door of the address I hunted, for the first time the true emotion that had kept me from even consciously thinking of Eileen, until Lisa recalled her directly to my attention, began to boil up in me. The scene in the forest clearing on New Earth rose again around me as vividly as a nightmare; and fear and rage began to burn in me like a fever.

For a moment I faltered—I almost stopped. But then the momentum I had built up by the long voyage this far carried me on to the doorway and I sounded the doorcall.

There was a second's eternity of waiting. Then the door opened and a middle-aged woman's face looked out. I stared down into it in shock, for it was not the face of my sister.

"Eileen . . ." I stammered. "I mean—Mrs. David Hall? Isn't she here?" Then I remembered that this woman could not know me. "I'm her brother—from Earth. Newsman Tam Olyn."

I was wearing cape and beret, of course, and in a way this was passport enough. But for the moment I had forgotten all about it. I remembered then as the woman fluttered a bit. She had probably never before seen a member of the Guild in the actual flesh.

"Why, she's moved," the woman said. "This place was too big for her alone. She's down a few levels and north of here. Just a minute, I'll get you her number."

She darted away. I heard her talking to a male voice for a moment, and then she came back with a slip of paper.

"Here," she said a little breathlessly. "I wrote it down for you. You go right along this corridor—oh, I see you've got a direction rod. Just set it then. It's not far."

"Thank you," I said.

"Not at all. We're glad to—well, I mustn't keep you, I suppose," she said, for I was already beginning to turn away. "Glad to be of service. Good-bye."

"Good-bye," I muttered. I was moving off down the corridor resetting the direction rod. It led me away and down and the door I finally pressed the call button on was well below ground level.

There was a longer wait this time. Then, at last, the door slid back—and my sister stood there.

"Tam," she said.

She did not seem to have changed at all. There was no sign of change or grief upon her, and my mind leaped suddenly with hope. But when she simply continued to stand there, looking at me, the hope sank once more. I could do nothing but wait. I stood there also.

"Come in," she said finally, but without much change in tone. She stood aside and I walked in. The door slid closed behind me.

I looked around, shocked out of my emotion for the moment by what I saw. The gray-draped room was no bigger than the first-class compartment I had occupied on the spaceship coming there.

"What're you doing living here?" I burst out.

She looked at me without any response to my shock.

"It's cheaper," she said indifferently.

"But you don't need to save money!" I said. "I got that arrangement made for your inheritance from Mathias—it was all set with an Earth-working Cassidan to transfer funds from his family back here to you. You mean"—for the thought had never occurred to me before—"there's been some hitch at this end? Hasn't his family been paying you?"

"Yes," she said calmly enough. "But there's Dave's family now to take care of, too."

"Family?" I stared stupidly at her.

"Dave's younger brother's still in school—never mind." She stood still. Nor had she asked me to sit down. "It's too long a story, Tam. What've you come here for?"

I stared at her.

"Eileen," I said pleadingly. She only waited. "Look," I said, snatching at the straw of our earlier subject, "even if you're helping out Dave's family, there's no problem anymore. I'm a full Guild member now. I can supply you with anything in the way of funds you need."

"No." She shook her head.

"In heaven's name, why not? I tell you I've got unlimited—"

"I don't want anything from you, Tam," she said. "Thank you anyway. But we're doing fine, Dave's family and myself. I've got a good job."

"Eileen!"

"I asked you once, Tam," she said, still unmoved. "Why've you come here?"

If she had been changed to stone, there could not have been a greater difference in her from the sister I had known. She was no one I knew. She was like a perfect stranger to me.

"To see you," I said. "I thought—you might like to know—"

"I know all about it," she said, with no emotion at all. "I was told all about it. They said you were wounded, too; but you're well now, aren't you, Tam?"

"Yes," I said, helplessly. "I'm well now. My knee's a little stiff. They say it'll stay that way."

"That's too bad," she said.

"Damn it, Eileen!" I burst out. "Don't just stand there talking to me as if you don't know me! I'm your brother!"

"No." She shook her head. "The only relatives I have now—the only relatives I want now—are Dave's family. They need me. You don't and never did, Tam. You were always sufficient for yourself, by yourself.''

"Eileen!'' I said, pleadingly. "Look, I know you must blame me—partly at least—for Dave's death.''

"No,'' she answered. "You can't help being what you are. It was my fault, all these years, for trying to convince myself that you were something different from what you are. I thought there was something about you that Mathias never got to, something that just needed a chance to come out. It was that I was counting on when I asked you to help me decide about Jamie. And when you wrote you were going to help Dave, I was sure that what I'd always thought was in you was finally coming to the front. But I was wrong both times.''

"Eileen!'' I cried. "It wasn't my fault we ran into a madman, Dave and I. Maybe I should have done something different—but I did try to make him leave me after I got shot, only he wouldn't. Don't you understand, it *wasn't all my fault*!''

"Of course it wasn't, Tam,'' she said. I stared at her. "That's why I don't blame you. You're no more responsible for what you do than a police dog that's been trained to attack anyone who moves. You're what Uncle Mathias made you, Tam—a destroyer. It's not your fault, but that doesn't change anything. In spite of all the fighting you did with him, Mathias' teaching about *Destruct* filled you up, Tam, and didn't leave anything.''

"You can't say that!'' I shouted at her. "It's not true. Give me just one more chance, Eileen, and I'll show you! I tell you, it's not true!''

"Yes, it is,'' she said. "I know you, Tam, better

than anyone alive. And I've known this about you for a long time. I just wouldn't let myself believe it. But I have to, now—for the sake of Dave's family, who need me. I couldn't help Dave, but I can help them— as long as I never see you again. If I let you come close to them, through me, you'll destroy them, too.''

She stopped talking then and stood looking at me. I opened my mouth to answer her, but I could think of nothing to say. We stood looking at each other across a couple of feet of distance that was a wider, deeper space and gulf than I had ever encountered in my life.

''You'd better go, then, Tam,'' she said at last.

Her words stirred me numbly to life again.

''Yes,'' I said dully. ''I guess I'd better.''

I turned away from her. As I stepped toward the door I think I still hoped she might stop me and call me back. But there was no movement or sound behind me; and as I went out the door I glanced back for a final time over my shoulder.

She had not moved. She was still standing where she had been, like a stranger, waiting for me to go.

So I went. And I returned to the spaceport alone. Alone, alone, alone. . . .

CHAPTER 16 ■

I got on the first ship out for Earth. I had priority now over all but people with diplomatic status, and I used it. I bumped someone with a prior reservation and found myself once more alone in a first-class compartment, while the ship I was on shifted, stopped to calculate its position, and shifted again between the stars.

That closed cabin was like a sanctuary, a hermit's cell to me, a chrysalis in which I could lock and reshape myself before entering once more into the worlds of men in a different dimension. For I had been stripped to the very core of my old self and no single self-delusion remained, that I could see, to cover me.

Mathias had cleaned the most of the flesh of self-delusion off my bones early, of course. But here and there a shred had stuck—like the rain-washed memory of the ruins of the Parthenon that I used to gaze at in the vision screens as a boy after Mathias' deadly dialectic had stripped away one more shred of nerve or sinew. Just by being there, above the dark, windowless house, the Parthenon had seemed to my young mind to refute all Mathias' arguments.

It had been, once—and therefore he must be wrong, I used to comfort myself in thinking. It had existed, once it had been, and if the men of Earth were no more than Mathias said, it never could have been built. But it had *been*—that was what I saw now. For in the end it was no more than ruins and the dark defeatism of Mathias endured. So, at last now I came to it—I endured, in Mathias' image, and the dreams of glory and rightness somehow, in some way, for those born on Earth in spite of those changed and greater children of younger worlds, were ruins, like the Parthenon, filed away with other childish delusions, filed and forgotten in the rain.

What was it Lisa had said? If I had only understood her, I thought now, I could have foreseen this moment and saved myself the pain of hoping that Eileen might have forgiven me for Dave's death. Lisa had mentioned two portals, that there were only two portals left to me, and she was one of them. I understood what those portals were now. They were doorways through which love could get at me.

Love—the deadly sickness that robbed the strength from men. Not just carnal love, but any weak hungering for affection, for beauty, for hope of wonders to come. For I remembered now that there was one thing I had never been able to do. I had never been able to hurt Mathias, to shame, or even trouble him. And why not? Because he was as pure in health as any sterilized body. He loved not only no one, but nothing. And so, by giving away the universe, he had gained it, for the universe was nothing, too; and in that perfect symmetry of nothing into nothing he rested, like a stone, content.

With that understanding, I suddenly realized I could drink again. On the way here, I had not been able to do so because of my feeling of guilt and hope, and because of the tattered bits of corruptible, love-susceptible flesh still clinging to the pure skeleton of Mathias' philosophy in me. But now—

I laughed out loud in the empty compartment. Because then, on the way to Cassida when I most needed that anesthesia of liquor, I had not been able to use it. And now that I did not need it at all, I could swim in it if I wanted.

Always provided I had a due care for the respectableness of my professional position and did not overdo in public. But there was no reason keeping me back from getting drunk privately in my compartment right now if I wanted to. In fact, there was every reason to do just that. For this was an occasion for celebration—the hour of my deliverance from the weaknesses of the flesh and mind that caused pain to all ordinary men.

I ordered a bottle, a glass and ice; and I toasted myself in the mirror of my compartment, across from the lounge seat in which I sat, with the bottle at my elbow.

"Slainte, Tam Olyn bach!" I said to myself; for it was Scotch I had ordered, and all the Scot and Irish of my ancestors was frothing metaphorically in my veins at the moment. I drank deeply.

The good liquor burned inside me and spread

comfortably through me; and after a little while, as I went on drinking, the close walls of the compartment moved back away from me for some distance while the wide memory of how I had ridden the lightning, under Padma's hypnotic influence, that day at the Encyclopedia, came back to me.

Once more I felt the power and the fury that had come into me then, and for the first time I became aware of how I now stood, with no more human weaknesses to hold me back, to temper my use of that lightning. For the first time I saw possibilities in that use and the power of *Destruct*. Possibilities to which what Mathias had done, or even I had accomplished before now, were child's play.

I drank, dreaming of things that were possible. And, after a while, I fell asleep, or passed out, whichever it was; and I dreamed literally.

It was a dream I passed into from waking with no seeming transition. Suddenly, I was there—and *there* was someplace on a stony hillside, between the mountains and the western sea, in a small house of stone, chinked with turf and dirt. A small, one-room house with no fireplace, but a primitive hearth with walls on each side leading up to a hole in the roof for the smoke to get out. On the wall near the fire, on two wooden pegs driven into cracks between stones, hung my one valuable possession.

It was the family weapon, the true, original claymore—*claidheamh mōr*, the "great sword." Over four feet long it was, straight and double-edged and wide of blade, not tapering to the point. Its hilt had only a simple crossbar with the guards turned down. Altogether it was a two-handed broadsword carefully kept wrapped in greased rags and laid on its pegs, for it had no sheath.

But, at the time of my dream, I had taken it down and unwrapped it, for there was a man I was to meet in three days' time, some half a day's walk away. For two days the sky was fair, the sun bright but cold, and I sat out on the beach, sharpening the long sword's two edges with a gray stone from the beach, smoothed by the sea. On the morning of the third day it was overcast and with the dawn a light rain began falling. So I wrapped the sword in a corner of the long, rectangular plaid I had wound about me, and went to keep my appointment.

The rain blew cold and wet in my face and the wind was cold, but under the thick, almost oily wool of the plaid, my sword and I were dry, and a fine, fierce joy rose in me, a wondrous feeling greater than I had ever felt before. I could taste it as a wolf must taste hot blood in his mouth, for there was no feeling to compare to this—that I was going at last to my revenge.

And then I woke. I saw the bottle almost empty and felt the heavy, sluggish feeling of drunkenness; but the joy of my dream was still with me. So I stretched out on the lounge seat and fell asleep again.

This time I did not dream.

When I woke, I could feel no trace of a hangover. My mind was cold and clear and free. I could remember, as if it had been just the second before I had dreamed it, the terrible joy I had felt, going sword in hand to my meeting in the rain. And, at once, I saw my way clear before me.

I had sealed the two portals that remained—that meant I had stripped love from me. But now to replace it I had found this wine-rich joy of revenge. I almost laughed out loud as I thought about it, because I remembered what the Friendly Groupman had said, before he left me with the bodies of those he had massacred.

"What I have writ upon these men is beyond the power of you or any man to erase."

Oh, it was true enough. I could not erase that exact, particular writing of his. But I—alone among sixteen worlds of people—had it in my power and skill to erase something far greater than that. I could erase the instruments that made such writing. I was a rider and master of the lightning; and with that I could destroy the culture and people of both the Friendly worlds together. Already, I saw glimmerings of the method by which it could be done.

By the time my spaceship reached Earth, the basic outline of my plans was essentially made.

CHAPTER 17 ■

My immediate goal was a quick return to New Earth,
where Eldest Bright, having ransomed free the troops
Kensie Graeme's forces had captured, had immediately reinforced them. The reinforced unit had been
encamped outside Moreton, the North Partition capital, as an occupation force in demand of interstellar
credits due the Friendly Worlds for troops hired by
the now defunct rebel government.

But there was a matter to be taken care of before
I could go directly to New Earth. First, I needed a
sanction and a seal for what I intended to do. For,
once you were a full member of the Newsman's Guild
there was no higher authority over you—except for
the fifteen members that made up the Guild Council
to watchdog the Creed of Impartiality under which
we operated, and to set Guild policy, to which all
members must conform.

I made an appointment to see Piers Leaf, Chairman of that Council. It was a bright morning in April in St. Louis, just across the city from the Final Encyclopedia, that I finally found myself facing him across a wide, neatly bare oak desk in his office on the top floor of the Guild Hall.

"You've come a long way pretty fast for someone so young, Tam," he said, after he had ordered and received coffee for both of us. He was a dry-mannered, small man in his late fifties, who never left the Solar System nowadays and seldom left Earth, because of the public-relations aspect of his Chairmanship. "Don't tell me you still aren't satisfied? What do you want now?"

"I want a seat on the Council," I said.

He was lifting his coffee cup to his lips when I spoke. He went right on lifting without a pause. But the sudden glance he shot me over the rim of his cup was as sharp as a falcon's. But all he said was:

"Do you? Why?"

"I'll tell you," I said. "Maybe you've noticed I seem to have a knack for being where the news-stories are."

He set his cup down precisely in the center of its saucer.

"That, Tam," he said mildly, "is why you're wearing the cape permanently now. We expect certain things from members, you know."

"Yes," I said. "But I think mine may be a little bit out of the ordinary—oh," I said, as his eyebrows rose suddenly, "I'm not claiming some kind of precognition. I just think I happen to have a talent for a little more insight into the possibilities of situations than other members."

His eyebrows came down. He frowned slightly.

"I know," I said, "that sounds like boasting. But, just stop and suppose I have what I claim. Wouldn't a talent like that be highly useful to the Council in its policy decisions for the Guild?"

He looked at me sharply.

"Maybe," he said, "if it was true—and it worked every time—and a number of other things."

"But if I could convince you of all those ifs, you'd sponsor me for the next opening on the Council?"

He laughed.

"I might," he said. "But how are you going to prove it to me?"

"I'll make a prediction," I said. "A prediction calling—if it comes true—for a major policy decision by the Council."

"All right," he said. He was still smiling. "Predict, then."

"The Exotics," I said, "are at work to wipe out the Friendlies."

The smile went away. For a moment he stared at me.

"What do you mean by that?" he demanded. "The Exotics can't be out to wipe out anyone. It's not only against everything they say they believe in, but no one can *wipe out* two whole worlds of people and a complete way of life. What do you mean by 'wipe out,' anyway?"

"Just about what you'd think," I answered. "Tear down the Friendly culture as a working theocracy, break both worlds financially, and leave only a couple of stony planets filled with starving people who'll either have to change their way of life or emigrate to other worlds."

He stared at me. For a long moment neither of us said anything.

"What," he said, finally, "gave you this fantastic idea?"

"A hunch. My insight," I said. "Plus the fact that it was a Dorsai Field Commander, Kensie Graeme, lent to the Cassidan levies at the last moment, that defeated the Friendly forces there."

"Why," said Piers, "that's the sort of thing that could happen in any war, anywhere, between any two armies."

"Not exactly," I said. "Kensie's decision to sweep around the north end of the Friendly line and take the Friendlies in the rear wouldn't have worked so successfully at all if Eldest Bright hadn't the day before taken command and ordered a Friendly attack on the south end of Kensie's line. There's a double coincidence here. An Exotic Commander appears and does just the right thing at the moment when the Friendly forces take the very action that makes them vulnerable."

Piers turned and reached for the phone on his desk.

"Don't bother checking," I said. "I already have. The decision to borrow Kensie from the Exotics was taken independently on the spur of the moment by the Cassidan Levies Command, and there was no way Kensie's Intelligence Unit could have known in advance about the attack Bright had ordered."

"Then it's coincidence." Piers scowled at me. "Or that Dorsai genius for tactics we all know they have."

"Don't you think Dorsai genius may have been a little overrated? And I don't buy the coincidence. It's too large," I said.

"Then what?" demanded Piers. "How do you explain it?"

"My hunch—my insight—suggests that the Exotics have some way of predicting what the Friendlies will do in advance. You spoke of Dorsai military genius—how about the Exotic psychological genius?"

"Yes, but—" Piers broke off, suddenly thoughtful. "The whole thing's fantastic." He looked once more at me. "What do you suggest we do about it?"

"Let me dig into it," I said. "If I'm right, three years from now will see Exotic troops fighting Friendlies. Not as hirelings in some other-planet war, but in a direct test of Exotic-Friendly strength." I paused. "And if I turn out to be right, you sponsor me to replace the next Council member dying or retiring."

Once more, the dry little man sat staring at me for a long minute.

"Tam," he said finally. "I don't believe a word of it. But look into it as much as you want; I'll answer for Council backing for you on that—if the question comes up. And if it comes off anything like you say, come talk to me again."

"I will," I said, getting up and smiling at him.

He shook his head, remaining in his seat, but said nothing.

"I'll hope to see you again before too long," I said. And I went out.

It was a tiny burr I had stuck onto him, to irritate his mind in the direction I wanted him to speculate. But Piers Leaf had the misfortune of having a highly intelligent and creative mind; otherwise he would not have been Chairman of the Council. It was the kind of mind that refused to let go of a question until it had settled it one way or another. If it could not disprove the question, it was likely to start finding evidence to prove it—even in places where others could not see such proof at all.

And this particular burr would have nearly three years to stick and work itself into the fabric of Leaf's picture of things. I was content to wait for that, while I went ahead with other matters.

I had to spend a couple of weeks on Earth, bringing some order back to my personal business affairs there; but at the end of that time I took ship for New Earth once more.

The Friendlies, as I said, having bought back the troops they had lost as prisoners to the Cassidan forces under Kensie Graeme, had immediately reinforced them and encamped them outside the North Partition capital of Moreton, as an occupation force in demand of interplanetary credits due them.

The credits due, of course, were from the government of the now defeated and nonexistent North Partition rebels who had hired them. But, while there was nothing exactly legal about it, this was not uncommon practice between the stars, to hold a world ransom for any debt contracted off-world by any of its people.

The reason, of course, was that special currency between worlds which was the services of individual human units, whether as psychiatrists or soldiers. A debt contracted for the services of such units by one world from another had to be paid by the debtor world, and could not be repudiated by a change of governments. Governments would have proved too easy to change, if that had been a way out of inter-planetary debts.

In practice, it was a winner-pay-all matter, if con-flicting interests on a single world hired help from off-world. Something like the reverse of a civil suit-at-law to recover monetary damages, where the loser is required to pay the court costs of the winner. Of-ficially, what had happened was that the Friendly government, being unpaid for the soldiers it had lent the rebel government, had declared war on New Earth as a world, until New Earth as a world should make up the bad debt contracted by some of her in-habitants.

In actuality, no hostilities were involved, and pay-ment would, after a due amount of haggling, be forthcoming from those New Earth governments most directly involved. In this case, the South Par-tition government, mainly, since it had been the win-ner. But meanwhile, Friendly troops were in occupation upon New Earth soil; and it was in self-assignment to write a series of feature articles about this that I arrived there, some eight months after I had left.

I got in to see their Field Commander with no trouble this time. It was evident among the bubble-plastic buildings of the cantonment they had set up in an open area that the Friendly military were under orders to give as little irritation to non-Friendlies as possible. I heard no cant spoken by any of the sol-diers, from the cantonment gate clear into and in-cluding the office of the Field Commander himself. But in spite of the fact he "youed" instead of "thoued" me, he was not happy to see me.

"Field Commander Wassel," he introduced himself. "Sit down, Newsman Olyn. I've heard about you."

He was a man in his late forties or early fifties with close-cropped, pure gray hair. He was built as square as the lower half of a Dutch door and had a heavy, square jaw which had no trouble looking grim. It was looking grim now, for all he was trying to appear unconcerned—and I knew the cause of the worry that was making his expression a rebel against his intentions.

"I supposed you would have," I said, grim enough in my own way. "So I'll make one point clear by reminding you right from the start of the impartiality of the Interstellar News Services."

He had sat back down.

"We know about that," he said, "and I'm not suggesting any bias on your part against us, either, Newsman. We regret the death of your brother-in-law and your own wounding. But I'd like to point out that the News Services, in sending you, of all Guild members, to do a series of articles on our occupation of this New Earth territory—"

"Let me make myself perfectly clear!" I broke in on him. "I chose to do this assignment, Commander. I asked to be able to do it!"

By this time his face was grim as a bulldog's, with little pretense remaining. I stared as bitterly straight across his desk into his eyes.

"I see you don't understand, Commander." I rapped the words out in as metallic a tone as I could; and—to my ear, at least—the tone was good. "My parents died when I was young. I was raised by an uncle and it was the goal of my life to be a Newsman. To me, the News Services are more important than any institution or human being on any of the sixteen civilized worlds. The Creed of the members of the Guild is carried in my heart, Commander. And the keystone article of that Creed is impartiality—the crushing down, the wiping out of any personal feeling where that might conflict with or influence to the slightest degree the work of a Newsman.''

He continued to look grim at me from across the desk; and, gradually it seemed to me, a hint of doubt crept into that iron visage of his.

''Mr. Olyn,'' he said at last; and the more neutral title was a tentative lightening of the formal sword's-point attitude with which we had begun our talk. ''Are you trying to tell me that you're here to do these articles as proof of your lack of bias toward us?''

''Toward you, or any people or things,'' I said, ''in accordance with the Newsman's Creed. This series will be a public testimony to our Creed, and consequently to the benefit of all who wear the cloak.''

He did not believe me even then, I think. His good sense warred with what I was telling him; and the assumption of selflessness on my part must have had a boastful ring in the mouth of someone he knew to be a non-Friendly.

But, at the same time, I was talking his language. The harsh joy of self-sacrifice, the stoic amputation of my own personal feelings in the pursuit of my duty rang true to the beliefs he had lived with all his own life.

''I see,'' he said at last. He got to his feet and extended his hand across the desk as I rose, too.

"Well, Newsman, I cannot say that we are pleased to see you here, even now. But we will cooperate with you within reason as much as possible. Though any series reflecting the fact that we are here as unwelcome visitors upon a foreign planet is bound to do us harm in the eyes of the people of the sixteen worlds."

"I don't think so this time," I said shortly as I shook hands. He let go of my hand and looked at me with a sudden renewal of suspicion.

"What I plan to do is an editorial series," I explained. "It'll be titled *The Case for Occupation by the Friendly Troops on New Earth*, and it'll restrict itself completely to exploring the attitudes and positions of you and your men in the occupation force."

He stared at me.

"Good afternoon," I said.

I went out, hearing his half-mumbled "Good afternoon" behind me. I left him, I knew, completely uncertain as to whether he was sitting on a carton of high explosive or not.

But, as I knew he would, he began to come around, when the first of the articles in the series began to appear in the Interstellar News releases. There is a difference between an ordinary article of reportage and an editorial article. In an editorial article, you can present the case for the Devil; and as long as you dissociate yourself from it personally, you can preserve your reputation of a freedom from bias.

I presented the case for the Friendlies, in the Friendlies' own terms and utterances. It was the first time in years that the Friendly soldiers had been written about in the Interstellar News without adverse criticism; and, of course, to the Friendlies, all adverse criticism implied a bias against them. For they knew of no half-measures in their own way of life and recognized none in outsiders. By the time I was halfway through the series, Field Commander Wassel and all his occupation forces had taken me as close to their grim hearts as a non-Friendly could be taken.

Of course, the series evoked a howl from the New Earthians that *their* side of the occupation also be written up. And a very good Newsman named Moha Skanosky was assigned by the Guild to do just that.

But I had had the first innings at bat in the public eye; and the articles had so strong an effect that they almost convinced *me*, their writer. There is a magic in words when they are handled, and when I had finished the series I was almost ready to find in myself some excuse and sympathy for these unyielding men of a Spartan faith.

But there was a *claidheamh mōr*, unsharpened and unslaked, hanging on the stone walls of my soul, that would not bend to any such weakness.

CHAPTER 18 ■

*Still, I was under the close observation of my peers
in the Guild; and on my return to St. Louis on Earth,
among my other mail was a note from Piers Leaf.*

Dear Tam:
Your series was an admirable job. But, bearing
in mind what we talked about the last time we
met, I would think that straight reporting might
build a better professional record for you than
dealing in background material of this sort.
With best wishes for your future—

P.L.

It was a plain enough cautioning not to be observed
involving myself personally in the situation I had told
him I would investigate. It might have caused me to
put off for a month or so the trip I had planned to

Ste. Marie. But just then Donal Graeme, who had accepted the position of War Chief for the Friendlies, carried out his first subsurface extrication of a Friendly expeditionary force from Coby, the airless mining world in the same system as the Exotic worlds and Ste. Marie. As a result of that rescue, the Exotic mercenary command was severely shaken up, to be reorganized under the command of Geneve bar-Colmain.

Despite widespread admiration for Graeme's skill, the public saw the situation as an unexpected pardon for Friendly forces who had been the aggressors on Coby. With the general liking for the Exotics on the other twelve worlds, what attention my series of articles had obtained was completely wiped out. In this I was well content. What I hoped to gain from their publication, I had already gained in the relaxation of enmity and suspicion of me personally by Field Commander Wassel and his occupation force.

I went to Ste. Marie, a small but fertile world which, with Coby and a few uninhabited bits of rock like Zombri, shared the Procyon system with the Exotic worlds, Mara and Kultis. My official purpose of visit was to see what effect the Coby military debacle had had on this suburban planet with its largely Roman Catholic, predominantly rural population.

While there were no official connections between them, except a mutual-aid pact, Ste. Marie was by necessity of spatial geography almost a ward of the larger, more powerful Exotic worlds. Like anyone with rich and powerful neighbors Ste. Marie, in her government and affairs, pretty much rose and fell with Exotic fortunes. It would be interesting to the reading public of the sixteen worlds to see how the

Exotic reversal on Coby had caused the winds of opinion and politics to blow on Ste. Marie.

As anyone might expect, it had caused them to blow contrary. After some five days of pulling strings, I finally arranged an interview with Marcus O'Doyne, past-President and political power in the so-called Blue Front, the out-of-power political party of Ste. Marie. It took less than half an eye to see that he was bursting with ill-contained joy.

We met in his hotel suite in Blauvain, the capital of Ste. Marie. He was of no more than average height, but his head was outsized, heavy-boned and powerful-featured under wavy white hair. It sat awkwardly on his plump and fairly narrow shoulders; and he had a habit of booming his voice out with the ring of a platform speaker, during ordinary conversation, that did not endear him to me. His faded blue eyes gleamed as he spoke.

". . . Woken them up, by—*George*!" he said, once we were seated in overplump chairs in the sitting room of his hotel suite with drinks in our hands. He paused, catching his breath stagily a little before coming out with emphasis on the "—*George*!" as if he wished me to notice that he had been about to use the name of the deity, but had recollected himself in time. It was, I began to find out, a regular trick of his, this catching himself from profanity or obscenity as if in the nick of time.

"—the common people—the rural people," he said leaning confidentially toward me. "They were asleep here. They've been asleep for years. Lulled to sleep by those sons of—*Belial* on the Exotics. But that business on Coby woke them up. Opened their eyes!"

175 ■

"Lulled to sleep—how?" I asked.

"Song and dance, song and dance!" O'Doyne rocked back and forth on the couch. "Stage-show magic! Headshrinker's tactics—oh, a thousand and one things, Newsman. You wouldn't believe it!"

"My readers might," I said. "How about citing some instances?"

"Why—*darn* your readers! Yes, I say—*darn* your readers!" He rocked forward again, glaring proudly at me. "It's the common inhabitant of my own world I'm concerned with! The common inhabitant. *He* knows what instances, what coercions, what wrongs! We're not a sideshow here, Mr. Olyn, though maybe you think so! No, I say—*darn* your readers, and—*darn* you! I'll get no man in trouble with those robed—*babies* by citing exact instances."

"You don't give me much to write about, in that case," I said. "Suppose we shift our ground a little, then. I understand that you claim that the people of the present government are maintained in power only by Exotic pressures on Ste. Marie?"

"They are appeasers, plain and simple, Mr. Olyn. The government—no, no! Call them the Green Front, which is all they are! They claim to represent all the people of Ste. Marie. They—You know our political situation, here?"

"I understand," I said, "that your constitution laid out your planet originally into political districts of equal areas, with two representatives to a planetary government from each district. Now I understand your party claims that the growth of city population has allowed the rural districts to control the cities, since a city like Blauvain with half a million inhabitants has no more representation than a district with three or four thousand people in it?''

"Exactly, exactly!'' O'Doyne rocked forward and boomed confidentially at me. "The need for reapportionment is acute, as it always has been in such historic situations. But will the Green Front vote themselves out of power? Not likely! Only a bold move—only a grass-roots' revolution can get them out of power and our own party, representing the common man, the ignored man, the disenfranchised man of the cities, into government.''

"You think such a grass-roots' revolution is possible at the present time?'' I adjusted downward the volume control on my recorder.

"Before Coby, I would have said—*no*! Much as I would have hoped for such a thing—no! But, since Coby—'' He stopped and rocked triumphantly backward, looking at me significantly.

"Since Coby?'' I prompted, since significant looks and significant silences were no use to me in doing a job of straight reporting. But O'Doyne had a politician's caution about talking himself into a corner.

"Why, since Coby,'' he said, "it's become apparent—apparent to any thinking man of this world—that Ste. Marie may have to go it alone. That we may have to do without the parasitic, controlling hand of the Exotics. And where are men to be found who can steer this troubled ship of Ste. Marie through the stormy trials of the future? In the cities, Newsman! In the ranks of those of us who have always fought for the common man. In our own Blue Front party!''

"I understand,'' I said. "But under your constitution wouldn't a change of representatives require an election? And can't an election only be called for by a majority vote of the current representatives? And don't the Green Front have that majority now, so that they are unlikely to call an election that would put most of them out of office?''

"True!" he boomed. "True!" He rocked back and forth, glaring at me with the same broad hint of significance.

"Then," I said, "I don't see how the grass-roots' revolution you talk about is possible, Mr. O'Doyne."

"Anything is possible!" he answered. "To the common man, nothing is impossible! The straws are in the wind, the wind of change is in the air. Who can deny it?"

I shut off my recorder.

"I see," I said, "we're getting nowhere. Perhaps we could make a little better progress off the record?"

"Off the record! Absolutely! Indeed—absolutely!" he said heartily. "I'm as willing to answer questions off the record as on, Newsman. And you understand why? Because to me, on—on and off—are one and the same. One and the same!"

"Well, then," I said, "how about some of these straws in the wind? Off the record, can you give me an example?"

He rocked toward me and lowered his voice.

"There are—gatherings, even in the rural areas," he muttered. "Stirrings of unrest—this much I can tell you. If you ask me for places—names—why, no. I won't tell you."

"Then you're leaving me with nothing but vague hints. I can't make a story out of that," I said. "And you'd like a story written on this situation, I suppose?"

"Yes, but—" His powerful jaw set. "I won't tell you. I won't risk—I won't tell you!"

"I see," I said. I waited for a long minute. He opened his mouth, closed it, and then fidgeted upon the couch. "Perhaps," I said slowly, "perhaps there's a way out of this."

He flashed a glance almost of suspicion at me, from under white eyebrows.

"Perhaps I could tell you instead," I said quietly. "You wouldn't have to confirm anything. And of course, as I say, even my own remarks would be off the record."

"You—tell me?" He stared hard at me.

"Why not?" I said easily. He was too good a public man to let his bafflement show on his face, but he continued to stare at me. "In the News Services we've got our own avenues of information; and from these we can build up a general picture, even if some parts are missing. Now, speaking hypothetically of course, the general picture on Ste. Marie at this moment seems to be pretty much the way you've described it. Stirrings of unrest, gatherings and rumblings of discontent with the present—you might say, puppet—government."

"Yes," he rumbled. "Yes, the very word. That's what it is, a—*darn* puppet government!"

"At the same time," I went on, "as we've already discussed, this puppet government is well able to subdue any kind of local uprising, and is not about to call an election that will remove it from power; and—barring the calling of such an election—there seems no constitutional way of changing the status quo. The highly able and selfless leaders that Ste. Marie might otherwise—I say *might*, being neutral myself, of course—find among the Blue Front, seem legally committed to remaining private citizens without the power to save their world from foreign influence.''

"Yes," he muttered, staring at me. "Yes."

"Consequently, what course remains open to those who would save Ste. Marie from her present government?" I went on. "Since all legal avenues of recourse are stopped up, the only way left, it may seem to brave men, strong men, is to set aside normal procedure in such times of trial. If there are no constitutional ways to remove the men presently holding the reins of government, they may end up being removed otherwise, for the ostensible good of the whole world of Ste. Marie and everyone on it.''

He stared at me. His lips moved a little, but he said nothing. Under the white eyebrows, his faded blue eyes seemed to be popping slightly.

"In short—a bloodless coup d'état, a direct and forcible removal from office of these bad leaders seems to be the only solution left for those who believe this planet needs saving. Now, we know—''

"Wait—" broke in O'Doyne, booming. "I must tell you here and now, Newsman, that my silence mustn't be construed as giving consent to any such speculation. You shall not report—''

"Please," I interrupted in my turn, holding up a hand. He subsided rather more easily than one might have expected. "This is all perfectly theoretical supposition on my part. I don't suppose it has anything to do with the real situation." I hesitated. "The only question in this projection of the situation—theoretical situation—is the matter of implementation. We realize that as far as numbers and equipment, forces of the Blue Front outnumbered a hundred to one in the last election is hardly to be compared with the planetary forces of the Ste. Marie Government.''

''Our support—our grass-roots' support—''

''Oh, of course,'' I said. ''Still, there's the question of actually taking any physically effective action in the situation. That would take equipment and men—particularly men. By which I mean, of course, military men able either to train raw native troops, or themselves to take powerful action—''

''Mr. Olyn,'' said O'Doyne, ''I must protest such talk. I must reject such talk. I must''—he had gotten up to pace the room, and I saw him going back and forth, with his arms waving—''I must refuse to listen to such talk.''

''Forgive me,'' I said. ''As I mentioned, I'm only playing with a hypothetical situation. But the point I'm trying to get at—''

''The point you're trying to get at doesn't concern me, Newsman!'' said O'Doyne, halting in front of me with his face stern. ''The point doesn't concern us in the Blue Front.''

''Of course not,'' I said soothingly. ''I know it doesn't. Of course, the whole matter is impossible.''

''Impossible?'' O'Doyne stiffened. ''What's impossible?''

''Why, the whole matter of a coup d'état,'' I said. ''It's obvious. Any such thing would require outside help—the business of militarily trained men, for example. Such military men would have to be supplied by some other world—and what other world would be willing to lend valuable troops on speculation to an obscure out-of-power political party on Ste. Marie?''

I let my voice dwindle off and sat smiling, gazing at him, as if I expected him to answer my final question. And he sat staring back at me as if he expected me to answer it myself. It must have been a good twenty seconds that we sat in mutually expectant silence before I broke it once more, getting up as I did so.

"Obviously," I said, with a touch of regret in my voice, "none. So I must conclude we'll be seeing no marked change of government or alteration in relations with the Exotics after all on Ste. Marie in the near future. Well"—and I held out my hand—"I must apologize for being the one to cut this interview short, Mr. O'Doyne; but I see I've lost track of the time. I'm due at Government house across the city in fifteen minutes, for an interview with the President, to get the other side of the picture; and then I'll have to rush to get back to the spaceport in time to leave this evening for Earth."

He rose automatically and shook my hand.

"Not at all," he began. His voice rose to a boom momentarily, and then faltered back to ordinary tones. "Not at all—it's been a pleasure acquainting you with the true situation here, Newsman." He let go of my hand, almost regretfully.

"Good-bye, then," I said.

I turned to go and I was halfway to the door when his voice broke out again behind me.

"Newsman Olyn—"

I stopped and turned.

"Yes?" I said.

"I feel"—his voice boomed out suddenly—"I have

a duty to ask you—a duty to the Blue Front, a duty to my party to require you to tell me of any rumors you might have heard concerning the identity of any world—any world—ready to come to the aid of good government here on St. Marie. *We* are your readers here, too, on this world, Newsman. You also owe us information. Have you heard of some world which is—reported, rumored, what have you—to be ready to extend aid to a grass-roots' movement on Ste. Marie, to throw off the Exotic yoke and ensure equal representation among our people?''

I looked back at him. I let him wait for a second or two.

''No,'' I said. ''No, Mr. O'Doyne, I haven't.''

He stood, unmoving, as if my words had fixed him in position, legs spread a little wide, chin high, challenging me.

''I'm sorry,'' I said. ''Good-bye.''

I went out. I do not think he even answered my farewell.

I went across to Government house and spent a twenty minutes full of reassuring, pleasant platitudes in interview with Charles Perrinni, President of the Ste. Marie government. Then I returned, by way of New San Marcos and Joseph's Town to the spaceport and the spaceliner for Earth.

I paused only to check my mail on Earth and then transshipped immediately for Harmony, and the site on that planet of the United Council of Churches, which together governed both Friendly worlds of Harmony and Association. I spent five days in the city there, cooling my heels in the offices and wardrooms of minor officers of their so-called Public Relations Bureau.

On the sixth day, a note I had sent immediately on arriving to Field Commander Wassel paid its dividend. I was taken to the Council building, itself; and, after being searched for weapons—there were some violent sectarian differences between Church groups on the Friendly worlds themselves, and they made no exceptions, evidently, even for Newsmen— I was admitted to a lofty-ceilinged office with bare walls. There, surrounded by a few straight-backed chairs, in the middle of the black-and-white tile of the floor, sat a heavy desk with the seated man behind it dressed entirely in black.

The only white things about him were his face and hands. All else was covered. But his shoulders were as square and broad as a barn door and above them his white face had eyes as black as the clothing, which seemed to blaze at me. He got up and came around the desk, towering half a head over me, to offer his hand.

"God be with you," he said.

Our hands met. There was the hint of a hard touch of amusement in the thin line of his straight mouth; and the glance of his eyes seemed to probe me like twin doctor's scalpels. He held my hand, not hard, but with the hint of a strength that could crush my fingers as if in a vise, if he chose.

I was face to face, at last, with the Eldest of that Council of Elders who ruled the combined churches of Harmony and Association, him who was called Bright, First among the Friendlies.

CHAPTER 19 ■

*"You come well recommended by Field Commander
Wassel,"* he said after he had shaken my hand. *"An
unusual thing for a Newsman."* It was a statement,
not a sneer; and I obeyed his invitation—almost more
order than invitation—to sit, as he went back around
to sit down behind his desk. He faced me across it.

There was power in the man, the promise of a
black flame. Like the promise, it suddenly occurred
to me, of the flame latent in the gunpowder, stored
in 1687 by the Turks within the Parthenon, when a
shell fired by the Venetian army under Morosini exploded the black grains and blew out the center of
that white temple. There had always been a special
dark corner of hatred in me for that shell and that
army—for if the Parthenon had been living refutation
of Mathias' darkness to me as a boy, the destruction

wrought by that shell had been evidence of how that darkness conquered, even in the heart of light.

So, viewing Eldest Bright, I connected him in my mind with that old hate, though I was careful to shield my feelings from his eyes. Only in Padma had I felt such a penetrating power of gaze, before now— and there was a man here, too, behind the gaze.

For the eyes themselves were the eyes of a Torquemada, that prime mover of the Inquisition in ancient Spain—as others had remarked before me; for the Friendly Churches were not without their own repressors and extinguishers of heresy. But behind those eyes moved the political intelligence of a mind that knew when to leash or when to loose the powers of two planets. For the first time I realized the feeling of someone who, stepping into the lion's cage alone for the first time, hears the steel door click shut behind him.

For the first time, also, since I had stood in the Index Room of the Final Encyclopedia and loosened the hinges of my knees—for what if this man had *no* weaknesses; and in trying to control him, I only gave my plans away?

But the habits of a thousand interviews were coming to my rescue and even as the doubts struck and clung to me, my tongue was working automatically.

". . . the utmost in cooperation from Field Commander Wassel and his men on New Earth," I said. "I appreciated it highly."

"I, too," said Bright harshly, his eyes burning upon me, "appreciated a Newsman without bias. Otherwise you wouldn't be here in my office interviewing me. The work of the Lord between the stars leaves me little time for providing amusement for the ungodly of seven systems. Now, what's the reason for this interview?''

"I've been thinking of making a project," I said, "of revealing the Friendlies in a better light to people on the other worlds—"

"To prove your loyalty to the Creed of your profession—as Wassel said?" interrupted Bright.

"Why, yes," I said. I stiffened slightly in my chair. "I was orphaned at an early age; and the dream of my growing years was to join the News Services—"

"Don't waste my time, Newsman!" Bright's hard voice chopped like an axe across the unfinished section of my sentence. He got to his feet once more, suddenly, as if the energy in him was too great to be contained, and prowled around his desk to stand looking down at me, thumbs hooked in the belt at his narrow waist, his bony, middle-aged face bent above me. "What's your Creed to me, who move in the light of God's word?"

"We all move in our own lights, in our own way," I said. He was standing so close above me that I could not get to my feet to face him as my instincts urged me. It was as if he held me physically pinned in my chair, beneath him. "If it weren't for my Creed I wouldn't be here now. Perhaps you don't know what happened to me and my brother-in-law at the hands of one of your Groupmen on New Earth—"

"I know." The two words were merciless. "You'll have been apologized to, some time since, for that. Listen to me, Newsman." His thin lips quirked slightly in a sour smile. "You are not Anointed of the Lord."

"No," I said.

"In those who follow God's word, there may be a cause to believe that they act from faith in something more than their own selfish interests. But in those without the Light, how can there be any faith to anything but themselves?" The quirking smile on his own lips mocked his own words, mocked at the canting phrases in which he called me a liar—and dared me to deny the sophistication in him that had permitted him to see through me.

I stiffened this time with a look of outrage.

"You're sneering at my Newsman's Creed only because it isn't your own!" I snapped at him.

My outburst moved neither him nor his quirk of a smile.

"The Lord would not choose a fool to be Eldest over the Council of our Churches," he said—and turning his back on me, walked back around to sit down once more behind his desk. "You should have thought of that before you came to Harmony, Newsman. But at any rate you know it now."

I stared at him, almost blinded by the sudden brilliance of my own understanding. Yes, I knew it now—and in knowing it, suddenly saw how he had delivered himself out of his own mouth into my hands.

I had been afraid that he might turn out to have no weakness of which I could take advantage as I had taken advantage of lesser men and women with my words. And it was true—he had no ordinary weakness. But by the same token he had an extraordinary one. For his weakness was his strength, that same sophistication that had lifted him to be ruler and leader of his people. His weakness was that to have become what he was, he had to be as fanatic as the worst of them were—but with something more, as well. He had to have the extra strength that made him able to lay his fanaticism aside, when it came to interfere in his dealing with the leaders of other worlds—with his equals and opposites between the stars. It was this, *this* he had unknowingly admitted to me just now.

Unlike the furious-eyed, black-clad ones about him, he was not limited to the fanatic's view of the universe that painted everything in colors of either pure black or pure white. He was able to perceive and deal in shades between—in shades of gray, as well. In short, he could be a politician when he chose—and, as a politician, I could deal with him.

As a politician, I could lead him into a politician's error.

I crumpled. I let the stiffness go out of me suddenly as I sat in my chair with his eyes newly upon me. And I heaved a long, shuddering breath.

"You're right," I said in a dead voice. I got to my feet. "Well, it's no use now. I'll be going—"

"Go?" His voice cracked like a rifle shot, stopping me. "Did I say the interview was over? Sit down!"

Hastily I sat down again. I was trying to look pale, and I think I succeeded. For all I had suddenly understood him, I was still in the lion's cage, and he was still the lion.

"Now," he said, staring at me, "what did you really hope to gain from me—and from us who are the Chosen of God on these two worlds?"

I wet my lips.

"Speak up," he said. He did not raise his voice,

but the low, carrying tones of it promised retribution
on his part if I did not obey.

"The Council—" I muttered.

"Council? The Council of our Elders? What about
it?"

"Not that," I said, looking down at the floor.
"The Council of the Newsman's Guild. I wanted a
seat on it. You Friendlies could be the reason I could
get it. After Dave—after what happened to my
brother-in-law—my showing with Wassel that I could
do my job without bias even to you people—that's
been getting me attention, even in the Guild. If I
could go on with that—if I could raise public opinion
in the other seven systems in your favor—it'd raise
me, too, in the public eye. And in the Guild."

I stopped speaking. Slowly I looked up at him. He
was staring at me with harsh humor.

"Confession cleanses the soul even of such as
you," he said grimly. "Tell me, you've given thought
to the improvement of our public image among the
cast-aside of the Lord on the other worlds?"

"Why, that depends," I said. "I'd have to look
around here for story material. First—"

"Never mind that now!"

He rose once more behind his desk and his eyes
commanded me to rise also, so I did.

"We'll go into this in a few days," he said. His
Torquemada's smile saluted me. "Good-day for the
present, Newsman."

"Good—day," I managed to say. I turned and
went out, shakily.

Nor was the shakiness entirely assumed. My legs
felt weak, as if from tense balancing on the edge of

a precipice, and a dry tongue clung to the roof of my dry mouth.

I puttered around the town the next few days, ostensibly picking up background material. Then, on the fourth day after I had seen Eldest Bright, I was called once more to his office. He was standing when I came in, and he remained standing, halfway between the door and his desk.

"Newsman," he said abruptly, as I came in, "it occurs to me that you can't favor us in your news reports without your fellow Guild members noticing that favoring. If this is so, what good are you to me?"

"I didn't say I'd favor you," I answered indignantly. "But if you show me something favorable on which I can report, I can report on it."

"Yes." He looked hard at me with the black flames of his eyes. "Come and look at our people, then."

He led me out of his office and down an elevator tube to a garage where a staff car was waiting. We got in and its driver took us out of the Council City, through a countryside that was bare and stony, but neatly divided into farms.

"Observe," said Bright dryly as we went through a small town that was hardly more than a village. "We grow only one crop thickly on our poor worlds—and those are the bodies of our young men, to be hired out as soldiers that our people may not starve and our Faith endure. What disfigures these young men and the other people we pass that those on the other worlds should resent them so strongly, even while hiring them to fight and die in their foreign wars?"

I turned and saw his eyes on me with grim amusement, once again.

"Their—attitudes," I said cautiously.

Bright laughed, a short lion's cough of a laugh deep in his chest.

"Attitudes!" he said harshly. "Put a plain word to it, Newsman! Not attitudes—*pride! Pride!* Bone-poor, skilled only in hand toil and weapon-handling, as these people you see are—still they look as if from lofty mountains down on the dust-born slugs who hire them, knowing that those employers may be rich in worldly wealth and furniture, fat in foodstuffs and padded in soft raiment—yet when all peoples pass alike beyond the shadow of the grave, then they, who have wallowed in power and wealth, will not be endured even to stand, cap in hand, below those gates of silver and of gold which we, who have suffered and are Anointed, pass singing through."

He smiled at me, his savage, predator's smile, across the width of the staff car.

"What can you find in all you see here," he said, "to teach a proper humbleness and a welcome to those who hire the Bespoken of the Lord?"

He was mocking me again. But I had seen through him on that first visit in his office, and the subtle path to my own end was becoming clearer as we talked. So his mockery bothered me less and less.

"It isn't pride or humbleness on either side that I can do much about," I said. "Besides, that isn't what you need. You don't care what employers think of your troops, as long as they hire them. And employers will hire them, if you can make your people merely bearable—not necessarily lovable, but bearable."

"Stop here, driver!" interrupted Bright; and the car pulled to a halt.

We were in a small village. Sober, black-clad people moved between the buildings of bubble-plastic—temporary structures which would long since on other worlds have been replaced with more sophisticated and attractive housing.

"Where are we?" I asked.

"A lesser town called Remembered-of-the-Lord," he answered, and dropped the window on his side of the car. "And here comes someone you know."

In fact, a slim figure in a Force-Leader's uniform was approaching the car. It reached us, stooped slightly, and the face of Jamethon Black looked calmly in on both of us.

"Sir?" he said to Bright.

"This officer," said Bright, to me, "seemed qualified once for high service in the ranks of us who served God's will. But six years past, he was attracted by a daughter of a foreign world who would not have him; and since then he has seemed to lose his will to rise in rank among us." He turned to Jamethon. "Force-Leader," he said. "You have seen this man twice. Once in his home on Earth six years ago, when you sought his sister in marriage; and again last year on New Earth when he sought from you a pass to protect his assistant between the battle lines. Tell me, what do you know about him?"

Jamethon's eyes looked across the interior of the car into mine.

"Only that he loved his sister and wanted a better life for her, perhaps, than I could give her," said Jamethon in a voice as calm as his face. "And that he wished his brother-in-law well, and sought protection for him.'' He turned to look directly into the eyes of Bright. ''I believe him to be an honest man and a good one, Eldest.''

''I did not ask for your beliefs!'' snapped Bright.

''As you wish,'' said Jamethon, still calmly facing the older man; and I felt a rage swelling up inside me so that I thought that I would burst out with it, no matter what the consequences.

Rage against Jamethon, it was. For not only had he the effrontery to recommend me to Bright as an honest man and a good one, but because there was something else about him that was like a slap in the face. For a moment, I could not identify it. And then it came to me. *He* was not afraid of Bright. And I had been so, in that first interview.

Yet I was a Newsman, with the immunity of the Guild behind me; and he was a mere Force-Leader facing his own Commander-in-Chief, the Warlord of two worlds, of which Jamethon's was only one. How could he—? And then it came to me, so that I almost ground my teeth in fury and frustration. For it was with Jamethon no different than it had been with the Groupman on New Earth who had denied me a pass to keep Dave safe. That Groupman had been instantly ready to obey that Bright, who was the Eldest, but felt in himself no need to bow before that other Bright, who was merely the man.

In the same way now Bright held the life of Jamethon in his hand, but unlike the way it had been with me, in holding this he held the lesser part of the young man before him, rather than the greater.

''Your leave home here is ended, Force-Leader,'' Bright said sharply. ''Tell your family to send on your effects to Council City and join us now. I'm appointing you aide and assistant to this Newsman from now on. And we'll promote you Commandant to make the post worthwhile.''

"Sir," said Jamethon emotionlessly with an inclination of his head. He stepped back into the building from which he had just emerged, before coming back out a few moments later to join us. Bright ordered the staff car turned about and so we returned to the city and his office.

When we got back there, Bright turned me loose with Jamethon to get acquainted with the Friendly situation in and around Council City. Consequently, the two of us, Jamethon and I, did a certain amount of sightseeing, though not much, and I returned early to my hotel.

It required very little in the way of perception to see that Jamethon had been assigned to act as a spy upon me while performing the functions of an aide. However, I said nothing about it, and Jamethon said nothing at all, so that, almost strangely, we two moved around Council City, and its related neighborhood, in the days that followed like a couple of ghosts, or men under a vow not to speak to each other. It was a strange silence of mutual consent that agreed that the only things worth talking about between us—Eileen, and Dave and the rest—would reward any discussion only with a pain that would make the discussion unprofitable.

Meanwhile, I was summoned from time to time to the office of Eldest Bright. He saw me more or less briefly on these occasions and spoke of little that was to the point of my announced reason for being on the Friendlies and in partnership with him. It was as if he were waiting for something to happen. And eventually I understood what that was. He had set Jamethon to check me out, while he himself checked out the interstellar situation which, as Eldest of the Friendly Worlds, he faced alone, searching for the situation and the moment in which he could best make use of this self-seeking Newsman who had offered to improve the public image of his people.

Once I had realized this, I was reassured, seeing how, interview by interview, day by day, he came closer as I wanted to the heart of the matter. That heart was the moment in which he might ask my advice, must ask me to tell him what he should do about me and with me.

Day by day and interview by interview, he became apparently more relaxed and trusting in his words with me—and more questioning.

"What is it they like to read, on those other worlds, Newsman?" he asked one day. "Just what is it they most like to hear about?"

"Heroes, of course," I answered as lightly as he had questioned. "That's why the Dorsai make good copy—and to a certain extent the Exotics."

A shadow which may or may not have been intentional passed across his face at the mention of the Exotics.

"The ungodly," he muttered. But that was all. A day or so later he brought the subject of heroes up again.

"What makes heroes in the public's eyes?" he asked.

"Usually," I said, "the conquering of some older, already established strong man, villain or hero." He was looking at me agreeably, and I took a venture. "For example, if your Friendly troops should face up to an equal number of Dorsai and outfight them—''

The agreeableness was abruptly wiped out by an expression I had never seen on his face before. For a second he all but gaped at me. Then he flashed me a stare as smoking and hot as liquid basalt from a volcano's throat.

''Do you take me for a fool?'' he snapped. Then his face changed, and he looked at me curiously. ''—Or are you simply one yourself?''

He gazed at me for a long, long moment. Finally he nodded.

''Yes,'' he said, as if to himself. ''That's it—the man's a fool. An Earth-born fool.''

He turned on his heel, and that ended our interview for the day.

I did not mind his taking me for a fool. It was that much more insurance against the moment when I would make any move to delude *him*. But, for the life of me, I could not understand what had brought such an unusual reaction from him. And that bothered me. Surely my suggestion about the Dorsai could not have been so farfetched? I was tempted to ask Jamethon, but discretion as the better part of valor held me wisely back.

Meanwhile the day came when Bright finally approached the question I knew he must ask me sooner or later.

''Newsman,'' he said. He was standing, legs spread, hands locked together behind his back, looking out through the floor-to-ceiling window of his office at the Government Center and Council City, below. His back was to me.

''Yes, Eldest?'' I answered. He had called me once

more to his office, and I had just walked through the door. He spun around at the sound of my voice to stare flamingly at me.

"You said once that heroes are made by their defeat of some older, established heroes. You mentioned as examples of older heroes in the public gaze the Dorsai—and the Exotics."

"That's right," I said, coming up to him.

"The ungodly on the Exotics," he said, as if he mused to himself. "They use hired troops. What good to defeat hirelings—even if that were possible and easy?"

"Why not rescue someone in distress, then?" I said lightly. "That sort of thing would give you a good, new public image. Your Friendlies haven't been known much for doing that sort of thing."

He flicked a hard glance at me.

"Who should we rescue?" he demanded.

"Why," I said, "there're always small groups of people who, rightly or wrongly, think they're being imposed on by the larger groups around them. Tell me, don't you ever get approached by small dissident groups wanting to hire your soldiers on speculation for revolt against their established government—" I broke off. "Why, of course you do. I was forgetting New Earth and the North Partition of Altland."

"We gained little credit in the eyes of the other worlds by way of our business with the North Partition," said Bright, harshly. "As you well know!"

"Oh, but the sides were about equal there," I said. "What you've got to do is help out some really tiny minority against some selfish giant of a majority— say, something like the miners on Coby against the mine owners."

"Coby? The miners?" He darted me a hard glance, but this was a glance I had been waiting for all these days and I met it blandly. He turned and strode over to stand behind his desk. He reached down and half-lifted a sheet of paper—it looked like a letter—that lay on his desk. "As it happens, I have had an appeal for aid on a purely speculative basis by a group—"

He broke off, laid the paper down and lifted his head to look at me.

"A group like the Coby miners?" I said. "It's not the miners themselves?"

"No," he said. "Not the miners." He stood silent a moment, then he came back around the desk and offered me his hand. "I understand you're about to leave."

"I am?" I said.

"Have I been misinformed?" said Bright. His eyes burned into mine. "I heard that you were leaving for Earth on a spaceliner this evening. I understood passage had already been booked by you."

"Why—yes," I said, reading the message clear in the tone of his voice. "I guess I just forgot. Yes, I'm on my way."

"Have a good trip," said Bright. "I'm glad we could come to a friendly understanding. You can count on us in the future. And we'll take the liberty of counting on you in return."

"Please do," I said. "And the sooner the better."

"It will be soon enough," said Bright.

We said good-bye again and I left for my hotel. There, I found my things had already been packed; and, as Bright had said, passage had already been booked for me on a spaceliner leaving that evening for Earth. Jamethon was nowhere to be seen.

Five hours later, I was once more between the stars, shifting on my way back toward Earth.

Five weeks later, the Blue Front on Ste. Marie, having been secretly supplied with arms and men by the Friendly worlds, erupted in a short but bloody revolt that replaced the legal government with the Blue Front leaders.

CHAPTER 20 ■

This time I did not ask for an interview with Piers Leaf. He sent to ask for me. As I went through the Guild Hall and up the elevator tube to his office, heads turned among the cloaked members I passed. For in the two years since the Blue Front leaders had seized power on Ste. Marie, much had changed for me.

I had had my hour of torment in that last interview with my sister. And I had had, while returning from that to Earth, the first dream of my revenge. Afterward, I had taken the two steps, one on Ste. Marie, one on Harmony, to set that revenge in motion. But still, even with those things done, I had not yet changed inside me. For change takes time.

It was the last two years that had really changed me—that had brought Piers Leaf to call upon me, that had caused the heads above the capes to turn as

I passed. For in those years the power of my understanding had come full upon me, in such measure that it now seemed by contrast to have been a weak, newborn and latent thing, even up through the moment in which I shook hands and said farewell to Eldest Bright, three years before.

I had dreamed my primitive dream of a revenge, sword in hand, going to a meeting in the rain. Then for the first time, I had felt the pull of it, but the reality I felt now was far stronger, stronger than meat or drink or love—or life itself.

They are fools that think that wealth or women or strong drink or even drugs can buy the most in effort out of the soul of a man. These things offer pale pleasures compared to that which is greatest of them all, that task which demands from him more than his utmost strength, that absorbs him, bone and sinew and brain and hope and fear and dreams—and still calls for more.

They are fools who think otherwise. No great effort was ever bought. No painting, no music, no poem, no cathedral in stone, no church, no state was ever raised into being for payment of any kind. No Parthenon, no Thermopylae was ever built or fought for pay or glory; no Bukhara sacked, or China ground beneath Mongol heel, for loot or power alone. The payment for the doing of these things was itself the doing of them.

To wield oneself—to use oneself as a tool in one's own hand—and so to make or break that which no one else can build or ruin—*that* is the greatest pleasure known to man! To one who has felt the chisel in his hand and set free the angel prisoned in the marble block, or to one who has felt the sword in hand and set homeless the soul that a moment before lived in the body of his mortal enemy—to these both come alike the taste of that rare food spread only for demons or for gods.

As it had come to me, these two and more than two years past.

I had dreamed of holding the lightning in my hand over the sixteen worlds and bending them all to my will. Now, I held that lightning, in sober fact, and read it. My abilities had hardened in me; and I *knew* now what failure of a wheat harvest on Freiland must mean in the long run to those who needed but could not pay for professional education on Cassida. I saw the movements of those like William of Ceta, Project Blaine of Venus, and Sayona the Bond, of both Exotic Worlds—all of whom bent and altered the shape of things happening between the stars—and I read their results-to-be clearly. And with this knowledge I moved to where the news would be, and wrote it even as it was only beginning to happen, until my fellow Guild members began to think me half-devil or half-seer.

But I cared nothing for their thoughts. I cared only for the secret taste of my waiting revenge, the feel of the hidden sword in my grasp—the tool of my *Destruct!*

For now I had no doubts left. I did not love him for it, but Mathias had seen me clearly—and from his grave, I worked the will of his anti-faith, but with a power he could never have imagined.

Now, however, I was at Piers Leaf's office. He was standing in the door of it, waiting for me, for from below they would have warned him I was on my way up. He took my hand in a handshake and held it to

draw me inside his office and close the door behind
us. We sat down not at his desk, but to one side on
the floats of a sofa and an overstuffed chair; and he
poured drinks for us both with fingers that seemed
thinned by sudden age.

"You've heard, Tam?" he said without preamble.
"Morgan Chu Thompson is dead."

"I've heard," I said. "And a seat on the Council
is now vacant."

"Yes." He drank a little from his glass and set it
down again. He rubbed a hand wearily over his face.
"Morgan was an old friend of mine."

"I know," I said, though I felt nothing for him at
all. "It must be hard on you."

"We were the same age—" He broke off, and
smiled at me a little wanly. "I imagine you're expecting me to sponsor you for the empty seat?"

"I think," I said, "the Guild members might think
it a little odd if you didn't, the way things have been
going for me for some time now."

He nodded but at the same time he hardly seemed
to hear me. He picked up his drink and sipped at it
again, without interest, and set it down.

"Nearly three years ago," he said, "you came in
here to see me with a prediction. You remember
that?"

I smiled.

"You could hardly forget it, I suppose," he said.
"Well, Tam—" He stopped and sighed heavily. He
seemed to be having trouble getting down to what he
wished to say. But I was old and experienced in patience nowadays. I waited. "We've had time to see
things work out and it seems to me, you were both
right—and wrong."

"Wrong?" I repeated.

"Why, yes," he said. "It was your theory that the Exotics were out to destroy the Friendly culture on Harmony and Association. But look at how things have gone since then."

"Oh?" I said. "How?—For example?"

"Why," he said, "it's been plain for nearly a generation now that the fanaticism of the Friendlies—acts of unreasoning violence like that massacre that took your brother-in-law's life on New Earth three years ago—were turning opinion on the fourteen other worlds against the Friendlies. To the point where they were losing the chance to hire out their young men as mercenary soldiers. But anyone with half an eye could see that was something the Friendlies were doing to themselves simply by being the way they are. The Exotics couldn't be to blame for that."

"No," I said. "I suppose not."

"Of course not." He sipped at his drink again, a little more heartily this time. "I think that was why I felt so much doubt when you told me that the Exotics were out to get the Friendlies. It just didn't ring right. But then it turned out to be Friendly troops and equipment backing that Blue Front revolution on Ste. Marie, right in the Exotics' back yard under the Procyon suns. And I had to admit there seemed to be something going on between the Friendlies and the Exotics." He stopped and looked at me.

"Thank you," I said.

"But the Blue Front didn't last," he went on.

"It seemed to have a great deal of popular support at first," I interrupted.

"Yes, yes." Piers brushed my interruption aside.

"But you know how it is in situations like that. There's always a chip on the shoulder where a bigger, richer neighbor's concerned—next door or on the next world, whichever. The point is, the Ste. Marians were bound to see through the Blue Front shortly and toss them out—make them an illegal party as they are now. That was bound to happen. There were only a handful of those Blue Front people, anyway, and they were mostly crackpots. Besides, Ste. Marie isn't set up to go it alone, financially or any other way, in the shadow of two rich worlds like Mara and Kultis. The Blue Front thing was bound to fail—anyone outside the picture had to see that."

"I suppose so," I said.

"You know so!" said Piers. "Don't tell me anyone with the perception you've demonstrated couldn't see that from the start, Tam. I saw it myself. But what I didn't see—and apparently you didn't either—was that, inevitably, once the Blue Front was kicked out, the Friendlies would put in an occupation force on Ste. Marie to back up their claim for payment from the legal government for the help they'd given the Blue Front. And that under the mutual assistance treaty that had always existed between the Exotics and the legal government of Ste. Marie, the Exotics would *have* to reply to the Ste. Marians' call for help to oust the Friendly occupation forces—since Ste. Marie couldn't pay the kind of bill the Friendlies were presenting."

"Yes," I said. "I foresaw that, too."

He darted a sharp glance at me.

"You did?" he said. "Then how could you think that—" He broke off, suddenly thoughtful.

"The point is," I said easily, "that the Exotic expeditionary forces haven't been having too much trouble pushing the Friendly forces back into a corner and cutting them up. They've stopped for the winter season now; but unless Eldest Bright and his council send reinforcements, the soldiers they have on Ste. Marie will probably have to surrender to the Exotic troops this spring. They can't afford to send reinforcements but they have to anyway—''

''No,'' said Piers, ''they don't.'' He looked at me strangely. ''You're about to claim, I suppose, that this whole situation was an Exotic maneuver to bleed the Friendlies twice—both for their help to the Blue Front, and again in the cost of sending reinforcements.''

I smiled inside, for he was coming to the very point I had intended to come to three years ago— only I had planned that *he* should tell *me* about it, not I, him.

''Isn't it?'' I said, pretending astonishment.

''No,'' said Piers strongly. ''Just opposite. Bright and his council intend to leave their expeditionary force to be either captured or slaughtered—preferably slaughtered. The result will be just what you were about to claim in the eyes of the fourteen worlds. The principle that any world can be held ransom for debts incurred by its inhabitants is a vital—if not legally recognized—part of the interstellar financial structure. But the Exotics, in conquering the Friendlies on Ste. Marie, will be rejecting it. The fact that the Exotics are bound by their treaty to answer Ste. Marie's appeal for help won't alter things. Bright will only need to go hunting for help from Ceta, Newton and all the tight-contract worlds to form a league to bring the Exotics to their knees.''

He broke off and stared at me.

"Do you see what I'm driving at now? Do you understand now why I said you were both right—in your notion of an Exotic-Friendly vendetta—and wrong? Do you see," he asked, "*now*, how you were wrong?"

I deliberately stared back at him for a moment before I answered.

"Yes," I said. I nodded. "I see now. It's not the Exotics who are out to get the Friendlies. It's the Friendlies who're out to get the Exotics."

"Exactly!" said Piers. "The wealth and specialized knowledge of the Exotics has been the pivot of the association of the loose-contract worlds that allowed them to balance off against the obvious advantage of trading trained people like sacks of wheat, which gives the tight-contract worlds their strength. If the Exotics are broken, the balance of power between the two groups of worlds is destroyed. And only that balance has let our Old World of Earth stand aloof from both groups. Now, she'll be drawn into one group or another—and whoever gets her will control *our* Guild, and the up until now impartiality of our News Services."

He stopped talking and sat back, as if worn out. Then he straightened up again.

"You know what group'll get Earth if the Friendlies win," he said, "the tight-contract group. So—where do we, we in the Guild, stand now, Tam?"

I stared back at him, giving him time to believe that his words were sinking into me. But, in reality, I was tasting at last the first slight flavor of my revenge. Here he was, at last, at the point to which I had set out to bring him, a point at which it seemed the Guild faced either the destruction of its high principle of impartiality, forcing it to take sides against the Friendly worlds; or its eventual capture by that partisan group of worlds to which the tight-contract Friendlies belonged. I let him wait, and think himself helpless for a little while. Then I answered him slowly.

"If the Friendlies can destroy the Exotics," I said, "then possibly the Exotics can destroy the Friendlies. Any situation like this has to have the possibility of tilting with equal force either way. Now if, without compromising our impartiality, I could go to Ste. Marie for the spring offensive, it might be that this ability of mine to see a little deeper into the situation than others can, might help that tilt."

Piers stared at me, his face a little white.

"What do you mean?" he said at last. "You can't openly side with the Exotics—you don't mean that?"

"Of course not," I answered. "But I might easily see something that they could turn to their advantage to get out of the situation. If so, I could make sure that they see it, too. There's nothing certain of success about this; but, as you said, otherwise, where do we stand now?"

He hesitated. He reached for his glass on the table and, as he picked it up, his hand shook a little. It took little insight to know what he was thinking. What I was suggesting was a violation of the spirit of the law of impartiality in the Guild, if not the letter of it. We would be choosing sides—but Piers was thinking that perhaps for the sake of the Guild we should do just that, while the choice was still in our own hands.

"Do you have any actual evidence that Eldest

Bright means to leave his occupation forces cut up as they are?'' I asked as he hesitated. ''Do we know for sure he won't reinforce them?''

''I've got contacts on Harmony trying to get evidence right now—'' he was beginning to answer when his desk phone chimed. He pressed a button and it lit up with the face of Tom Lassiri, his secretary.

''Sir,'' said Tom. ''Call from the Final Encyclopedia. For Newsman Olyn. From a Miss Lisa Kant. She says it's a matter of the utmost emergency.''

''I'll take it,'' I said, even as Piers nodded. For my heart had lurched in my chest for some reason which I had no time to examine. The screen cleared and Lisa's face formed on it.

''Tam!'' she said, without any other greeting. ''Tam, come quick. Mark Torre's been shot by an assassin! He's dying, in spite of anything the doctors can do. And he wants to speak to you—to you, Tam, before it's too late! Oh, Tam, hurry! Hurry as fast as you can!''

''Coming,'' I said.

And I went. There was no time to ask myself why I should answer to her summons. The sound of her voice lifted me out of my chair and headed me out of Piers's office as if some great hand was laid upon my shoulders. I just—went.

CHAPTER 21 ■

Lisa met me at the lobby entrance to the Final En-cyclopedia, where I had first caught sight of her years before. She took me into the quarters of Mark Torre by the strange maze and the moving room by which she had taken me there previously; and on the way she told me what had happened.

It had been the inevitable danger for which the maze and the rest of it had been set up originally—the expected, reasonless, statistically fatal chance that had finally caught up with Mark Torre. The building of the Final Encyclopedia had from its very begin-ning triggered fears latent in the minds of unstable people on all the sixteen civilized worlds of men. Because the Encyclopedia's purpose was aimed at a mystery that could be neither defined nor easily ex-pressed, it had induced a terror in psychotics both on Earth and elsewhere.

And one of these had finally gotten to Mark Torre—a poor paranoiac who had kept his illness hidden from even his own family while in his mind he fostered and grew the delusion that the Final Encyclopedia was to be a great Brain, taking over the wills of all humanity. We passed his body lying on the floor of the office, when at last Lisa and I reached it, a stick-thin, white-haired, gentle-faced old man with blood on his forehead.

He had, Lisa told me, been admitted by mistake. A new physician was supposed to have been admitted to see Mark Torre that afternoon. By some mistake, this gentle-looking, elderly, well-dressed man had been admitted instead. He had fired twice at Mark and once at himself, killing himself instantly. Mark, with two spring-gun slivers in his lungs, was still alive, but sinking fast.

Lisa brought me at last to him, lying still on his back on the blood-stained coverlet of a large bed in a bedroom just off the office. The clothing had been taken from his upper body and a large white bandage like a bandolier angled across his chest. His eyes were closed and sunken, so that his jutting nose and hard chin seemed to thrust upward almost as if in furious resentment of the death that was slowly and finally dragging his hard-struggling spirit down under its dark waters.

But it was not his face that I remember best. It was the unexpected width of chest and shoulder, and length of naked arm he showed, lying there. I was reminded suddenly, out of the forgotten past of my boyhood history studies, of the witness to the assassinated Abraham Lincoln, lying wounded and dying on the couch, and how that witness had been startled by the power of muscle and bone revealed in the unclothed upper body of the President.

So it was with Mark Torre. In his case, the muscle had largely wasted away through long illness and lack of use, but the width and length of bone showed the physical strength that he must have had as a young man. There were other people in the room, several of them physicians; but they made way for us as Lisa brought me up to the bedside.

She bent and spoke softly to him.

"Mark," she said. "Mark!"

For several seconds I did not think he would answer. I remember even thinking that perhaps he was already dead. But then the sunken eyes opened, wandered, and focused on Lisa.

"Tam's here, Mark," she said. She moved aside to let me get closer to the bed, and looked over her shoulder at me. "Bend down, Tam. Get close to him," she said.

I moved in, and I bent down. His eyes gazed at me. I was not sure whether he recognized me or not; but then his lips moved and I heard the ghost of a whisper, rattling deep in the wasted cavern of his once-broad chest.

"Tam—"

"Yes," I said. I found I had taken hold of one of his hands with one of mine. I did not know why. The long bones were cool and strengthless in my grasp.

"Son . . ." he whispered, so faintly that I could hardly hear him. But at the same time, all in a flash, without moving a muscle, I went rigid and cold, cold as if I had been dipped in ice, with a sudden, terrible fury.

How dare he? How dare he call *me* "son"? I'd given him no leave, or right or encouragement to do that to me—me, whom he hardly knew. Me, who had nothing in common with him, or his work, or anything he stood for. How dare he call me "*son*"?

But he was still whispering. He had two more words to add to that terrible, that unfair, word by which he had addressed me.

". . . take over. . . ."

And then his eyes closed, and his lips stopped moving, though the slow, slow stir of his chest showed that he still lived. I dropped his hand and turned and rushed out of the bedroom. I found myself in the office; and there I stopped in spite of myself, bewildered, for the doorway out, of course, was still camouflaged and hidden.

Lisa caught up with me there.

"Tam?" She put a hand on my arm and made me look at her. Her face told me she had heard him and that she was asking me now what I was going to do. I started to burst out that I was going to do no such thing as the old man had said, that I owed him nothing, and her nothing. Why, it had not even been a question he had put to me! He had not even asked me—he had *told* me to take over.

But no words came out of me. My mouth was open, but I could not seem to speak. I think I must have panted like a cornered wolf. And then the phone chimed on Mark's desk to break the spell that held us.

She was standing beside the desk; automatically her hand went out to the phone and turned it on, though she did not look down at the face which formed in the screen.

"Hello?" said a tiny voice from the instrument. "Hello? Is anyone there? I'd like to speak to Newsman Tam Olyn, if he's there. It's urgent. Hello? Is anyone there?"

It was the voice of Piers Leaf. I tore my gaze away from Lisa and bent down to the set.

"Oh, there you are, Tam," said Piers out of the screen. "Look, I don't want you to waste time covering the Torre assassination. We've got plenty of good men here to do that. I think you ought to get to Ste. Marie right away." He paused, looking at me significantly in the screen. "You understand? That information I was waiting for has just come in. I was right, an order's been issued."

Suddenly it was back again, washing out everything that had laid its hold upon me in the past few minutes—my long-sought plan and hunger for revenge. Like a great wave, it broke over me once more, washing away all the claims of Mark Torre and Lisa that had clung to me just now, threatening to trap me in this place.

"No further shipments?" I said sharply. "That's what the order said? No more coming?"

He nodded.

"And I think you ought to leave now because the forecast calls for a weather break within the week there," he said. "Tam, do you think—"

"I'm on my way," I interrupted. "Have my papers and equipment waiting for me at the spaceport."

I clicked off and turned to face Lisa once more. She gazed at me with eyes that shook me like a blow; but I was too strong for her now, and I thrust off their effect.

"How do I get out of here?" I demanded. "I've got to leave. Now!"

"Tam!" she cried.

"I've got to go, I tell you!" I thrust past her. "Where's that door out of here? Where—"

She slipped past me as I was pawing at the walls of the room and touched something. The door opened to my right; and I turned swiftly into it.

"Tam!"

Her voice stopped me for a final time. I checked and looked back over my shoulder at her.

"You're coming back," she said. It was not a question. She said it the way he, Mark Torre, had said it. She was not asking me; she was telling me; and for a last time it shook me once more to my deepest depths.

But then the dark and mounting power, that wave which was my longing for my revenge, tore me loose again and sent me hurtling on, through the doorway into the farther room.

"I'll be back," I assured her.

It was an easy, simple lie. Then the door I had come through closed behind me and the whole room moved about me, carrying me away.

CHAPTER 22 ■

As I got off the spaceliner on Ste. Marie, the little breeze from the higher pressure of the ship's atmosphere at my back was like a hand from the darkness behind me, shoving me into the dark day and the rain. My Newsman's cloak covered me. The wet chill of the day wrapped around me but did not enter me. I was like the naked claymore of my dream, wrapped and hidden in the plaid, sharpened on a stone, and carried now at last to the meeting for which it had been guarded over three years of waiting.

A meeting in the cold rain of spring. I felt it cold as old blood on my hands and tasteless on my lips. Above, the sky was low and clouds were flowing to the east. The rain fell steadily.

The sound of it was like a rolling of drums as I went down the outside landing stairs, the multitude of raindrops sounding their own end against the unyielding concrete all around. The concrete stretched far from the ship in every direction, hiding the earth, as bare and clean as the last page of an account book before the final entry. At its far edge, the spaceport terminal stood like a single gravestone. The curtains of falling water between it and me thinned and thickened like the smoke of battle, but could not hide it entirely from my sight.

It was the same rain that falls in all places and on all worlds. It had fallen like this on Athens on the dark, unhappy house of Mathias, and on the ruins of the Parthenon as I saw it from my bedroom vision screen.

I listened to it now as I went down the landing stairs, drumming on the great ship behind me which had shifted me free between the stars—from Old Earth to this second smallest of the worlds, this small terraformed planet under the Procyon suns—and drumming hollowly upon the Credentials case sliding down the conveyor belt beside me. That case now meant nothing to me—neither my papers nor the Credentials of Impartiality I had carried four years now and worked so hard to earn. Now I thought less of these than of the name of the man I should find dispatching groundcars at the edge of the field. If, that is, he was actually the man my Earth informants had named to me. And if they had not lied.

"Your luggage, sir?"

I woke from my thoughts and the rain. I had reached the concrete. The debarking officer smiled at me. He was older than I, though he looked younger. As he smiled, some beads of moisture broke and spilled like tears from the brown visor-edge of his cap onto the tally sheet he held.

"Send it to the Friendly compound," I said. "I'll take the Credentials case."

I took it up from the conveyor belt and turned to walk off. The man standing in a dispatcher's uniform by the first groundcar in line did fit the description.

"Name, sir?" he said. "Business on Ste. Marie?"

If he had been described to me, I must have been described to him. But I was prepared to humor him.

"Newsman Tam Olyn," I said. "Old Earth resident and Interstellar News Services Guild Representative. I'm here to cover the Friendly-Exotic conflict." I opened my case and gave him my papers.

"Fine, Mr. Olyn." He handed them back to me, damp from the rain. He turned away to open the door of the car beside him and set the automatic pilot. "Follow the highway straight to Joseph's Town. Put it on automatic at the city limits and the car'll take you to the Friendly compound."

"All right," I said. "Just a minute."

He turned back. He had a young, good-looking face with a little mustache and he looked at me with a bright blankness. "Sir?"

"Help me get in the car."

"Oh, I'm sorry, sir." He came quickly over to me. "I didn't realize your leg—"

"Damp stiffens it," I said. He adjusted the seat and I got my left leg in behind the steering column. He started to turn away.

"Wait a minute," I said again. I was out of patience. "You're Walter Imera, aren't you?"

"Yes, sir," he said softly.

"Look at me," I said. "You've got some information for me, haven't you?"

He turned slowly back to face me. His face was still blank.

"No, sir."

I waited a long moment, looking at him.

"All right," I said then, reaching for the car door. "I guess you know I'll get the information anyway. And they'll believe you told me."

His little mustache began to look like it was painted on.

"Wait," he said. "You've got to understand. Information like that's not part of your news, is it? I've got a family—"

"And I haven't," I said. I felt nothing for him.

"But you don't understand. They'd kill me. That's the sort of organization the Blue Front is now, here on Ste. Marie. What d'you want to know about them for? I didn't understand you meant—"

"All right," I said. I reached for the car door.

"Wait." He held out a hand to me in the rain. "How do I know you can make them leave me alone if I tell you?"

"They may be back in power here someday," I said. "Not even outlawed political groups want to antagonize the Interstellar News Services." I started to close the door once more.

"All right," he said quickly. "All right. You go to New San Marcos. The Wallace Street Jewelers there. It's just beyond Joseph's Town, where the Friendly compound is you're going to." He licked his lips. "You'll tell them about me?"

"I'll tell them." I looked at him. Above the edge of the blue uniform collar on the right side of his neck I could see an inch or two of fine silver chain, bright against winter-pale skin. The crucifix attached to it would be down under his shirt. "The Friendly soldiers have been here two years now. How do people like them?"

He grinned a little. His color was coming back.

"Oh, like anybody," he said. "You just have to understand them. They've got their own ways."

I felt the ache in my stiff leg where the doctors on New Earth had taken the needle from the spring-rifle out of it three years before.

"Yes, they have," I said. "Shut the door."

He shut it. I drove off.

There was some religious medal on the car's instrument panel. One of the Friendly soldiers would have ripped it off and thrown it away, or refused the car. And so it gave me a particular pleasure to leave it where it was, though it meant no more to me than it would to him. It was not just because of Dave and the other prisoners they had shot down on New Earth. It was simply because there are some duties that have a small element of pleasure. After the illusions of childhood are gone and there is nothing left but duties, such pleasures are welcome. Fanatics, when all is said and done, are no worse than mad dogs.

But mad dogs have to be destroyed; it is simple common sense.

And you return to common sense after a while in life, inevitably. When the wild dreams of justice and progress are all dead and buried, when the painful beatings of feeling inside you are finally stilled, then it becomes best to be still, unliving, and unyielding as—the blade of a sword sharpened on a stone. The rain through which such a blade is carried to its using does not stain it, any more than the blood in which it is bathed at last. Rain and blood are alike to sharpened iron.

I drove for half an hour past wooded hills and plowed meadows. The furrows of the fields were black in the rain. I thought it a kinder black than some other shades I had seen. At last I reached the outskirts of Joseph's Town.

The autopilot of the car threaded me through a small, neat, typical Ste. Marie city of about a hundred thousand people. We came out on the far side into a cleared area, beyond which lifted the massive, sloping concrete walls of a military compound.

A Friendly noncom stopped my car at the gate with his black spring-rifle and opened the car door at my left.

"Thou hast business here?"

His voice was harsh and high in his nose. The cloth tabs of a Groupman edged his collar. Above them his forty-year-old face was lean and graven with lines. Both face and hands, the only uncovered parts of him, looked unnaturally white against the black cloth and rifle.

I opened the case beside me and handed him my papers.

"My Credentials," I said. "I'm here to see your acting Commander of Expeditionary Forces, Commandant Jamethon Black."

"Move over, then," he said nasally. "I must drive thee."

I moved.

He got in and took the stick. We drove through the gate and turned down an approach alley. I could see an interior square at the alley's far end. The close

concrete walls on either side of us echoed the sound
of our passage as we went. I heard drill commands
growing louder as we approached the square. When
we rolled out into it, soldiers were drawn up in ranks
for their midday service, in the rain.

The Groupman left me and went in the entrance
of what seemed to be an office set in the wall on one
side of the square. I looked over the soldiers standing
in formation. They stood at present-arms, their position of worship under field conditions; and as I
watched, the officer facing them, with his back to a
wall, led them into the words of their Battle Hymn.

> Soldier, ask not—now or ever,
> Where to war your banners go.
> Anarch's legions all surround us.
> Strike! And do not count the blow!

I sat trying not to listen. There was no musical ac-
companiment, no religious furniture or symbols except the thin shape of the cross whitewashed on the
gray wall behind the officer. The massed male voices
rose and fell slowly in the dark, sad hymn that promised them only pain, and suffering, and sorrow. At
last, the final line mourned its harsh prayer for a
battle death, and they ordered arms.

A Groupman dismissed the ranks as the officer
walked past my car without looking at me, and
passed in through the entrance where my noncommissioned guide had disappeared. As he passed I
saw the officer was Jamethon.

A moment later the guide came for me. Limping
a little on my stiffened leg, I followed him to an
inner room with the lights on above a single desk.

Jamethon rose and nodded as the door closed behind me. He wore the faded tabs of a Commandant on his uniform lapels.

As I handed my Credentials across the desk to him, the glare of the light over the desk came full in my eyes, blinding me. I stepped back and blinked at his blurred face. As it came back into focus I saw it for a moment as if it were older, harsher, twisted and engraved with the lines of years of fanaticism, like a face I remembered standing over the murdered prisoners on New Earth.

Then my eyes refocused completely, and I saw him as he actually was. Dark-faced, but thin with the thinness of youth rather than that of starvation. He was not the face burned in my memory. His features were regular to the point of being handsome, his eyes tired and shadowed; and I saw the straight, weary line of his mouth above the still, self-controlled stiffness of his body, smaller and slighter than mine.

He held the Credentials without looking at them. His mouth quirked a little, dryly and wearily, at the corners. "And no doubt, Mr. Olyn," he said, "you've got another pocket filled with authorities from the Exotic worlds to interview the mercenary soldiers and officers they've hired from the Dorsai and a dozen other worlds to oppose God's Chosen in War?"

I smiled. Because it was good to find him as strong as that, to add to my pleasure of breaking him.

CHAPTER 23 ■

I looked across the ten feet or so of distance that separated us. The Friendly Groupman who had killed the prisoners on New Earth had also spoken of God's Chosen.

"If you'll look under the papers directed at you," I said, "you'll find them. The News Services and its people are impartial. We don't take sides."

"Right," said the dark young face opposing me, "takes sides."

"Yes, Commandant," I said. "That's right. Only sometimes it's a matter of debate where Right is. You and your troops here now are invaders on the world of a planetary system your ancestors never colonized. And opposing you are mercenary troops hired by two worlds that not only belong under the Procyon suns but have a commitment to defend the smaller worlds of their system—of which Ste. Marie is one. I'm not sure Right is on your side.''

He shook his head slightly and said, ''We expect small understanding from those not Chosen.'' He transferred his gaze from me to the papers in his hand.

''Mind if I sit down?'' I said. ''I've got a bad leg.''

''By all means.'' He nodded to a chair beside his desk and as I sat down, seated himself. I looked across the papers on the desk before him and saw, standing to one side, the solidograph of one of the windowless high-peaked churches the Friendlies build. It was a legitimate token for him to own, but there just happened to be three people, an older man and woman and a young girl of about fourteen, in the foreground of the image. All three of them bore a family resemblance to Jamethon. Glancing up from my Credentials he saw me looking at them; and his gaze shifted momentarily to the graph and away again, as if he would protect it.

''I'm required, I see,'' he said, drawing my eyes back to him, ''to provide you with cooperation and facilities. We'll find quarters for you here. Do you need a car and driver?''

''Thanks,'' I said. ''That commercial car outside will do. And I'll manage my own driving.''

''As you like.'' He detached the papers directed to him, passed the rest back to me and leaned toward a grille in his desktop. ''Groupman.''

''Sir,'' the grille answered promptly.

''Quarters for a single male civilian. Parking assignment for a civilian vehicle, personnel.''

''Sir.''

The voice from the grille clicked off. Jamethon Black looked across his desk at me. I got the idea he was waiting for my departure.

"Commandant," I said, putting my Credentials back in their case, "two years ago your Elders of the United Churches on Harmony and Association found the planetary government of Ste. Marie in default of certain disputed balances of credit, so they sent an expedition in here to occupy and enforce payment. Of that expedition, how much in the way of men and equipment do you have left?"

"That, Mr. Olyn," he said, "is restricted military information."

"However"—and I closed the case—"you, with the regular rank of Commandant, are acting Commander of Forces for the remnants of your expedition. That position calls for someone about five ranks higher than you. Do you expect such an officer to arrive and take charge?"

"I'm afraid you'd have to ask that question of Headquarters on Harmony, Mr. Olyn."

"Do you expect reinforcements of personnel and more supplies?"

"If I did"—his voice was level—"I would have to consider that restricted information, too."

"You know that it's been pretty widely mentioned that your General Staff on Harmony has decided that this expedition to Ste. Marie is a lost cause? But that to avoid loss of face they prefer you here to be cut up, instead of withdrawing you and your men."

"I see," he said.

"You wouldn't care to comment?"

His dark, young, expressionless face did not change. "Not in the case of rumors, Mr. Olyn."

"One last question then. Do you plan to retreat westward, or surrender when the spring offensive of the Exotic mercenary forces begins to move against you?"

"The Chosen in War never retreat," he said. "Neither do they abandon, or suffer abandonment by, their Brothers in the Lord." He stood up. "I have work I must get back to, Mr. Olyn."

I stood up, too. I was taller than he was, older, and heavier-boned. It was only his almost unnatural composure that enabled him to maintain his appearance of being my equal or better.

"I'll talk to you later, perhaps, when you've got more time," I said.

"Certainly." I heard the office door open behind me. "Groupman," he said, speaking past me, "take care of Mr. Olyn."

The Groupman he had turned me over to found me a small concrete cubicle with a single high window, a camp bed and a uniform cabinet. He left me for a moment and returned with a signed pass.

"Thanks," I said as I took it. "Where do I find the Headquarters of the Exotic forces?"

"Our latest advice, sir," he said, "is that they're ninety kilometers east of here. New San Marcos." He was my height, but, like most of them, half a dozen years younger than I, with an innocence that contrasted with the strange air of control they all had.

"San Marcos." I looked at him. "I suppose you enlisted men know your General Headquarters on Harmony has decided against wasting replacements for you?"

"No, sir," he said. I might have commented on the rain for all the reaction he showed. Even these boys were still strong and unbroken. "Is there some-what else?"

"No," I said. "Thanks."

He went out. And I went out, to get in my car and head ninety kilometers east to New San Marcos. I reached it in about three-quarters of an hour. But I did not go directly to find the Exotic Field Head-quarters. I had other fish to fry.

These took me to the Wallace Street Jewelers. There, three shallow steps down from street level, an opaqued door let me into a long, dim-lighted room filled with glass cases. There was a small elderly man at the back of the store behind the final case and I saw him eyeing my correspondent's cloak and badge as I got closer.

"Sir?" he said as I stopped across the case from him. He raised gray, narrow old eyes in a strangely smooth face to look at me.

"I think you know what I represent," I said. "All worlds know the News Services. We're not con-cerned with local politics."

"Sir?"

"You'll find out how I learned your address any-way." I kept on smiling at him. "So I'll tell you it was from a spaceport auto-dispatcher named Imera. I promised him protection for telling me. We'd ap-preciate it if he remains well and whole."

"I'm afraid—" He put his hands on the glass top of the case. They were veined with the years. "You wanted to buy something?"

"I'm willing to pay in good will," I said, "for information."

His hands slid off the countertop.

"Sir." He sighed a little. "I'm afraid you're in the wrong store."

"I'm sure I am," I said. "But your store'll have to do. We'll pretend it's the right store and I'm talking to someone who's a member of the Blue Front."

He shook his head slowly and stepped back from the case.

"The Blue Front is illegal," he said. "Good-bye, sir."

"In a moment. I've got a few things to say first."

"Then I'm sorry." He retreated toward some drapes covering a doorway. "I can't listen. No one will come into this room with you, sir, as long as you talk like that."

He slipped through the drapes and was gone. I looked around the long, empty room.

"Well," I said a little more loudly, "I guess I'll have to speak to the walls. I'm sure the walls can hear me."

I paused. There was no sound.

"All right," I said. "I'm a correspondent. All I'm interested in is information. Our assessment of the military situation here on Ste. Marie"—and here I told the truth—"shows the Friendly Expeditionary Forces abandoned by their home headquarters and certain to be overrun by the Exotic forces as soon as the ground dries enough for heavy equipment to move."

There was still no answer, but the back of my neck knew they were listening and watching me.

"As a result," I went on—and here I lied, though they would have no way of knowing—"we consider it inevitable that the Friendly Command here will have got in contact with the Blue Front. Assassination of enemy commanders is expressly in violation of the Mercenaries' Code and the Articles of Civilized Warfare—but civilians could do what soldiers could not.''

Still there was no sound or movement beyond the drapes.

''A news representative,'' I said, ''carries Credentials of Impartiality. You know how highly these are held. I only want to ask a few questions. And the answers will be kept confidential.''

For a last time I waited, and there was still no answer. I turned and went up the long room and out. It was not until I was well out on to the street that I let the feeling of triumph within spread out and warm me.

They would take the bait. People of their sort always did. I found my car and drove to Exotic Headquarters.

These were outside the town. There a mercenary Commandant named Janol Marat took me in charge. He conducted me to the bubble structure of their HQ building. There was a feel of purpose, there, a sure and cheerful air of activity. They were well armed, well trained. After the Friendlies it jumped at me. I said so to Janol.

''We've got a Dorsai Commander and we outnumber the opposition.'' He grinned at me. He had a deeply tanned, long face that went into creases as his lips curved up. ''That makes everybody pretty optimistic. Besides, our Commander gets promoted if he wins. Back to the Exotics and staff rank—out of field combat for good. It's good business for us to win.''

I laughed and he laughed.

''Tell me more, though,'' I said. ''I want reasons

I can use in the stories I send back to News Services.''

''Well''—he answered the snappy salute of a passing Groupman, a Cassidan by the look of him—''I guess you might mention the usual—the fact our Exotic employers don't permit themselves to use violence and consequently they're always rather generous than otherwise when it comes to paying for men and equipment. And the OutBond—that's the Exotic Ambassador to Ste. Marie, you know—''

''I know.''

''He replaced the former OutBond here three years ago. Anyway, he's something special, even for someone from Mara or Kultis. He's an expert in ontogenetic calculations. If that means much to you. It's all over my head.'' Janol pointed. ''Here's the Field Commander's office. He's Kensie Graeme.''

''Graeme?'' I said, frowning. I could have admitted to knowing about Kensie Graeme, but I wanted Janol's reactions to him. ''Sounds familiar.'' We approached the office building. ''Graeme . . .''

''You're probably thinking of another member of the same family.'' Janol took the bait. ''Donal Graeme. A nephew. Kensie is Donal's uncle. Not as spectacular as the young Graeme, but I'll bet you'll like him better than you would the nephew. Kensie's got two men's likableness.'' He looked at me, grinning slightly again.

''That supposed to mean something special?'' I said.

''That's right,'' said Janol. ''His own likableness and his twin brother's, too. Meet Ian Graeme sometime when you're in Blauvain. That's where the Exotic embassy is, east of here. Ian's a dark man.''

We walked into the office.

"I can't get used," I said, "to how so many Dorsai seem related."

"Neither can I. Actually, I guess it's because there really aren't so many of them. The Dorsai's a small world, and those that live more than a few years—" Janol stopped by a Commandant sitting at a desk. "Can we see the Old Man, Hari? This is a Newsman from the Interstellar News Services."

"Why, I guess so." The other looked at his desk signal board. "The OutBond's with him, but he's just leaving now. Go on in."

Janol led me between the desks. A door at the back of the room opened before we reached it and a calm-faced man of middle age wearing an Exotic's blue robe, and close-cropped white hair, came out. His odd, hazel-colored eyes met mine.

It was Padma.

"Sir," said Janol to Padma, "this is—"

"Tam Olyn. I know," said Padma softly. He smiled up at me, and those eyes of his seemed to catch light for a moment and blind me. "I was sorry to learn about your brother-in-law, Tam."

I went quite cool all over. I had been ready to walk on, but now I stood stock still and looked at him.

"My brother-in-law?" I said.

"The young man who died near Dhores on New Earth."

"Oh, yes," I said between stiff lips. "I'm surprised that you'd know."

"I know because of you, Tam." Once more the hazel eyes of Padma seemed to catch light. "Have you forgotten? I told you once that we have a science called ontogenetics, by which we calculate the probabilities of human actions in present and future situations. You've been an important factor in those calculations for some time.'' He smiled. ''That's why I was expecting to meet you here, and now. We've calculated you into our present situation here on Ste. Marie, Tam.''

''Have you?'' I said. ''Have you? That's interesting.''

''I thought it would be,'' said Padma softly. ''To you, especially. Someone like a Newsman, like yourself, would find it interesting.''

''It is,'' I said. ''It sounds like you know more than I do about what I'm going to be doing here.''

''We've got calculations,'' said Padma in his soft voice, ''to that effect. Come see me in Blauvain, Tam, and I'll show you.''

''I'll do that,'' I said.

''You'll be very welcome.'' Padma inclined his head. His blue robe whispered on the floor as he turned and went out of the room.

''This way,'' said Janol, touching my elbow. I started as if I had just wakened from a deep sleep. ''The Commander's in here.''

I followed him automatically into an inner office. Kensie Graeme stood up as we came through the door. For the first time I stood face to face with this great, lean man in field uniform, with a heavy-boned, but open, smiling face under black, slightly curly hair. That peculiar golden warmth of personality—a strange thing in a Dorsai—seemed to flow out from him as he rose to meet me and his long-fingered, powerful hand swallowed mine in a handshake.

''Come on in,'' he said. ''Let me fix you up with a drink. Janol,'' he added to my mercenary Commandant from New Earth, "no need for you to stick around. Go on to chow. And tell the rest of them in the outer office to knock off."

Janol saluted and went. I sat down as Graeme turned to a small bar cabinet behind his desk. And for the first time in three years, under the magic of the unusual fighting man opposite me, a little peace came into my soul. With someone like this on my side, I could not lose.

CHAPTER 24 ■

"Credentials?" asked Graeme as soon as we were settled with drinks of Dorsai whisky—which is a fine whisky—in our hands.

I passed my papers over. He glanced through them, picking out the letters from Sayona, the Bond of Kultis, to "Commander—Ste. Marie Field Forces." He looked these over and put them aside. He handed me back the Credentials folder.

"You stopped at Joseph's Town first?" he said.

I nodded. I saw him looking at my face, and his own sobered.

"You don't like the Friendlies," he said.

His words took my breath away. I had come prepared to fence for an opening to tell him. It was too sudden. I looked away.

I did not dare answer right away. I could not. There was either too much or too little to say if I let it come out without thinking. Then I got a grip on myself.

"If I do anything at all with the rest of my life," I said, slowly, "it'll be to do everything in my power to remove the Friendlies and all they stand for from the community of civilized human beings."

I looked back up at him. He was sitting with one massive elbow on his desktop, watching me.

"That's a pretty harsh point of view, isn't it?"

"No harsher than theirs."

"Do you think so?" he said seriously. "I wouldn't say so."

"I thought," I said, "you were the one who was fighting them."

"Why, yes." He smiled a little. "But we're soldiers on both sides."

"I don't think they think that way."

He shook his head a little.

"What makes you say that?" he said.

"I've seen them," I answered. "I got caught up front in the lines near Dhores on New Earth, three years ago. You remember that conflict." I tapped my stiff knee. "I got shot and I couldn't navigate. The Cassidans around me began to retreat—they were mercenaries, and the troops opposing them were Friendlies hired out as mercenaries."

I stopped and took a drink of the whisky. When I took the glass away, Graeme had not moved. He sat as if waiting.

"There was a young Cassidan, a buck soldier," I said. "I was doing a series on the campaign from an individual point of view. I'd picked him for my individual. It was a natural choice. You see"—I drank again, and emptied the glass—"my younger sister went out on contract as an accountant to Cassida five years before that, and she'd married him. He was my brother-in-law.''

Graeme took the glass from my hand and silently replenished it.

"He wasn't actually a military man," I said. "He was studying shift mechanics and he had about three years to go. But he stood low on one of the competitive examinations at a time when Cassida owed a contractual balance of troops to New Earth." I took a deep breath. "Well, to make a long story short, he ended up on New Earth in this same campaign I was covering. Because of the series I was writing, I got him assigned to me. We both thought it was a good deal for him, that he'd be safer that way."

I drank some more of the whisky.

"But," I said, "you know, there's always a better story a little deeper in the combat zone. We got caught up front one day when the Cassidan troops were retreating. I picked up a needle through the kneecap. The Friendly armor was moving up and things were getting hot. The soldiers around us took off toward the rear in a hurry, but Dave tried to carry me, because he thought the Friendly armor would fry me before they had time to notice I was a noncombatant. Well"—I took another deep breath—"the Friendly ground troops caught us. They took us to a sort of clearing where they had a lot of prisoners and kept us there for a while. Then a Groupman—one of their fanatic types, a tall, starved-looking soldier about my age—came up with orders they were to reform for a fresh attack."

I stopped and took another drink. But I could not taste it.

"That meant they couldn't spare men to guard the prisoners. They'd have to turn them loose back of the Friendly lines. The Groupman said that wouldn't work. They'd have to make sure the prisoners couldn't endanger them."

Graeme was still watching me.

"I didn't understand. I didn't even catch on when the other Friendlies—none of them were noncoms like the Groupman—objected." I put my glass on the desk beside me and stared at the wall of the office, seeing it all over again, as plainly as if I looked through a window at it. "I remember how the Groupman pulled himself up straight. I saw his eyes. As if he'd been insulted by the others' objecting.

" 'Are they Chosen of God?' he shouted at them. 'Are they of the Chosen?' "

I looked across at Kensie Graeme and saw him still motionless, still watching me, his own glass small in one big hand.

"You understand?" I said to him. "As if because the prisoners weren't Friendlies, they weren't quite human. As if they were some lower order it was all right to kill." I shook suddenly. "And he did it! I sat there against a tree, safe because of my News Correspondent's uniform, and watched him shoot them down. All of them. I sat there and looked at Dave, and he looked at me, sitting there, as the Groupman shot him!"

I quit all at once. I hadn't meant to have it all come out like that. It was just that I'd been able to tell no one who would understand how helpless I had been. But something about Graeme had given me the idea he would understand.

"Yes," he said after a moment, and took and filled

my glass again. "That sort of thing's very bad. Was the Groupman found and tried under the Mercenaries' Code?"

"After it was too late, yes."

He nodded and looked past me at the wall. "They aren't all like that, of course."

"There's enough to give them a reputation for it."

"Unfortunately, yes. Well"—he smiled slightly at me—"we'll try and keep that sort of thing out of this campaign."

"Tell me something," I said, putting my glass down. "Does that sort of thing—as you put it—ever happen to the Friendlies themselves?"

Something took place then in the atmosphere of the room. There was a little pause before he answered. I felt my heart beat slowly, three times, as I waited for him to speak.

He said at last, "No, it doesn't."

"Why not?" I said.

The feeling in the room became stronger. And I realized I had gone too fast. I had been sitting talking to him as a man and forgetting what else he was. Now I began to forget that he was a man and became conscious of him as a Dorsai—an individual as human as I was, but trained all his life, and bred down the generations to a difference. He did not move or change the tone of his voice, or any such thing; but somehow he seemed to move off some distance from me, up into a higher, colder, stonier land into which I could venture only at my peril.

I remembered what was said about his people from that small, cold, stony-mountained world: that if the Dorsai chose to withdraw their fighting men from the services of all the other worlds, and challenge those other worlds, not the combined might of the rest of civilization could stand against them. I had never really believed that before. I had never even really thought much about it. But sitting there just then, because of what was happening in the room, suddenly it became real to me. I could feel the knowledge, cold as a wind blowing on me off a glacier, that it was true; and then he answered my question.

"Because," said Kensie Graeme, "anything like that is specifically prohibited by Article Two of the Mercenaries' Code."

Then he broke out abruptly into a smile and what I had just felt in the room withdrew. I breathed again.

"Well," he said, putting his glass down empty on the desk, "how about joining us in the Officers' Mess for something to eat?"

I had dinner with them and the meal was very pleasant. They wanted to put me up for the night, but I could feel myself being pulled back to that cold, joyless compound near Joseph's Town, where all that waited for me was a sort of cold and bitter satisfaction at being among my enemies.

I went back.

It was about eleven P.M. when I drove through the gate of the compound and parked, just as a figure came out of the entrance to Jamethon's headquarters. The square was dim-lighted with only a few spotlights about the walls, their light lost in the rain-wet pavement. For a moment I did not recognize the figure—and then I saw it was Jamethon.

He would have passed by me at some little distance, but I got out of my car and went to meet him. He stopped when I stepped in front of him.

"Mr. Olyn," he said evenly. In the darkness I could not make out the expression of his face.

"I've got a question to ask," I said, smiling in the darkness.

"It's late for questions."

"This won't take long." I strained to catch the look on his face, but it was all in shadow. "I've been visiting the Exotic camp. Their commander's a Dorsai. I suppose you know that?"

"Yes." I could barely see the movement of his lips.

"We got to talking. A question came up and I thought I'd ask you, Commandant. Do you ever order your men to kill prisoners?"

An odd, short silence came between us. Then he answered.

"The killing or abuse of prisoners of war," he said without emotion, "is forbidden by Article Two of the Mercenaries' Code."

"But you aren't mercenaries here, are you? You're native troops in service to your own True Church and Elders."

"Mr. Olyn," he said, while I still strained without success to make out the expression of his shadowed face—and it seemed that the words came slowly, though the tone of the voice that spoke them remained as calm as ever, "My Lord has set me to be His servant and a leader among men of war. In neither of those tasks will I fail Him."

And with that he turned, his face still shadowed and hidden from me, and passed around me and went on.

Alone, I went back inside to my quarters, undressed and lay down on the hard and narrow bed they had given me. The rain outside had stopped at last. Through my open, unglazed window I could see a few stars showing.

I lay there getting ready to sleep and making mental notes on what I would need to do next day. The meeting with Padma had jolted me sharply. Strangely, somehow I had almost managed to forget that his calculations of human actions could apply to me personally. It shook me now to be reminded of that. I would have to find out more about how much his science of ontogenetics knew and could predict. If necessary, from Padma himself. But I would start first with ordinary reference sources.

No one, I thought, would ordinarily entertain the fantastic thought that one man like myself could destroy a culture involving the populations of two worlds. No one, except perhaps a Padma. What I knew, he with his calculations might have discovered. And that was that the Friendly worlds of Harmony and Association were facing a decision that would mean life or death to their way of living. A very small thing could tip the scales they weighed on. I went over my plan, nursing it in my mind.

For there was a new wind blowing between the stars.

Two hundred years before we had all been men of Earth—Old Earth, the mother planet which was my native soil. One people.

Then, with the movement out to new worlds, the human race had "splintered," to use an Exotic term. Every small social fragment and psychological type had drawn apart by itself, and joined others like it and progressed toward specialized types. Until we had half a dozen fragments of human types—the warrior on the Dorsai, the philosopher on the Exotic worlds, the hard scientist on Newton, Cassida and Venus, and so forth.

Isolation had bred specific types. Then a growing intercommunication between the younger worlds, now established, and an ever-increasing rate of technological advance had forced specialization. The trade between the worlds was the trade of skilled minds. Generals from the Dorsai were worth their exchange rate in psychiatrists from the Exotics. Communications men like myself from Old Earth bought spaceship designers from Cassida. And so it had been for the last hundred years.

But now the worlds were drifting together. Economics was fusing the race into one whole again. And the struggle on each world was to gain the advantages of that fusion while holding on to as much as possible of their own ways.

Compromise was necessary—but the harsh, stiff-necked Friendly religion forbade compromise and had made many enemies. Already public opinion moved against the Friendlies on other worlds. Discredit them, smear them, publicly here in this campaign, and they would not be able to hire out their soldiers. They would lose the balance of trade they needed to hire the skilled specialists trained by the special facilities of other worlds, and which they needed to keep their own two poor-in-natural-resources worlds alive. They would die.

As young Dave had died. Slowly. In the dark.

In the darkness now, as I thought of it, it rose up before me once again. It had been only midafternoon when we were taken prisoner, but by the time the

Groupman came with his orders for our guards to move up, the sun was almost down.

I remembered how, after they left, after it was all over and I was left alone, I crawled to the bodies in the clearing. And how I had found Dave among them; and he was not quite gone. He was wounded in the body and I could not stop the bleeding.

It would not have helped if I had, they told me afterward. But then it seemed that it would have. So I tried. But finally I gave up and by that time it was quite dark. I only held him and did not know he was dead until he began to grow cold. And that was when I had begun to change into what my uncle had always tried to make me. I felt myself die inside. Dave and my sister were to have been my family, the only family I had ever had hopes of keeping. Instead, I could only sit there in the darkness, holding him and hearing the blood from his red-soaked clothing falling drop by drop, slowly, on the dead variform oak leaves beneath us.

I lay there now in the Friendly compound, unable to sleep and remembering. And after a while I heard the soldiers marching, forming in the square for midnight service.

I lay on my back, listening to them. Their marching feet stopped at last. The single window of my room was over my bed, high in the wall against which the left side of my cot was set. It was unglazed and the night air with its sounds came freely through it along with the dim light from the square which painted a pale rectangle on the opposite wall of my room. I lay watching that rectangle and listening to the service outside; and I heard the duty officer lead them in a prayer for worthiness. After that they sang their battle hymn again, and I lay hearing it this time all the way through.

> Soldier, ask not—now, or ever,
> Where to war your banners go.
> Anarch's legions all surround us.
> Strike—and do not count the blow.
>
> Glory, honor, praise and profit,
> Are but toys of tinsel worth.
> Render up your work, unasking,
> Leave the human clay to earth.
>
> Blood and sorrow, pain unending,
> Are the portion of us all.
> Grasp the naked sword, opposing.
> Gladly in the battle fall.
>
> So shall we, anointed soldiers,
> Stand at last before the Throne.
> Baptized in our wounds, red-flowing,
> Sealed unto our Lord—alone!

After that they dispersed to cots no different from mine.

I lay there listening to the silence in the square and the measured dripping of a rainspout outside by my window, its slow drops falling after the rain, one by one, uncounted in the darkness.

CHAPTER 25 ■

After the day I landed, there was no more rain. Day
by day the fields dried. Soon they would be firm
underneath the weight of heavy surface-war equipment, and everyone knew that then the Exotic spring
offensive would get under way. Meanwhile both Exotic and Friendly troops were in training.

During the next few weeks, I was busy about my
newswork—mostly feature and small stories on the
soldiers and the native people. I had dispatches to
send and I sent them faithfully. A correspondent is
only as good as his contacts; I made contacts everywhere but among the Friendly troops. These remained aloof, though I talked to many of them. They
refused to show fear or doubt.

I heard these Friendly soldiers were generally un-
dertrained because the suicidal tactics of their officers kept their ranks always filled with green

replacements. But the ones here were the remnants of an expeditionary force six times their present numbers. They were all veterans, though most of them were in their teens. Only here and there, among the noncoms and more often among the commissioned officers, I saw the prototype of the noncom who had ordered the prisoners shot on New Earth. Here, the men of this type looked like rabid gray wolves mixed among polite, well-schooled young dogs just out of puppyhood. It was a temptation to think that they alone were what I had set out to destroy.

To fight that temptation I told myself that Alexander the Great had led expeditions against the hill tribes and ruled in Pella, capital of Macedonia, and ordered men put to death when he was sixteen. But still the Friendly soldiers looked young to me. I could not help contrasting them with the adult, experienced mercenaries in Kensie Graeme's forces. For the Exotics, in obedience to their principles, would hire no drafted troops or soldiers who were not in uniform of their own free will.

Meanwhile I had heard no word from the Blue Front. But by the time two weeks had gone, I had my own connections in New San Marcos, and at the beginning of the third week one of these brought me word that the jeweler's shop in Wallace Street there had closed its door, had pulled its blinds and emptied the long room of stock and fixtures, and moved or gone out of business. That was all I needed to know.

For the next few days, I stayed in the vicinity of Jamethon Black himself, and by the end of the week my watching him paid off.

At ten o'clock that Friday night I was on a catwalk just above my quarters and under the sentry-walk of the walls, watching as three civilians with Blue Front written all over them drove into the square, got out and went into Jamethon's office.

They stayed a little over an hour. When they left, I went back down to bed. That night I slept soundly.

The next morning I got up early, and there was mail for me. A message had come by spaceliner from the director of News Services back on Earth, personally congratulating me on my dispatches. Once, three years before, this would have meant a great deal to me. Now I only worried that they would decide I had made the situation here newsworthy enough to require extra people being sent out to help me. I could not risk having other news personnel here now to see what I was doing.

I got in my car and headed east along the highway to New San Marcos and the Exotic Headquarters. The Friendly troops were already out in the field; eighteen kilometers east of Joseph's Town, I was stopped by a squad of five young soldiers with no noncom over them. They recognized me.

"In God's name, Mr. Olyn," said the first one to reach my car, bending down to speak to me through the open window at my left shoulder. "You cannot go through."

"Mind if I ask why?" I said.

He turned and pointed out and down into a little valley between two wooded hills at our left.

"Tactical survey in progress."

I looked. The little valley or meadow was perhaps a hundred yards wide between the wooded slopes, and it wound away from me and curved to disappear to my right. At the edge of the wooded slopes, where they met open meadow, there were lilac bushes with blossoms several days old. The meadow itself was green and fair with the young chartreuse grass of early summer and the white and purple of the lilacs, and the variform oaks behind the lilacs were fuzzy in outline, with small, new leaves.

In the middle of all this, in the center of the meadow, were black-clad figures moving about with computing devices, measuring and figuring the possibilities of death from every angle. In the very center of the meadow for some reason they had set up marking stakes—a single stake, then a stake in front of that with two stakes on either side of it, and one more stake in line before these. Farther on was another single stake, down, as if fallen on the grass and discarded.

I looked back up into the lean young face of the soldier.

"Getting ready to defeat the Exotics?" I said.

He took it as if it had been a straightforward question, with no irony in my voice at all.

"Yes, sir," he said seriously. I looked at him and at the taut skin and clear eyes of the rest.

"Ever think you might lose?"

"No, Mr. Olyn." He shook his head solemnly. "No man loses who goes to battle for the Lord." He saw that I needed to be convinced, and he went about it earnestly. "He hath set His hand upon His soldiers. And all that is possible to them is victory—or sometimes death. And what is death?"

He looked to his fellow soldiers and they all nodded.

"What is death?" they echoed.

I looked at them. They stood there asking me and each other what was death as if they were talking about some hard but necessary job.

I had an answer for them, but I did not say it. Death was a Groupman, one of their own kind, giving orders to soldiers just like themselves to assassinate prisoners. That was death.

"Call an officer," I said. "My pass lets me through here."

"I regret, sir," said the one who had been talking to me, "we cannot leave our posts to summon an officer. One will come soon."

I had a hunch what "soon" meant, and I was right. It was high noon before a Force-Leader came by to order them to chow and let me through.

As I pulled into Kensie Graeme's Headquarters, the sun was low, patterning the ground with the long shadows of trees. Yet it was as if the camp were just waking up. I did not need experience to see the Exotics were beginning to move at last against Jamethon.

I found Janol Marat, the New Earth Commandant.

"I've got to see Field Commander Graeme," I said.

He shook his head, for all that we now knew each other well.

"Not now, Tam. I'm sorry."

"Janol," I said, "this isn't for an interview. It's a matter of life and death. I mean that. I've got to see Kensie."

He stared at me. I stared back.

"Wait here," he said. We were standing just inside the headquarters office. He went out and was gone for perhaps five minutes. I stood, listening to the wall clock ticking away. Then he came back.

"This way," he said.

He led me outside the back between the bubble roundness of the plastic buildings to a small structure half-hidden in some trees. When we stepped through its front entrance, I realized it was Kensie's personal quarters. We passed through a small sitting room into a combination bedroom and bath. Kensie had just stepped out of the shower and was getting into battle clothes. He looked at me curiously, then turned his gaze back on Janol.

"All right, Commandant," he said, "you can get back to your duties, now."

"Sir," said Janol, without looking at me.

He saluted and left.

"All right, Tam," Kensie said, pulling on a pair of uniform slacks. "What is it?"

"I know you're ready to move out," I said.

He looked at me a little humorously as he locked the waistband of his slacks. He had not yet put on his shirt, and in that relatively small room he loomed like a giant, like some irresistible natural force. His body was tanned like dark wood and the muscles lay in flat bands across his chest and shoulders. His belly was hollow and the cords in his arms came and went as he moved them. Once more I felt the particular, special element of the Dorsai in him. It was not even the fact that he was someone trained from birth to war, someone bred for battle. No, it was something living but untouchable—the same quality of difference to be found in the pure Exotic like Padma the OutBond, or in some Newtonian or Cassidan researchist. Something so much above and beyond the common form of man that it was like a serenity, a sense of conviction where his own type of thing was concerned that was so complete it made him beyond all weaknesses, untouchable, unconquerable.

I saw the slight, dark shadow of Jamethon in my mind's eye, standing opposed to such a man as this; and the thought of any victory for Jamethon was unthinkable, an impossibility.

But there was always danger.

"All right, I'll tell you what I came about," I said to Kensie. "I've just found out Black's been in touch with the Blue Front, a native terrorist political group with its headquarters in Blauvain. Three of them visited him last night. I saw them."

Kensie picked up his shirt and slid a long arm into one sleeve.

"I know," he said.

I stared at him.

"Don't you understand?" I said. "They're assassins. It's their stock in trade. And the one man they and Jamethon both could use out of the way is you."

He put his other arm in a sleeve.

"I know that," he said. "They want the present government here on Ste. Marie out of the way and themselves in power—which isn't possible with Exotic money hiring us to keep the peace here."

"They haven't had Jamethon's help."

"Have they got it now?" he asked, sealing the shirt closure between thumb and forefinger.

"The Friendlies are desperate," I said. "Even if reinforcements arrived tomorrow, Jamethon knows what his chances are with you ready to move. Assassins may be outlawed by the Conventions of War and the Mercenaries' Code, but you and I know the Friendlies."

Kensie looked at me oddly and picked up his jacket. "Do we?" he said.

I met his eyes. "Don't we?"

"Tam." He put on the jacket and closed it. "I know the men I have to fight. It's my business to know. But what makes you think you know them?"

"They're my business, too," I said. "Maybe you've forgotten. I'm a Newsman. People are my business, first, last and always."

"But you've got no use for the Friendlies."

"Should I?" I said. "I've been on all the worlds. I've seen the Cetan entrepreneur—and he wants his margin, but he's a human being. I've seen the Newtonian and the Venusian with their heads in the clouds, but if you yanked on their sleeves hard enough, you could pull them back to reality. I've seen Exotics like Padma at their mental parlor tricks, and the Freilander up to his ears in his own red tape. I've seen them from my own world of Old Earth, and Coby, and Venus and even from the Dorsai, like you. And I tell you they've all got one thing in common. Underneath it all they're human. Every one of them's human—they've just specialized in some one, valuable way."

"And the Friendlies haven't?"

"Fanaticism," I said. "Is that valuable? It's just the opposite. What's good, what's even permissible about blind, deaf, dumb, unthinking faith that doesn't let a man reason for himself?"

"How do you know they don't reason?" Kensie asked. He was standing facing me now.

"Maybe some of them do," I said. "Maybe the young ones, before the poison's had time to work in. What good does that do, as long as the culture exists?"

A sudden silence came into the room.

"What are you talking about?" said Kensie.

"I mean you want the assassins," I said. "You don't want the Friendly troops. Prove that Jamethon Black has broken the Conventions of War by arranging with them to kill you; and you can win Ste. Marie for the Exotics without firing a shot."

"And how would I do that?"

"Use me," I said. "I've got a pipeline to the political group the assassins represent. Let me go to them as your representative and outbid Jamethon. You can offer them recognition by the present government now. Padma and the present Ste. Marie government heads would have to back you up if you could clean the planet of Friendlies that easily."

He looked at me with no expression at all.

"And what would I be supposed to buy with this?" he said.

"Sworn testimony they'd been hired to assassinate you. As many of them as needed could testify."

"No Court of Interplanetary Inquiry would believe people like that," Kensie said.

"Ah," I said, and I could not help smiling. "But they'd believe me as a News Service Representative when I backed up every word that was said."

There was a new silence. His face had no expression at all.

"I see," he said.

He walked past me into the salon. I followed him. He went to his phone, put his finger on a stud and spoke into an imageless gray screen.

"Janol," he said.

He turned away from the screen, crossed the room

to an arms cabinet and began putting on his battle harness. He moved deliberately and neither looked nor spoke in my direction. After a few long minutes, the building entrance slid aside and Janol stepped in.

"Sir?" said the officer.

"Mr. Olyn stays here until further orders."

"Yes, sir," said Janol.

Graeme went out.

I stood numb, staring at the entrance through which he had left. I could not believe that he would violate the Conventions so far himself as not only to disregard me, but to put me essentially under arrest to keep me from doing anything further about the situation.

I turned to Janol. He was looking at me with a sort of wry sympathy on his long, brown face.

"Is the OutBond here in camp?" I asked him.

"No." He came up to me. "He's back in the Exotic Embassy in Blauvain. Be a good fella now and sit down, why don't you? We might as well kill the next few hours pleasantly."

We were standing face to face; I hit him in the stomach.

I had done a little boxing as an undergraduate on the college level. I mention this not to make myself out a sort of muscular hero, but to explain why I had sense enough not to try for his jaw. Graeme could probably have found the knockout point there without even thinking, but I was no Dorsai. The area below a man's breastbone is relatively large, soft, handy and generally just fine for amateurs. And I did know something about how to punch.

For all that, Janol was not knocked out. He went over on the floor and lay there doubled up with his eyes still open. But he was not ready to get up right away. I turned and went quickly out of the building.

The camp was busy. Nobody stopped me. I got back into my car, and five minutes later I was free on the darkening road for Blauvain.

CHAPTER 26 ■

From New San Marcos to Blauvain and Padma's Embassy was fourteen hundred kilometers. I should have made it in six hours, but a bridge was washed out and I took fourteen.

It was after eight the following morning when I burst into the half-park, half-building that was the embassy.

"Padma," I said. "Is he still—"

"Yes, Mr. Olyn," said the girl receptionist. "He's expecting you."

She smiled above her blue robe. I did not mind. I was too busy being glad Padma had not already taken off for the fringe areas of the conflict.

She took me down and around a corner and turned me over to a young male Exotic, who introduced himself as one of Padma's secretaries. He took me a short distance and introduced me to another secretary, a middle-aged man this time, who led me through several rooms and then directed me down a long corridor and around a corner, beyond which he said was the entrance to the office area where Padma worked at the moment. Then he left me.

I followed his direction. But when I stepped through that entrance it was not into a room, but into another short corridor. And I stopped dead. For what I suddenly thought I saw coming at me was Kensie Graeme—Kensie with murder on his mind.

But the man who looked like Kensie merely glanced at me and dismissed me, continuing to come on. Then I knew.

Of course, he was not Kensie. He was Kensie's twin brother, Ian, Commander of Garrison Forces for the Exotics here in Blauvain. He strode toward me; and I began once more to walk toward him, but the shock stayed with me until we had passed one another.

I do not think anyone could have come on him like that, in my position, and not been hit the same way. From Janol, at different times, I had gathered how Ian was the converse of Kensie. Not in a military sense—they were both magnificent specimens of Dorsai officers—but in the matter of their individual natures.

Kensie had had a profound effect on me from the first moment, with his cheerful nature and the warmth of being that at times obscured the very fact that he was Dorsai. When the pressure of military affairs was not directly on him he seemed all sunshine; you could warm yourself in his presence as you might in the sun. Ian, his physical duplicate, striding toward me like some two-eyed Odin, was all shadow.

Here at last was the Dorsai legend come to life. Here was the grim man with the iron heart and the dark and solitary soul. In the powerful fortress of his body, what was essentially Ian dwelt as isolated as a hermit on a mountain. He was the fierce and lonely Highlandman of his distant ancestry, come to life again.

Not law, not ethics, but the trust of the given word, clan-loyalty and the duty of the blood feud held sway in Ian. He was a man who would cross hell to pay a debt for good or ill; and in that moment when I saw him coming toward me and recognized him at last, I suddenly thanked whatever gods were left that he had no debt with me.

Then we had passed each other, and he was gone around a corner.

Rumor had it, I remembered, that the blackness around him never lightened except in Kensie's presence, that he was truly his twin brother's other half. And that if he should ever lose the light that Kensie's bright presence shed on him, he would be doomed to his own lightlessness forever.

It was a statement I was to remember at a later time, as I was to remember seeing him come toward me in that moment.

But now I forgot him as I went forward through another entrance into what looked like a small conservatory and saw the gentle face and short-cropped white hair of Padma above his blue robe.

"Come in, Mr. Olyn," he said, getting up, "and come along with me."

He turned and walked out through an archway of

purple clematis blooms. I followed him, and found a small courtyard all but filled with the elliptical shape of a sedan air-car. Padma was already climbing into one of the seats facing the controls. He held the door for me.

"Where are we going?" I asked as I got in.

He touched the autopilot panel; the ship rose in the air. He left it to its own navigation and pivoted his chair about to face me.

"To Commander Graeme's headquarters in the field," he answered.

His eyes were the same light hazel color, but they seemed to catch and swim with the sunlight striking through the transparent top of the air-car as we reached altitude and began to move horizontally. I could not read them or the expression on his face.

"I see," I said. "Of course, I know a call from Graeme's HQ could get to you much faster than I could by ground-car from the same spot. But I hope you aren't thinking of having him kidnap me or something like that. I have Credentials of Impartiality protecting me as a Newsman, as well as authorizations from both the Friendly and the Exotic worlds. And I don't intend to be held responsible for any conclusions drawn by Graeme after the conversation the two of us had earlier this morning—alone."

Padma sat still in his air-car seat, facing me. His hands were folded in his lap together, pale against the blue robe, but with strong sinews showing under the skin of their backs.

"You're coming with me now by my decision, not Kensie Graeme's."

"I want to know why," I said tensely.

"Because," he said slowly, "you are very dangerous." And he sat still, looking at me with unwavering eyes.

I waited for him to go on, but he did not. "Dangerous?" I said. "Dangerous to whom?"

"To the future of all of us."

I stared at him, then I laughed. I was angry.

"Cut it out!" I said.

He shook his head slowly, his eyes never leaving my face. I was baffled by those eyes. Innocent and open as a child's, but I could not see through them into the man himself.

"All right," I said. "Tell me, why am I dangerous?"

"Because you want to destroy a vital part of the human race. And you know how."

There was a short silence. The air-car fled on through the skies without a sound.

"Now that's an odd notion," I said slowly and calmly. "I wonder where you got it?"

"From our ontogenetic calculations," said Padma as calmly as I had spoken. "And it's not a notion, Tam. As you know yourself."

"Oh, yes," I said. "Ontogenetics. I was going to look that up."

"You did look it up, didn't you, Tam?"

"Did I?" I said. "I guess I did, at that. It didn't seem very clear to me, though, as I remember. Something about evolution."

"Ontogenetics," said Padma, "is the study of the effect of evolution upon the interacting forces of human society."

"Am I an interacting force?"

"At the moment and for the past several years,

yes,'' said Padma. "And possibly for some years into the future. But possibly not.''

"That sounds almost like a threat.''

"In a sense it is.'' Padma's eyes caught the light as I watched them. "You're capable of destroying yourself as well as others.''

"I'd hate to do that.''

"Then,'' said Padma, "you'd better listen to me.''

"Why, of course,'' I said. "That's my business, listening. Tell me all about ontogenetics—and myself.''

He made an adjustment in the controls, then swung his seat back to face mine once more.

"The human race,'' said Padma, "broke up in an evolutionary explosion at the moment in history when interstellar colonization became practical.'' He sat watching me. I kept my face attentive. "This happened for reasons stemming from racial instinct which we haven't completely charted yet, but which was essentially self-protective in nature.''

I reached into my jacket pocket.

"Perhaps I'd better take a few notes,'' I said.

"If you want to,'' said Padma, unperturbed. "Out of that explosion came cultures individually devoted to single facets of the human personality. The fighting, combative facet became the Dorsai. The facet which surrendered the individual wholly to some faith or other became the Friendly. The philosophical facet created the Exotic culture to which I belong. We call these Splinter Cultures.''

"Oh, yes,'' I said. "I know about Splinter Cultures.''

"You know about them, Tam, but you don't know them.''

"I don't?"

"No," said Padma, "because you, like all our ancestors, are from Earth. You're old full-spectrum man. The Splinter peoples are evolutionarily advanced over you."

I felt a little twist of bitter anger knot suddenly inside me. His voice woke the echo of Mathias' voice in my memory.

"Oh? I'm afraid I don't see that."

"Because you don't want to," said Padma. "If you did, you'd have to admit that they were different from you and had to be judged by different standards."

"Different? How?"

"Different in a sense that all Splinter people, including myself, understand instinctively, but full-spectrum man has to extrapolate to imagine." Padma shifted a little in his seat. "You'll get some idea, Tam, if you imagine a member of a Splinter Culture to be a man like yourself, only with a monomania that shoves him wholly toward being one type of person. But with this difference: instead of all parts of his mental and physical self outside the limits of that monomania being ignored and atrophied as they would be with you—"

I interrupted, "Why specifically with me?"

"With any full-spectrum man, then," said Padma calmly. "These parts, instead of being atrophied, are altered to agree with and support the monomania, so that we don't have a sick man, but a healthy, different one."

"Healthy?" I said, seeing the Friendly Groupman who had killed Dave on New Earth again in my mind's eye.

"Healthy as a culture. Not as occasional crippled individuals of that culture. But as a culture."

"Sorry," I said. "I don't believe it."

"But you do, Tam," said Padma softly. "Unconsciously you do. Because you're planning to take advantage of the weakness such a culture must have to destroy it."

"And what weakness is that?"

"The obvious weakness that's the converse of any strength," said Padma. "The Splinter Cultures are not viable."

I must have blinked. I was honestly bewildered.

"Not viable? You mean they can't live on their own?"

"Of course not," said Padma. "Faced with an expansion into space, the human race reacted to the challenge of a different environment by trying to adapt to it. It adapted by trying out separately all the elements of its personality, to see which could survive best. Now that all elements—the Splinter Cultures—have survived and adapted, it's time for them to breed back into each other again, to produce a more hardy, universe-oriented human."

The air-car began to descend. We were nearing our destination.

"What's that got to do with me?" I said, at last.

"If you frustrate one of the Splinter Cultures, it can't adapt on its own as full-spectrum man would do. It will die. And when the race breeds back to a whole, that valuable element will be lost to the race."

"Maybe it'll be no loss," I said, softly in my turn.

"A vital loss," said Padma. "And I can prove it. You, a full-spectrum man, have in you an element from every Splinter Culture. If you admit this you can identify even with those you want to destroy. I have evidence to show you. Will you look at it?''

The ship touched ground; the door beside me opened. I got out with Padma and found Kensie waiting.

I looked from Padma to Kensie, who stood with us and a head taller than I, two heads taller than OutBond. Kensie looked back down at me with no particular expression. His eyes were not the eyes of his twin brother—but just then, for some reason, I could not meet them.

"I'm a Newsman," I said. "Of course my mind is open."

Padma turned and began walking toward the headquarters building. Kensie fell in with us and I think Janol and some of the others came along behind, though I didn't look back to make sure. We went to the inner office where I had first met Graeme—just Kensie, Padma and myself. There was a file folder on Graeme's desk. He picked it up, extracted a photocopy of something and handed it to me as I came up to him.

I took it. There was no doubting its authenticity.

It was a memo from Eldest Bright, ranking Elder of the joint government of Harmony and Association, to the Friendly War Chief at the Defense X Center, on Harmony. It was dated two months previously. It was on the single-molecule sheet, where the legend cannot be tampered with or removed once it is on.

Be Informed, in God's Name—
—That since it does seem the Lord's Will that our Brothers on Ste. Marie make no success, it is

ordered that henceforth no more replacements or
personnel or supplies be sent them. For if our Captain does intend us the victory, surely we shall conquer without further expenditure. And if it be His
will that we conquer not, then surely it would be an
impiety to throw away the substance of God's
Churches in an attempt to frustrate that Will.

Be it further ordered that our Brothers on Ste.
Marie be spared the knowledge that no further
assistance is forthcoming, that they may bear witness to their faith in battle as ever, and God's
Churches be undismayed. Heed this Command,
in the Name of the Lord:

By order of him who is called—

Bright
Eldest Among The Chosen

I looked up from the memo. Both Graeme and
Padma were watching me.

"How'd you get hold of this?" I said. "No, of
course you won't tell me." The palms of my hands
were suddenly sweating so that the slick material of
the sheet in my fingers was slippery. I held it tightly,
and talked fast to keep their eyes on my face. "But
what about it? We already knew this, everybody
knew Bright had abandoned them. This just proves
it. Why even bother showing it to me?"

"I thought," said Padma, "it might move you just
a little. Perhaps enough to make you take a different
view of things."

I said, "I didn't say that wasn't possible. I tell you
a Newsman keeps an open mind at all times. Of
course"—I picked my words carefully—"if I could
study it—"

"I'd hoped you'd take it with you," said Padma. "Hoped?"

"If you dig into it and really understand what Bright means there, you might understand all the Friendlies differently. You might change your mind about them."

"I don't think so," I said. "But—"

"Let me ask you to do that much," said Padma. "Take the memo with you."

I stood for a moment, with Padma facing me and Kensie looming behind him, then shrugged and put the memo in my pocket.

"All right," I said. "I'll take it back to my quarters and think about it. I've got a groundcar here somewhere, haven't I?" And I looked at Kensie.

"Ten kilometers back," said Kensie. "You wouldn't get through anyway. We're moving up for the assault and the Friendlies are maneuvering to meet us."

"Take my air-car," said Padma. "The Embassy flags on it will help."

"All right," I said.

We went out together toward the air-car. I passed Janol in the outer office and he met my eyes coldly. I did not blame him. We walked to the air-car and I got in.

"You can send the air-car back whenever you're through with it," said Padma, as I stepped in through the entrance section of its top. "It's an Embassy loan to you, Tam. I won't worry about it."

"No," I said. "You needn't worry."

I closed the section and touched the controls.

It was a dream of an air-car. It went up into the

air as lightly as thought, and in a second I was two thousand feet up and well away from the spot. I made myself calm down, though, before I reached into my pocket and took the memo out.

I looked at it. My hand still trembled a little as I held it.

Here it was in my grasp at last. Proof of the evidence Piers Leaf had heard of back on Earth, and what I had been after from the start. And Padma himself had insisted I carry it away with me.

It was the lever, the Archimedes pry-bar which would move not one world but two. And push the Friendly peoples over the edge to extinction.

CHAPTER 27 ■

They were waiting for me. They converged on the air-car as I landed it in the interior square of the Friendlies' compound, all four of them with black rifles at the ready.

They were apparently the only ones left. Jamethon seemed to have turned out every other man of his remnant of a battle unit. And these were all men I recognized, case-hardened veterans. One was the Groupman who had been in the office that first night when I had come back from the Exotic camp and stepped in to speak to Jamethon, asking him if he ever ordered his men to kill prisoners. Another was a forty-year-old Force-Leader, the lowest commissioned rank, but acting Major—just as Jamethon, a Commandant, was acting as Expeditionary Field Commander, a position equivalent to Kensie Graeme's. The other two soldiers were noncommissioned, but similar. I knew them all. Ultrafanatics. And they knew me.

We understood each other.

"I have to see the Commandant," I said as I got out, before they could begin to question me.

"On what business?" said the Force-Leader. "This air-car hath no business here. Nor thyself."

I said, "I must see Commandant Black immediately. I wouldn't be here in a car flying the flags of the Exotic Embassy if it wasn't necessary."

They could not take the chance that my reason for seeing Black wasn't important, and I knew it. They argued a little, but I kept insisting I had to see the Commandant. Finally, the Force-Leader took me across into the same outer office where I had always waited to see Jamethon.

I faced Jamethon alone in the office.

He was putting on his battle harness, as I had seen Graeme putting on his earlier. On Graeme, the harness and the weapons it carried had looked like toys. On Jamethon's slight frame they looked almost too heavy to bear.

"Mr. Olyn," he said.

I walked across the room toward him, drawing the memo from my pocket as I came. He turned a little to face me, his fingers sealing the locks on his harness, jingling slightly with his weapons and his harness as he turned.

"You're taking the field against the Exotics," I said.

He nodded. I had never been this close to him before. From across the room I would have believed he was holding his usual stony expression, but standing just a few feet from him now I saw the tired wraith of a smile touch the corners of his straight mouth in that dark, young face for a second.

"That is my duty, Mr. Olyn."

"Some duty," I said. "When your superiors back on Harmony have already written you off their books."

"I've already told you," he said calmly. "The Chosen are not betrayed in the Lord, one by another."

"You're sure of that?" I said.

Once more I saw that little ghost of a weary smile.

"It's a subject, Mr. Olyn, on which I am more expert than you."

I looked into his eyes. They were exhausted but calm. I glanced aside at the desk where the picture of the church, the older man and woman and the young girl stood still.

"Your family?" I asked.

"Yes," he said.

"It seems to me you'd think of them in a time like this."

"I think of them quite often."

"But you're going to go out and get yourself killed just the same."

"Just the same," he said.

"Sure!" I said. "You would!" I had come in calm and in control of myself. But now it was as if a cork had been pulled on all that had been inside me since Dave's death. I began to shake. "Because that's the kind of hypocrites you are—all of you Friendlies. You're so lying, so rotten clear through with your own lies, if someone took them away from you there'd be nothing left. Would there? So you'd rather die now than admit committing suicide like this isn't the most glorious thing in the universe. You'd rather die than admit that you're just as full of doubts as anyone else, just as afraid."

I stepped right up to him. He did not move.

"Who're you trying to fool?" I said. "Who? I see through you just like the people on all the other worlds do! I know you know what a mumbo-jumbo your United Churches are. I know you know the way of life you sing of through your nose so much isn't what you claim it is. I know your Eldest Bright and his gang of narrow-minded old men are just a gang of world-hungry tyrants that don't give a damn for religion or anything as long as they get what they want. I know you know it—and I'm going to make you admit it!"

And I shoved the memo under his nose.

"Read it!"

He took it from me. I stepped back from him, shaking badly as I watched him.

He studied it for a long minute, while I held my breath. His face did not change. Then he handed it back to me.

"Can I give you a ride to meet Graeme?" I said. "We can get across the lines in the OutBond's air-car. You can get the surrender over with before any shooting breaks out."

He shook his head. He was looking at me in a particularly level way, with an expression I could not understand.

"What do you mean—no?"

"You'd better stay here," he said. "Even with ambassadorial flags, that air-car may be shot at over the lines." And he turned as if he would walk away from me, out the door.

"Where're you going?" I shouted at him. I got in front of him and pushed the memo before his eyes again. "That's real. You can't close your eyes to that!"

He stopped and looked at me. Then he reached out and took my wrist and put my arm and hand with the memo aside. His fingers were thin, but much stronger than I thought, so that I let the arm go down in front of him when I hadn't intended to do so.

"I know it's real. I'll have to warn you not to interfere with me any more, Mr. Olyn. I've got to go now." He stepped past me and walked toward the door.

"You're a liar!" I shouted after him. He kept on going. I had to stop him. I grabbed the solidograph from his desk and smashed it on the floor.

He turned like a cat and looked at the broken pieces at my feet.

"That's what you're doing!" I shouted, pointing at them.

He came back without a word and squatted down and carefully gathered up the pieces one by one. He put them into his pocket and got back to his feet, and raised his face at last to mine. And when I saw his eyes I stopped breathing.

"If my duty," he said in a low, controlled voice, "were not in this minute to—"

His voice stopped. I saw his eyes staring into me; and slowly I saw them change and the murder that was in them soften into something like wonder.

"Thou," he said softly, "thou hast no faith?"

I had opened my mouth to speak. But what he said stopped me. I stood as if punched in the stomach, without the breath for words. He stared at me.

"What made you think," he said, "that that memo would change my mind?"

"You read it!" I said. "Bright wrote you were a losing proposition here, so you weren't to get any more help. And no one was to tell you for fear you might surrender if you knew."

"Is that how you read it?" he said. "Like that?"

"How else? How else can you read it?"

"As it is written." He stood straight facing me now and his eyes never moved from mine. "You have read it without faith, leaving out the Name and the will of the Lord. Eldest Bright wrote not that we were to be abandoned here, but that since our cause was sore tried, we be put in the hands of our Captain and our God. And further he wrote that we should not be told of this, that none here should be tempted to a vain and special seeking of the martyr's crown. Look, Mr. Olyn. It's down there in black and white."

"But that's not what he meant! That's not what he meant!"

He shook his head. "Mr. Olyn, I can't leave you in such delusion."

I stared at him, for it was sympathy I saw in his face. For me.

"It's your own blindness that deludes you," he said. "You see nothing, and so believe no man can see. Our Lord is not just a name, but all things. That's why we have no ornament in our churches, scorning any painted screen between us and our God. Listen to me, Mr. Olyn. Those churches themselves are but tabernacles of the earth. Our Elders and Leaders, though they are Chosen and Anointed, are still but mortal men. To none of these things or people do we hearken in our faith, but to the very voice of God within us."

He paused. Somehow I could not speak.

"Suppose it was even as you think," he went on, even more gently. "Suppose that all you say was a fact, and that our Elders were but greedy tyrants, ourselves abandoned here by their selfish will and set to fulfill a false and prideful purpose. No." Jamethon's voice rose. "Let me attest as if it were only for myself. Suppose that you could give me proof that all our Elders lied, that our very Covenant was false. Suppose that you could prove to me"—his face lifted to mine and his voice drove at me—"that all was perversion and falsehood, and nowhere among the Chosen, not even in the house of my father, was there faith or hope! If you could prove to me that no miracle could save me, that no soul stood with me, and that opposed were all the legions of the universe, still I, I alone, Mr. Olyn, would go forward as I have been commanded, to the end of the universe, to the culmination of eternity. For without my faith I am but common earth. But with my faith, there is no power can stay me!"

He stopped speaking and turned about. I watched him walk across the room and out the door.

Still I stood there, as if I had been fastened in place—until I heard from outside, in the square of the compound, the sound of a military air-car starting up.

I broke out of my stasis then and ran out of the building.

As I burst into the square, the military air-car was just taking off. I could see Jamethon and his four hard-shell subordinates in it. And I yelled up into the air after them.

"That's all right for you, but what about your men?"

They could not hear me. I knew that. Uncontrollable tears were running down my face, but I screamed up into the air after him anyway.

"You're killing your men to prove your point! Can't you listen? You're murdering helpless men!"

Unheeding, the military air-car dwindled rapidly to the west and south, where the converging battle forces waited. And the heavy concrete walls and buildings about the empty compound threw back my words with a hollow, wild and mocking echo.

CHAPTER 28 ∎

I should have gone to the spaceport. Instead, I got back into the air-car and flew back across the lines looking for Graeme's Battle Command Center.

I was as little concerned about my own life just then as a Friendly. I think I was shot at once or twice, in spite of the ambassadorial flags on the air-car, but I don't remember exactly. Eventually I found the Command Center and descended.

Enlisted men surrounded me as I stepped out of the air-car. I showed my Credentials and went up to the battle screen, which had been set up in open air at the edge of shadow from some tall variform oaks. Graeme, Padma and his whole staff were grouped around it, watching the movements of their own and the Friendly troops reported on it. A continual low-voiced discussion of the movements went on, and a steady stream of information came from the communications center fifteen feet off.

The sun slanted steeply through the trees. It was almost noon and the day was bright and warm. No one looked at me for a long time; and then Janol, turning away from the screen, caught sight of me standing off at one side by the flat-topped shape of a tactics computer. His face went cold. He went on about what he was doing. But I must have been looking pretty bad, because after a while he came by with a canteen cup and set it down on the computer top.

"Drink that," he said shortly, and went off. I picked it up, found it was Dorsai whisky and swallowed it. I could not taste it, but evidently it did me some good, because in a few minutes the world began to sort itself out around me and I began to think again.

I went up to Janol. "Thanks."

"All right." He did not look at me, but went on with the papers on the field desk before him.

"Janol," I said. "Tell me what's going on."

"See for yourself," he said, still bent over his papers.

"I can't see for myself. You know that. Look— I'm sorry about what I did. But this is my job, too. Can't you tell me what's going on now and fight with me afterward?"

"You know I can't brawl with civilians." Then his face relaxed. "All right," he said, straightening up. "Come on."

He led me over to the battle screen, where Padma and Kensie were standing, and pointed to a sort of small triangle of darkness between two snakelike lines of light. Other spots and shapes of light ringed it about.

"These"—he pointed to the two snakelike lines—"are the Macintok and Sarah Rivers, where they come together, just about ten miles this side of Joseph's Town. It's fairly high ground, hills thick with cover, fairly open between them. Good territory for setting up a stubborn defense, bad area to get trapped in."

"Why?"

He pointed to the two river lines.

"Get backed up in here and you find yourself hung up on high bluffs over the river. There is no easy way across, no cover for retreating troops. It's nearly all open farmland the rest of the way, from the other sides of the rivers to Joseph's Town."

His finger moved back out from the point where the river lines came together, past the small area of darkness and into the surrounding shapes and rings of light.

"On the other hand, the approach to this territory from our position is through open country, too—narrow strips of farmland interspersed with a lot of swamp and marsh. It's a tight situation for either commander, if we commit to a battle here. The first one who has to backpedal will find himself in trouble in a hurry."

"Are you going to commit?"

"It depends. Black sent his light armor forward. Now he's pulling back into the high ground between the rivers. We're far superior in strength and equipment. There's no reason for us not to go in after him, as long as he's trapped himself—" Janol broke off.

"No reason?" I asked.

"Not from a tactical standpoint," Janol frowned at the screen. "We couldn't get into trouble unless we suddenly had to retreat. And we wouldn't do that unless he suddenly acquired some great tactical advantage that'd make it impossible for us to stay there."

I looked at his profile.

"Such as losing Graeme?" I said.

He transferred his frown to me. "There's no danger of that."

There was a certain change in the movement and the voices of the people around us. We both turned and looked.

Everybody was clustering around a screen. We moved in with the crowd and, looking between the shoulders of two of the officers of Graeme's staff, I saw on the screen the image of a small grassy meadow enclosed by wooded hills. In the center of the meadow, the Friendly flag floated its thin black cross on white background beside a long table on the grass. There were folding chairs on each side of the table, but only one person—a Friendly officer, standing on the table's far side as if waiting. There were the lilac bushes along the edge of the wooded hills where they came down in variform oak and ash to the meadow's edge; and the lavender blossoms were beginning to brown and darken for their season was almost at an end. So much difference had twenty-four hours made. Off to the left of the screen I could see the gray concrete of a highway.

"I know that place—" I started to say, turning to Janol.

"Quiet!" he said, holding up a finger. Around us,

everybody else had fallen still. Up near the front of our group a single voice was talking.

"—it's a truce table."

"Have they called?" said the voice of Kensie.

"No, sir."

"Well, let's go see." There was a stir up front. The group began to break up and I saw Kensie and Padma walking off toward the area where the air-cars were parked. I shoved myself through the thinning crowd like a process server, running after them.

I heard Janol shout behind me, but I paid no attention. Then I was up to Kensie and Padma, who turned.

"I want to go with you," I said.

"It's all right, Janol," Kensie said, looking past me. "You can leave him with us."

"Yes, sir." I could hear Janol turn and leave.

"So you want to come with me, Mr. Olyn?" Kensie said.

"I know that spot," I told him. "I drove by it yesterday. The Friendlies were taking tactical measurements all over that meadow and the hills on both sides. They weren't setting up truce talks."

Kensie looked at me for a long moment, as if he were taking some tactical measurements himself.

"Come on, then," he said. He turned to Padma. "You'll be staying here?"

"It's a combat zone. I'd better not." Padma turned his unwrinkled face to me. "Good luck, Mr. Olyn," he said, and walked away. I watched his blue-robed figure glide over the turf for a second, then turned to see Graeme halfway to the nearest military air-car. I hurried after him.

It was a battle car, not luxurious like the Out-

Bond's, and Kensie did not cruise at two thousand feet, but snaked it between the trees just a few feet above ground. The seats were cramped. His big frame overfilled his, crowding me where I sat. I felt the butt-plate of his spring-pistol grinding into my side with every movement he made on the controls.

We came at last to the edge of the wooded and hilly triangle occupied by the Friendlies and mounted a slope under the cover of the new-leaved variform oaks.

They were massive enough to have killed off most ground cover. Between their pillar-like trunks the ground was shaded and padded with the brown shapes of dead leaves. Near the crest of the hill, we came upon a unit of Exotic troops resting and waiting the orders to advance. Kensie got out of the car and returned the Force-Leader's salute.

"You've seen these tables the Friendlies set up?" Kensie asked.

"Yes, Commander. That officer they've got is still standing there. If you go just up over the crest of the slope here, you can see him—and the furniture."

"Good," said Kensie. "Keep your men here, Force-Leader. The Newsman and I'll go take a look."

He led the way up among the oak trees. At the top of the hill we looked down through about fifty yards more of trees and out into the meadow. It was two hundred yards across, the table right in the middle, the unmoving black figure of the Friendly officer standing on its far side.

"What do you think of it, Mr. Olyn?" asked Kensie, looking down through the trees.

"Why hasn't somebody shot him?" I asked.

He glanced sideways at me.

"There's plenty of time to shoot him," he said, "before he can get back to cover on the far side. If we have to shoot him at all. That wasn't what I wanted to know. You've seen the Friendly commander recently. Did he give you the impression he was ready to surrender?"

"No!" I said.

"I see," said Kensie.

"You don't really think he means to surrender? What makes you think something like that?"

"Truce tables are generally set up for the discussion of terms between opposing forces," he said.

"But he hasn't asked you to meet him?"

"No." Kensie watched the figure of the Friendly officer, motionless in the sunlight. "It might be against his principles to call for a discussion, but not to discuss—if we just happened to find ourselves across a table from one another."

He turned and signaled with his hand. The Force-Leader, who had been waiting down the slope behind us, came up.

"Sir?" he said to Kensie.

"Any Friendly strength in those trees across the way?"

"Four men, that's all, sir. Our scopes pick out their body heats clear and sharp. They aren't attempting to hide."

"I see." He paused. "Force-Leader."

"Sir?"

"Be good enough to go down there in the meadow and ask that Friendly officer what this is all about."

"Yes, sir."

We stood and watched as the Force-Leader went

stiff-legging it down the steep slope between the trees. He crossed the grass—it seemed very slowly—and came up to the Friendly officer.

They stood facing each other. They were talking but there was no way to hear their voices. The flag with its thin black cross whipped in the little breeze that was blowing there. Then the Force-Leader turned and climbed back toward us.

He stopped in front of Kensie and saluted. "Commander," he said, "the Commander of the Chosen Troops of God will meet with you in the field to discuss a surrender." He stopped to draw a fresh breath. "If you'll show yourself at the edge of the opposite woods at the same time; and you can approach the table together."

"Thank you, Force-Leader," said Kensie. He looked past his officer at the field and the table. "I think I'll go down."

"He doesn't mean it," I said.

"Force-Leader," said Kensie. "Form your men ready, just under the crown of the slope on the back side, here. If he surrenders, I'm going to insist he come back with me to this side immediately."

"Yes, sir."

"All this business without a regular call for parley may be because he wants to surrender first and break the news of it to his troops afterward. So get your men ready. If Black intends to present his officers with an accomplished fact, we don't want to let him down."

"He's not going to surrender," I said.

"Mr. Olyn," said Kensie, turning to me. "I suggest you go back behind the crest of the hill. The Force-Leader will see you're taken care of."

"No," I said. "I'm going down. If it's a truce parley to discuss surrender terms, there's no combat situation involved and I've got a perfect right to be there. If it isn't, what're you doing going down yourself?"

Kensie looked at me strangely for a moment.

"All right," he said. "Come with me."

Kensie and I turned and went down the sharply pitched slope between the trees. Our boot soles slipped until our heels dug in with every step downward. Coming through the lilacs I smelled the faint, sweet scent—almost gone now—of the decaying blossoms.

Across the meadow, directly in line with the table, four figures in black came forward as we came forward. One of them was Jamethon Black.

Kensie and Jamethon saluted each other.

"Commandant Black," said Kensie.

"Yes, Commander Graeme. I am indebted to you for meeting me here," said Jamethon.

"My duty and a pleasure, Commandant."

"I wished to discuss the terms of a surrender."

"I can offer you," said Kensie, "the customary terms extended to troops in your position under the Mercenaries' Code."

"You misunderstand me, sir," said Jamethon. "It was your surrender I came here to discuss."

The flag snapped.

Suddenly I saw the men in black measuring the field here, as I had seen them the day before. They had been right where we were now.

"I'm afraid the misunderstanding is mutual, Commandant," said Kensie. "I am in a superior tactical position and your defeat is normally certain. I have no need to surrender."

"You will not surrender?"

"No," said Kensie strongly.

All at once I saw the five stakes, in the position the Friendly noncoms, officers and Jamethon were now, and the stake up in front of them fallen down.

"Look out!" I shouted at Kensie—but I was far too late.

Things had already begun to happen. The Force-Leader had jerked back in front of Jamethon and all five of them were drawing their sidearms. I heard the flag snap again, and the sound of its rolling seemed to go on for a long time.

For the first time then I saw a man of the Dorsai in action. So swift was Kensie's reaction that it was eerily as if he had read Jamethon's mind in the instant before the Friendlies began to reach for their weapons. As their hands touched their sidearms, he was already in movement forward over the table and his spring-pistol was in his hand. He seemed to fly directly into the Force-Leader and the two of them went down together, but Kensie kept traveling. He rolled on off the Force-Leader, who now lay still in the grass. He came to his knees, fired, and dived forward, rolling again.

The Groupman on Jamethon's right went down. Jamethon and the remaining two were turned nearly full about now, trying to keep Kensie before them. The two that were left shoved themselves in front of Jamethon, their weapons not yet aimed. Kensie stopped moving as if he had run into a stone wall, came to his feet in a crouch, and fired twice more. The two Friendlies fell apart, one to each side.

Jamethon was facing Kensie now, and Jamethon's pistol was in his hand and aimed. Jamethon fired, and a light blue streak leaped through the air, but Kensie had dropped again. Lying on his side on the grass, propped on one elbow, he pressed the firing button on his spring-pistol twice.

Jamethon's sidearm sagged in his hand. He was backed up against the table now, and he put out his free hand to steady himself against the tabletop. He made another effort to lift his sidearm but he could not. It dropped from his hand. He bore more of his weight on the table, half-turning around, and his face came about to look in my direction. His face was as controlled as it had ever been, but there was something different about his eyes as he looked into mine and recognized me—something oddly like the look a man gives a competitor whom he has just beaten and who was no real threat to begin with. A little smile touched the corners of his thin lips. Like the smile of inner triumph.

"Mr. Olyn," he whispered. And then the life went out of his face and he fell beside the table.

Nearby explosions shook the ground under my feet. From the crest of the hill behind us the Force-Leader whom Kensie had left there was firing smoke bombs between us and the Friendly side of the meadow. A gray wall of smoke was rising between us and the far hillside, to screen us from the enemy. It towered up the blue sky like some impassable barrier, and under the looming height of it, only Kensie and I were standing.

On Jamethon's dead face there was a faint smile.

CHAPTER 29 ▓

In a daze I watched the Friendly troops surrender that same day. It was the one situation in which their officers felt justified in doing so.

Not even their Elders expected subordinates to fight a situation set up by a dead Field Commander for tactical reasons unexplained to his officers. And the live troops remaining were worth more than the indemnity charges for them that the Exotics would make.

I did not wait for the settlements. I had nothing to wait for. One moment the situation on this battlefield had been poised like some great, irresistible wave above all our heads, cresting, curling over and about to break downward with an impact that would reverberate through all the worlds of Man. Now, suddenly, it was no longer above us. There was nothing but a far-flooding silence, already draining away into the records of the past.

There was nothing for me. Nothing.

If Jamethon had succeeded in killing Kensie—even if as a result he had won a practically bloodless surrender of the Exotic troops—I might have done something damaging with the incident of the truce table. But he had only tried, and died, failing. Who could work up emotion against the Friendlies for that?

I took ship back to Earth like a man walking in a dream, asking myself why.

Back on Earth, I told my editors I was not in good shape physically; and they took one look at me and believed me. I took an indefinite leave from my job and sat around the News Services Center Library, at The Hague, searching blindly through piles of writings and reference material on the Friendlies, the Dorsai and the Exotic worlds. For what? I did not know. I also watched the news dispatches from Ste. Marie concerning the settlement, and drank too much while I watched.

I had the numb feeling of a soldier sentenced to death for failure on duty. Then in the news dispatches came the information that Jamethon's body would be returned to Harmony for burial; and I realized suddenly it was this I had been waiting for: the unnatural honoring by fanatics of the fanatic who with four henchmen had tried to assassinate the lone enemy commander under a truce flag. Things could still be written.

I shaved, showered, pulled myself together after a fashion and went to see about arrangements for passage to Harmony to cover the burial of Jamethon as a wrap-up.

The congratulations of Piers and word of my appointment to the Guild Council—that had reached me on Ste. Marie earlier—stood me in good stead. It got me a high-priority seat on the first spaceliner out.

Five days later I was on Harmony in that same little town, called Remembered-of-the-Lord, where Eldest Bright had taken me once before. The buildings in the town were still of concrete and bubbleplastic, unchanged by three years. But the stony soil of the farms about the town had been tilled, as the fields on Ste. Marie had been tilled when I got to that other world, for Harmony now was just entering the spring of its northern hemisphere. And it was raining as I drove from the spaceport of the town, as it had on Ste. Marie that first day. But the Friendly fields I saw did not show the rich darkness of the fields of Ste. Marie, only a thin, hard blackness in the wet that was like the color of Friendly uniforms.

I got to the church just as people were beginning to arrive. Under the dark, draining skies, the interior of the church was almost too dim to let me see my way about, for the Friendlies permit themselves no windows and no artificial lighting in their houses of worship. Gray light, cold wind and rain entered the doorless portal at the back of the church. Through the single rectangular opening in the roof watery sunlight filtered over Jamethon's body on a platform set up on trestles. A transparent cover had been set up to protect the body from the rain, which was channeled off the open space and ran down a drain in the back wall. But the elder conducting the Death

Service and anyone coming up to view the body was expected to stand exposed to sky and weather.

I got in line with the people moving slowly down the central aisle and past the body. To right and left of me the barriers at which the congregation would stand during the service were lost in gloom. The rafters of the steeply pitched roof were hidden in darkness. There was no music, but the low sound of voices individually praying to either side of me in the ranks of barriers and in the line blended into a sort of rhythmic undertone of sadness. Like Jamethon, the people were all very dark here, being of North African extraction. Dark into dark, they blended and were lost about me in the gloom.

I came up and passed at last by Jamethon. He looked as I remembered him. Death had shown no power to change him. He lay on his back, his hands at his sides, and his lips were as firm and straight as ever. Only his eyes were closed.

I was limping noticeably because of the dampness, and as I turned away from the body, I felt my elbow touched. I turned back sharply. I was not wearing my correspondent's uniform. I was in civilian clothes, so as to be inconspicuous.

I looked down into the face of the young girl in Jamethon's solidograph. In the gray, rainy light her unlined face was like something from the stained-glass window of an ancient cathedral back on Old Earth.

"You've been wounded," she said in a soft voice to me. "You must be one of the mercenaries who knew him on New Earth, before he was ordered to Harmony. His parents, who are mine as well, would find solace in the Lord by meeting you."

The wind blew rain down through the overhead opening all about me, and its icy feel sent a chill suddenly shooting through me, freezing me to my very bones.

"No!" I said. "I'm not. I didn't know him." And I turned sharply away from her and pushed my way into the crowd, back up the aisle.

After about fifteen feet, I realized what I was doing and slowed down. The girl was already lost in the darkness of the bodies behind me. I made my way more slowly toward the back of the church, where there was a little place to stand before the first ranks of the barriers began. I stood watching the people come in. They came and came, walking in their black clothing with their heads down and talking or praying in low voices.

I stood where I was, a little back from the entrance, half-numbed and dull-minded with the chill about me and the exhaustion I had brought with me from Earth. The voices droned about me. I almost dozed, standing there. I could not remember why I had come.

Then a girl's voice emerged from the jumble, bringing me back to full consciousness again.

". . . he did deny it, but I am sure he is one of those mercenaries who was with Jamethon on New Earth. He limps and can only be a soldier who hath been wounded."

It was the voice of Jamethon's sister, speaking with more of the Friendly cant on her tongue than she had used speaking to me, a stranger. I woke fully and saw her standing by the entrance only a few feet from me, half-facing two elder people whom I recognized as the older couple of Jamethon's solidograph. A bolt of pure, freezing horror shot through me.

"No!" I nearly shouted at them. "I don't know him. I never knew him. I don't understand what you're talking about!" And I turned and bolted out through the entrance of the church into the concealing rain.

I all but ran for about thirty or forty feet. Then I heard no footsteps behind me; I stopped.

I was alone in the open. The day was even darker now and the rain suddenly came down harder. It obscured everything around me with a drumming, shimmering curtain. I could not even see the ground-cars in the parking lot toward which I was facing; and for sure they could not see me from the church. I lifted my face up to the downpour and let it beat upon my cheeks and my closed eyelids.

"So," said a voice from behind me. "You did not know him?"

The words seemed to cut me down the middle, and I felt as a cornered wolf must feel. Like a wolf, I turned.

"Yes, I knew him!" I said.

Facing me was Padma, in a blue robe the rain did not seem to dampen. His empty hands that had never held a weapon in their life were clasped together before him. But the wolf part of me knew that as far as I was concerned, he was armed and a hunter.

"You?" I said. "What are you doing here?"

"It was calculated you would be here," said Padma softly. "So I am here, too. But why are *you* here, Tam? Among those people in there, there's sure to be at least a few fanatics who've heard the camp rumors of your responsibility in the matter of Jamethon's death and the Friendlies' surrender.''

"Rumors!" I said. "Who started them?"

"You did," Padma said. "By your actions on Ste. Marie." He gazed at me. "Didn't you know you were risking your life, coming here today?"

I opened my mouth to deny it. Then I realized I had known.

"What if someone should call out to them," said Padma, "that Tam Olyn, the Ste. Marie campaign Newsman, is here incognito?"

I looked at him with my wolf-feeling, grimly.

"Can you square it with your Exotic principles if you do?"

"We are misunderstood," answered Padma calmly. "We hire soldiers to fight for us not because of some moral commandment, but because our emotional perspective is lost if we become involved."

There was no fear left in me, only a hard, empty feeling.

"Call them then," I said.

Padma's strange hazel eyes watched me through the rain.

"If that was all that was needed," he said, "I could have sent word to them. I wouldn't have needed to come myself."

"Why did you come here?" My voice tore at my throat. "What do you on the Exotics care about me?"

"We care for every individual," said Padma. "But we care more for the race. And you're still dangerous to it. You're an unadmitted idealist, Tam, warped to destructive purpose. There is a law of conservation of energy in the pattern of cause and effect just as there is in other sciences. Your destructiveness was frustrated on Ste. Marie. Now what if it should turn inward to destroy you, or outward against the whole race of man?''

I laughed, and heard the harshness of my laughter.

"What're you going to do about it?" I said.

"Show you how the knife you hold cuts the hand that holds it as well as what you turn it against. I've got news for you, Tam. Kensie Graeme is dead."

"Dead?" The rain seemed to roar around me suddenly and the parking lot shifted unsubstantially under my feet.

"He was assassinated by three men of the Blue Front in Blauvain five days ago."

"Assassinated," I whispered. "Why?"

"Because the war was over," said Padma. "Because Jamethon's death and the surrender of the Friendly troops without the preliminary of a war that would tear up the countryside left the civilian population favorably disposed toward our troops. Because the Blue Front found themselves farther from power than ever, as a result of this favorable feeling. They hoped by killing Graeme to provoke his troops into retaliation against the civilian population, so that the Ste. Marie government would have to order them home to our Exotics, and stand unprotected to face a Blue Front revolt."

I stared at him.

"All things are interrelated," said Padma. "Kensie was slated for a final promotion to a desk command back on Mara or Kultis. He and his brother Ian would have been out of the wars for the rest of their professional lives. Because of Jamethon's death, which allowed the surrender of his troops without fighting, a situation was set up which led the Blue Front to assassinate Kensie. If you and Jamethon had not come into conflict on Ste. Marie, and Jamethon had not won, Kensie would be alive today. So our calculations show.''

''Jamethon and I?'' The breath went dry in my throat without warning, and the rain came down harder.

''Yes,'' said Padma. ''You were the factor that helped Jamethon to his solution.''

''I helped him?'' I said. ''*I* did?''

''He saw through you,'' said Padma. ''He saw through the revenge-bitter, destructive surface you thought was yourself, to the creative core that was so deep in the bone of you that even your uncle hadn't been able to eradicate it.''

The rain thundered between us. But Padma's every word came clearly through it to me.

''I don't believe you!'' I shouted. ''I don't believe he did anything like that!''

''I told you,'' said Padma, ''you didn't fully appreciate the evolutionary advances of our Splinter Cultures. Jamethon's faith was not the kind that can be shaken by outer things. If you had been in fact like your uncle Mathias, he would not even have listened to you. He would have dismissed you as a soulless man. As it was, he thought of you instead as a man possessed, a man speaking with what he would have called Satan's voice.''

''I don't believe it!'' I yelled.

''You do believe it,'' said Padma. ''You've got no choice except to believe it. Only because of it could Jamethon find his solution.''

''Solution!''

"He was a man ready to die for his faith. But as a commander he found it hard his men should go out to die for no other reasonable cause." Padma watched me, and the rain thinned for a moment. "But you offered him what he recognized as the Devil's choice—his life in this world, if he would surrender his faith and his men, to avoid the conflict that would end in his death and theirs."

"What crazy thinking was that?" I said. Inside the church, the praying had stopped, and a single strong, deep voice was beginning the burial service.

"Not crazy," said Padma. "The moment he realized this, his answer became simple. All he had to do was begin by denying whatever Satan offered. He must start with the absolute necessity of his own death."

"And that was a solution?" I tried to laugh but my throat hurt.

"It was the only solution," said Padma. "Once he decided that, he saw immediately that the one situation in which his men would permit themselves to surrender was if he was dead and they were in an untenable battlefield position, for reasons only he had known."

I felt the words go through me with a soundless shock.

"But he didn't mean to die!" I said.

"He left it to his God," said Padma. "He arranged it so only a miracle could save him."

"What're you talking about?" I stared at him. "He set up a truce table with a flag of truce. He took four men—"

"There was no flag. The men were overage martyrdom-seekers."

"He took four!" I shouted. "Four and one made five. The five of them against Kensie—one man. I stood there by that table and saw. Five against—"

"Tam."

The single word stopped me. Suddenly I began to be afraid. I did not want to hear what he was about to say. I was afraid I knew what he was going to tell me, that I had known it for some time. And I did not want to hear it, I did not want to hear him say it. The rain grew even stronger, driving upon us both and mercilessly on the concrete, but I heard every word relentlessly through all its sound and noise.

Padma's voice began to roar in my ears like the rain, and a feeling came over me like the helpless floating sensation that comes in high fever. "Did you think that Jamethon for a minute fooled himself as you deluded yourself? He was a product of a Splinter Culture. He recognized another in Kensie. Did you think that for a minute he thought that, barring a miracle, he and four overage fanatics could kill an armed, alert and ready man of the Dorsai—a man like Kensie Graeme—before they were gunned down and killed themselves?"

Themselves . . . themselves . . . themselves . . .

I rode off a long way on that word from the dark day and the rain. Like the rain and the wind behind the clouds it lifted me and carried me away at last to that high, hard and stony land I had glimpsed when I had asked Kensie Graeme that question about his ever allowing Friendly prisoners to be killed. It was this land I had always avoided, but to it I was come at last.

And I remembered.

From the beginning, I had known inside myself

that the fanatic who had killed Dave and the others was not the image of all Friendlies. Jamethon was no casual killer. I had tried to make him into one to shore up my own lie—to keep my eyes averted from the sight of that one man on the sixteen worlds I could not face. And that one man was not the Group-man who had massacred Dave and the others, not even Mathias.

It was myself.

Jamethon was no ordinary fanatic, no more than Kensie was an ordinary soldier, or Padma an ordinary philosopher. They were more than that, as secretly I had known all along, down inside myself where I need not face the knowledge. That was why they had not moved as I planned when I had tried to manipulate them. That was why, that was why.

The high, hard and stony land I had visioned was not only there for the Dorsai. It was there for all of them, a land where the tatters of falseness and illusion were stripped away by the clean cold wind of honest strength and conviction, where pretense drooped and died and all that could live was plain and pure.

It was there for them, for all those who embodied the pure metal of their Splinter Culture. And it was from that pure metal that their real strength came. They were beyond doubt—that was it; and above all skills of mind and body, this was what kept them undefeatable. For a man like Kensie would never be conquered. And Jamethon would never break his faith.

Had Jamethon not told me plainly so himself? Had he not said, "Let me testify for myself alone," and gone on to tell me that, even if his universe should crumble about him, even if all his God and his religion were proved false, what was in himself would not be touched.

No more, if armies about him retreated, leaving him alone, would Kensie abandon a duty or a post. Alone, he would remain to fight, though other armies came against him; for though they could kill him, they could not conquer him.

Nor, should all Padma's Exotic calculations and theories be overturned in an instant—proved untrue and groundless—would it move him from his belief in the upward-seeking evolution of the human spirit, in which service he labored.

They walked by right in that high and stony land— all of them. Dorsai, and Friendly, and Exotic. And I had been fool enough to enter it, to try to fight one of them there. No wonder I had been defeated, as Mathias always had said I would be. I had never had a hope of winning.

So I came back to the day and the downpour, like a broken straw of a man with my knees sagging under my own weight. The rain was slackening and Padma was holding me upright. As with Jamethon, I was dully amazed at the strength of his hands.

"Let me go," I mumbled.

"Where would you go, Tam?" he said.

"Any place," I muttered. "I'll get out of it. I'll go hole up somewhere and get out of it. I'll give up." I got my knees straightened finally under me.

"It's not that easy," said Padma, letting me go. "An action taken goes on reverberating forever. Cause never ceases its effects. You can't let go now, Tam. You can only change sides."

"Sides?" I said. The rain was dwindling fast about us. "What sides?" I stared at him drunkenly.

"The side of the force in man against his own evolution—which was your uncle's side," said Padma. "And the evolutionary side, which is ours." The rain was falling only lightly now and the day was brightening. A little pale sunlight filtered through the thinning clouds to illuminate more strongly the parking space around us. "Both are strong winds bending the fabric of human affairs even while that fabric is being woven. I told you long ago, Tam, that for someone like you there's no choice but to be effective upon the pattern one way or another. You have choice—not freedom. So, merely decide to turn your effect to the wind of evolution instead of to the force frustrating it."

I shook my head.

"No," I muttered. "It's no use. You know that. You saw. I moved heaven and earth and the politics of sixteen worlds against Jamethon—and he still won. I can't do anything. Just leave me alone."

"Even if I left you alone, events wouldn't," answered Padma. "Tam, open your eyes and look at things as they are. You're already involved. Listen to me." His hazel eyes caught what little light there was for a moment. "A force intruded on the pattern on Ste. Marie, in the shape of a unit warped by personal loss and oriented toward violence. That was you, Tam."

I tried to shake my head again, but I knew he was right.

"You were blocked in the direction of your conscious effort on Ste. Marie," Padma went on, "but the conservations of energies would not be balked.

When you were frustrated by Jamethon, the force you had brought to bear on the situation was not destroyed. It was only transmuted and left the pattern in the unit of another individual, now also warped by personal loss and oriented toward violent effect upon the pattern.''

I wet my lips.

''What other individual?''

''Ian Graeme.''

I stood, staring at him.

''Ian found his brother's three assassins hiding in a hotel room in Blauvain,'' said Padma. ''He killed them with his hands—and by so doing he calmed the mercenaries and frustrated the plans of the Blue Front to salvage something out of the situation. But then Ian resigned and went home to the Dorsai. He's charged now with the same sense of loss and bitterness you were charged with when you came to Ste. Marie.'' Padma hesitated. ''Now he has great causal potential. How it will expend itself within the future pattern remains to be seen.''

He paused again, watching me with his inescapable yellow gaze.

''You see, Tam,'' he went on after a moment, ''how no one like you can resign from effect upon the fabric of events? I tell you you can only change.'' His voice softened. ''Do I have to remind you now that you're still charged—only with a different force instead? You received the full impact and effect of Jamethon's self-sacrifice to save his men.''

His words were like a fist in the pit of my stomach—a blow as hard as the one I had given Janol Marat when I escaped from Kensie's camp on Ste.

Marie. In spite of the new, watery sunlight filtering down to us, I began to shiver.

It was so. I could not deny it. Jamethon, in giving his life up for a belief, where I had scorned all beliefs in my plan to twist things as I wanted them, had melted and changed me as lightning melts and changes the uplifted sword-blade that it strikes. I could not deny what had happened to me.

"It's no use," I said, still shivering. "It makes no difference. I'm not strong enough to do anything. I tell you, I moved everything against Jamethon, and he won."

"But Jamethon was wholehearted; and you were fighting against your true nature at the same time you fought him," said Padma. "Look at me, Tam!"

I looked at him. The hazel magnets of his eyes caught and anchored mine.

"The purpose for which on the Exotics it was calculated I should come to meet you here is still waiting for us," he said. "You remember, Tam, how in Mark Torre's office you accused me of hypnotizing you?"

I nodded.

"It wasn't hypnosis—or not quite hypnosis," he said. "All I did was to help you open a channel between your conscious and unconscious selves. Have you got the courage, after seeing what Jamethon did, to let me help you open it once again?"

His words hung on the air between us; and, balanced on the pinpoint of that moment, I heard the strong, proud-textured voice praying inside the church. I saw the sun trying to pierce through the thinning clouds overhead; and at the same time, in my mind's eye, I saw the dark walls of my valley as Padma had described them that day long ago back at the Encyclopedia. They were there still, high and close about me, shutting out the sunlight. Only, like a narrow doorway, still ahead of me, was there unshadowed light.

I thought of the place of lightning I had seen when Padma held up his finger to me that time before; and—weak, and broken and defeated as I felt now—the thought of entering that area of battle again filled me with a sick hopelessness. I was not strong enough to face lightning anymore. Maybe I never had been.

"For he hath been a soldier of his people, who are the People of the Lord, and a soldier of the Lord," the distant, single voice praying from the church came faintly to my ear, "and in no thing did he fail the Lord, who is our Lord, and the Lord of all strength and righteousness. Therefore, let him be taken up from us into the ranks of those who, having shed the mask of life, are blessed and welcomed unto the Lord."

I heard this, and suddenly the taste of homecoming, the taste of an undeniable return to an eternal home and unshakable certainty in the faith of my forefathers, was strong in my mouth. The ranks of those who would never falter closed comfortingly around me; and I, who also had not faltered, moved into step and went forward with them. In that second, for a second, then, I felt what Jamethon must have felt, faced with me and with the decision of life and death for himself on Ste. Marie. Only for a moment I felt it, but that was enough.

"Go ahead," I heard myself saying to Padma.

I saw his finger lifted toward me.

Into darkness, I went—into darkness and fury; a place of lightning, but not of open lightning any longer, but roiling murk and cloud and storm and thunder. Tossed and whirled, beaten downward by the rage and violence about me, I battled to lift, to fight my way up into the light and open air above the storm clouds. But my own efforts sent me tumbling, sent me whirling wildly, pitching downward instead of up—and, at last, I understood.

For the storm was my own inner storm, the storm of my making. It was the inner fury of violence and revenge and destruction that I had been building in myself all these years; and as I had turned the strengths of others against them, now it turned my own strength against me, pushing me down and down, ever farther into its darkness, until all light should be lost to me.

Down I went, for its power was greater than mine. Down I went, and down; but when I was lost at last in total darkness, and when I would have given up, I found I could not. Something other in me *would not*. It kept fighting back and fighting on. And then, I recognized this as well.

It was that which Mathias had never been able to kill in me as a boy. It was all of Earth and upward-striving man. It was Leonidas and his three hundred at Thermopylae. It was the wandering of the Israelites in the wilderness and their crossing of the Red Sea. It was the Parthenon on the Acropolis, white above Athens, and the windowless darkness of my uncle's house.

It was *this* in me—the unyielding spirit of all men—which would not yield now. Suddenly, in my battered, storm-beaten spirit, drowning in darkness, something leaped for wild joy. Because abruptly I saw that it was there for me, too—that high, stony land where the air was pure and the rags of pretense and trickery were stripped away by the unrelenting wind of faith.

I had attacked Jamethon in the area of his strength—out of my own inner area of weakness. *That* was what Padma had meant by saying I had been fighting myself, even while I was fighting Jamethon. That was why I had lost the conflict, pitting my unbelieving desire against his strong belief. But my defeat did not mean I was without a land of inner strength. It was there, it had been there, hidden in me all along!

Now I saw it clearly. And ringing like bells for a victory, then, I thought I heard once more the hoarse voice of Mark Torre, tolling at me in triumph; and the voice of Lisa, who, I saw now, had understood me better than I understood myself and never abandoned me. Lisa. And as I thought of her again, I began to hear them all.

All the millions, the billions of swarming voices— the voices of all human people since man first stood upright and walked on his hind legs. They were around me once more as they had been that day at the Transit Point of the Index Room of the Final Encyclopedia; and they closed about me like wings, bearing me up, up and unconquerable, through the roiling darkness, with the lift of a courage that was cousin to the courage of Kensie, with a faith that was father to the faith of Jamethon, with a search that was brother to the search of Padma.

With that, then, all my Mathias-induced envy and fear of the people of the Younger worlds was washed away from me, once and for all. I saw it, finally and squarely. If they had only one thing in actuality, I had all things in potential. Root stock, basic stock, Earth human that I was, I was part of all of them on the Younger worlds, and there was no one of them there that could not find an echo of themselves in me.

So I burst up at last through the darkness into the light—into the place of my original lightning, the endless void where the real battle lived, the battle of whole-hearted men against the ancient, alien dark that would keep us forever animals. And, distantly, as if down at the end of a long tunnel, I saw Padma standing under the strengthening light and dwindling rain of the parking lot speaking to me.

"Now you see," he said, "why the Encyclopedia has to have you. Only Mark Torre was able to bring it this far; and only you can finish the job, because the great mass of Earth's people can't yet see the vision of the future implicit in its being finished. You, who've bridged the gap in yourself between the people of the Splinter Cultures and the Earth-born, can build your vision into the Encyclopedia, so that when it's done, it can do as much for those who now can't see, and so begin the remodeling that will come when the Splinter Culture peoples turn back to recombine with Earth's basic stock into a new, evolved form of man."

His powerful gaze seemed to soften a little in the strengthening light. His smile grew a little sad.

"You'll live to see more of it than I will. Goodbye, Tam."

Without warning, then, I did see it. Suddenly it flowed together and clicked in my mind, the vision and the Encyclopedia as one reality. And, in the same moment, my coursing mind leaped full-throated onto the track of the opposition I would face in bringing about that reality.

Already they began to take shape in my head, out of my knowledge of my own world—the faces and the methods I would encounter. My mind raced on, caught up with them, and began to run on into plans ahead of them. Even now, I saw how I would work differently than had Mark Torre. I would keep his name as our emblem and only pretend the Encyclopedia continued to build on according to his forelaid plans for it. I would name myself as only one of a Board of Governors, who all in theory would have equal powers with me.

But actually I would be directing them, subtly, as I could; and I would be free, therefore, of the need for Torre's cumbersome protections against madmen like the one who had killed him. I would be free to move about Earth, even while I was directing the building, to locate and frustrate the efforts of those who would be trying to work against it. Already I could see now how I would begin to go about it.

But Padma was turning to leave me. I could not let him go like that. With an effort I tore my attention away from the future and came back to the day, the fading rain and the brightening light.

"Wait," I said. He stopped and turned back. It was hard for me to say it now that I had come to it. "You . . ." My tongue stumbled. "You didn't give up. You had faith in me, all this time."

"No," he said. I blinked at him, but he shook his head.

"I had to believe the results of my calculations." He smiled a little, almost ruefully. "And my calculations gave no real hope for you. Even at the locus point of Donal Graeme's party of Freiland, with five years' added information from the Encyclopedia, the possibility of your saving yourself seemed too small to plan for. Even on Mara, when we healed you, the calculations offered no hope for you."

"But—you stayed by me . . ." I stammered; staring at him.

"Not I. None of us. Only Lisa," he said. "She never gave you up from the first moment in Mark Torre's office. She told us she had felt something—something like a spark from you—when you were talking to her during the tour, even before you got to the Transit Room. She believed in you even after you turned her down at the Graeme locus; and when we set up to heal you on Mara, she insisted on being part of the process, so that we could bind her emotionally to you."

"Bind." The words made no sense.

"We sealed her emotional involvement with you, during the same process by which we repaired you. It made no difference to you, but it tied her to you irrevocably. Now, if she should ever lose you, she would suffer as greatly, or more greatly, than Ian Graeme suffered his loss of a mirror-twin at Kensie's death."

He stopped and stood watching me. But I still fumbled.

"I still don't—understand," I said. "You say it didn't affect me, what you did to her. What good, then—"

"None, as far as we could calculate then, or we've been able to interpret since. If she was bound to you, you were of course bound to her, as well. But it was like fastening a song-sparrow by a thread to the finger of a giant, as far as the relative massivity of your effect on the pattern, compared to hers. Only Lisa thought it would do some good.''

He turned.

''Good-bye, Tam,'' he said. Through the still misty, but brightening air I saw him walking alone toward the church, from which came the voice of the single speaker within, now announcing the number of the final hymn.

He left me standing, dumbfounded. But then, suddenly, I laughed out loud, because I suddenly realized I was wiser than he. Not all his Exotic calculations had been able to uncover why Lisa's binding herself to me could save me. But it had.

For it surged up in me now, my own strong love for her; and I recognized that all along my lonely self had returned that love of Lisa's, but would not admit it to myself. And for the sake of that love, I had wanted to live. A giant may carry a songbird without effort against all the beating of little wings. But if he cares for the creature he is tied to, he may be made to turn aside out of love where he could not be turned by force.

So, along that invisible cord binding us together, Lisa's faith had run to join with my faith, and I could not extinguish my own without extinguishing hers as well. Why else had I gone to her when she called me to come at Mark Torre's assassination? Even then I was turning to compromise my path with hers.

Seeing this now, the whole needle of my life's compass abruptly spun right about, a hundred and eighty degrees, and I saw everything suddenly straight and plain and simple in a new light. Nothing was changed for me, nothing of my hunger and my ambition and my drive, except that I was turned right about. I laughed out loud again at the simplicity of it; for I saw now that one aim was merely the converse of the other.

DESTRUCT : CONSTRUCT

CONSTRUCT—the clear and simple answer that I had longed for all those years to refute Mathias in his emptiness. It was this which I was born to do, *this* which was in the Parthenon, and the Encyclopedia, and all the sons of men.

I had been born, as were we all—even Mathias—if we did not go astray, a maker rather than a smasher, a creator, not a destroyer. Now, like one clean piece of metal, hammered free finally of impurities, I chimed clear through every atom and fiber of my being to the deep, unchanging frequency of the one true purpose in living. Dazed and weak, I turned away at last from the church, went to my car and got in. Now the rain was almost over and the sky was brightening faster. The faint mist of moisture fell, it seemed, more kindly; and the air was fresh and new.

I opened the car windows as I pulled out of the lot into the long road back to the spaceport. And through the open window beside me I heard them beginning to sing the final hymn inside the church.

It was the *Battle Hymn of the Friendly Soldiers* that they sang. As I drove away down the road the voices seemed to follow me strongly, not sounding slowly and mournfully as if in sadness and farewell, but strongly and triumphantly as in a marching song on the lips of those taking up a route at the beginning of a new day.

Soldier, ask not—now or ever!
Where to war your banners go! . . .

The singing followed me as I drove away. And as I got farther into the distance, the voices seemed to blend at last until they sounded like one voice alone, powerfully singing. Ahead the clouds were breaking. With the sun shining through, the patches of blue sky were like bright flags waving, like the banners of an army, marching forever forward into lands unknown.

I watched them as I drove forward toward where they blended at last into open sky; and for a long time I heard the singing behind me, as I drove to the spaceport and the ship for Earth and Lisa that waited in the sunlight for me there.